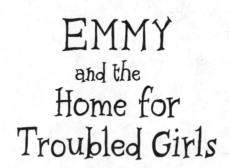

EMMY
and the
Home for
Troubled Girls

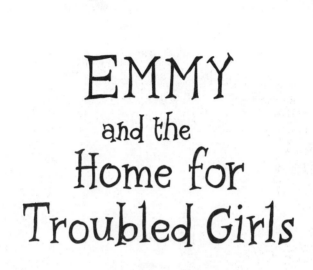

EMMY
and the
Home for
Troubled Girls

Lynne Jonell
Art by Jonathan Bean

HENRY HOLT AND COMPANY
NEW YORK

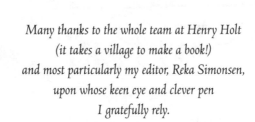

Many thanks to the whole team at Henry Holt
(it takes a village to make a book!)
and most particularly my editor, Reka Simonsen,
upon whose keen eye and clever pen
I gratefully rely.

Henry Holt and Company, LLC
Publishers since 1866
175 Fifth Avenue
New York, New York 10010
www.HenryHoltKids.com

Henry Holt® is a registered trademark of Henry Holt and Company, LLC.
Text copyright © 2008 by Lynne Jonell
Illustrations copyright © 2008 by Jonathan Bean
Distributed in Canada by H. B. Fenn and Company Ltd.

Library of Congress Cataloging-in-Publication Data
Jonell, Lynne.
Emmy and the Home for Troubled Girls / Lynne Jonell ; art by Jonathan Bean.—1st ed.
p.   cm.
Summary: Ten-year-old Emmy wants to be an ordinary girl, but the evil nanny Miss Barmy, now a
rat, has trapped five of her former charges, and when she uses them to steal jewels belonging to
Emmy's parents, it is up to Emmy, Joe, and their rodent friends to stop her.

ISBN-13: 978-0-8050-8151-0 / ISBN-10: 0-8050-8151-8
[1. Rodents—Fiction.   2. Kidnapping—Fiction.   3. Stealing—Fiction.   4. Nannies—
Fiction.   5. Humorous stories.]   I. Bean, Jonathan, ill.   II. Title.
PZ7.J675Ent 2008   [Fic]—dc22   2007041956
First Edition—2008

Printed in the United States of America on acid-free paper. ∞
1   3   5   7   9   10   8   6   4   2

To my dear brother Doug

In fond memory of
the infamous horseradish jelly-doughnut incident
and with many thanks
for making my childhood interesting
—L. J.

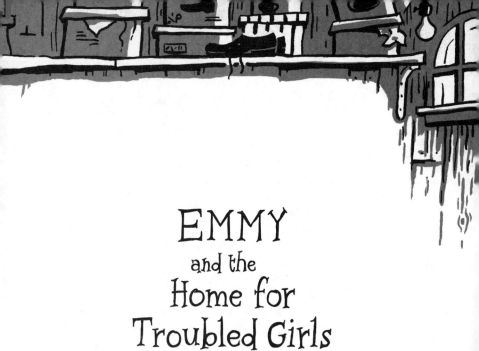

EMMY
and the
Home for
Troubled Girls

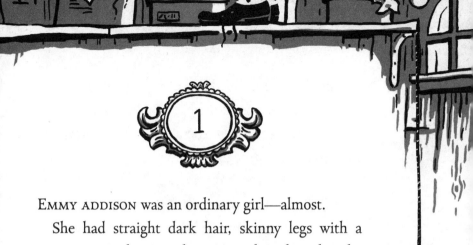

1

EMMY ADDISON was an ordinary girl—almost.

She had straight dark hair, skinny legs with a scrape on one knee, and no particular talent that she knew of. If you didn't count the fact that her parents were rich (very), her best friend was a boy (and a soccer star), and she could talk to rodents (and they talked back), she was very ordinary indeed.

She hadn't been ordinary for long, but even just a few weeks were enough to convince her that she didn't want to be any other way. Since the middle of May, her teacher had actually remembered her name at school. The other kids had played with her at recess. And her parents had eaten supper with her, and asked how her day had been, and reminded her to brush her teeth, in the most normal way possible.

Emmy didn't want it to end.

So she made a list of all the things an ordinary ten-and-a-half-year-old should do during the summer. She posted it beside her bedroom window—the

one in the turret—and she'd already managed to cross the first thing off the list. "Build a tree fort," it said, and just yesterday, she and her friend Joe had finished the best tree fort ever.

It was high—too high, her mother had worried, but her father had checked it for sturdiness, added a brace, and pronounced it safe. It was tucked snugly between three branches of the tallest oak in the woods behind Emmy's house, and from its platform she could look out over Grayson Lake and see sailboats skimming on Loon's Bay. Just now, though, she was flat on her stomach with her head hanging over the edge, watching Joe sprint up the path.

"Hiya!" Joe skidded to a stop beneath the big oak, a pale-haired boy in a blue soccer jersey and grass-stained shorts, and grinned up at Emmy, waiting.

"Password?" Emmy demanded.

"Oh, yeah. Um . . . Rat Fink?"

"No, that was yesterday's." Emmy propped her chin on her forearms.

Joe scratched his freckled nose. "Hamster Hocks?"

"Last week's."

Joe shot a glance over his shoulder. "Come on,

Emmy. I dodged my little brother two blocks ago, but he's faster on his pudgy feet than he used to be."

"It's Mouse Droppings," Emmy said resignedly, throwing down one end of the rope ladder. "You'd think you could remember a password you thought up yourself."

"Sorr-ry," said Joe, grabbing the rope. "I've remembered a message for you, though."

Emmy looked down at him warily. "Who from?"

"Mrs. Bunjee."

Emmy winced inwardly. How many girls, she wondered, got messages from chipmunks?

"She asked," Joe added, swaying as he climbed, "why you haven't come to visit. She has a new recipe for acorn soup, and says you're welcome anytime."

Emmy felt uncomfortable. She didn't want to seem ungrateful to the rodents who had helped her. Without the chipmunks, and the Rat, and all the rest, she would never have been able to get rid of Miss Barmy, the nanny who had nearly ruined her life.

But girls who visited chipmunks were—well, *weird*. It was okay for Joe; he was popular, he was the best athlete in the school, and everyone had known him since kindergarten; but for Emmy it was different.

3

She had been new at Grayson Lake Elementary last fall, when her parents had moved to the stone mansion on Loon's Bay. That was hard enough, but then Miss Barmy had used some unusual rodents to make Emmy's classmates, her teacher, and even her own parents forget that she existed. Emmy hadn't understood why her parents had suddenly seemed to stop caring about her or why all her attempts to make friends at school met with a blank stare.

If she hadn't discovered that Raston Rat, their fourth-grade class pet, had unusual powers, too; if she and Joe hadn't become friends, and shrunk to rat size; if they hadn't gone underground to Rodent City, where they joined forces with Professor Capybara and the chipmunks—then Miss Barmy might have succeeded in her plan to get rid of Emmy's parents, steal their money, and lock Emmy up for good in the Home for Troubled Girls.

But all had turned out well. Miss Barmy and her follower, Cheswick Vole, had been changed into rats themselves, Emmy's parents had become loving once more, and the kids at school had been as friendly as could be expected toward a girl they thought they'd just met. Still, though Emmy had had several weeks of being an ordinary kid, she had a lot of catching up to do before fifth grade.

She wanted to do regular ten-year-old things—go to birthday parties, and have sleepovers, and swim and bike and jump off swings in the park. She wanted to start fifth grade with a *hundred* friends— or, at any rate, more than one or two. She was going to be too busy this summer to spend time with a bunch of rodents, because she absolutely refused to go through another school year feeling lonely and invisible.

And of course there were a few more reasons why she wasn't keen on visiting Rodent City.

The tree house creaked as Joe clambered over the edge. "Free at last!"

"Did you win your game?" Emmy gazed idly at her house through the leaves, and her window in the topmost turret.

"Both games," said Joe gloomily. "So now we have to play two more tomorrow, before the championship." He rolled on his back to toss twigs at the large branch that overhung the platform. "At least I don't have to go to California on Monday. The soccer camp Dad tried to sign me up for was full."

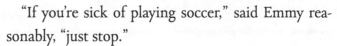

"If you're sick of playing soccer," said Emmy reasonably, "just stop."

"It's not that I don't want to play. I just don't want to play every stupid day all year long, that's all." Joe sat up abruptly, his eye caught by a knothole above him. "It's funny," he said, "but ever since that stuff happened—you know, shrinking and all—"

Emmy nodded impatiently. Of course she knew.

"I like to check out every rat-sized crack I see." He chinned himself on the overhanging branch and pressed his eye to the hole.

Emmy leaned back. "Can you see anything?"

"Too dark. Next time I'll bring a flashlight."

"We should have a box up here for that kind of stuff. Flashlights—"

"And batteries," added Joe, dropping down with a thump.

"Hammer and nails," Emmy said, "and Band-Aids."

"Comic books."

"Regular books, too," said Emmy, "especially ones about sailing—like *Swallows and Amazons*—"

"An astronomy book, so we can steer by the stars."

"I've got a telescope!" Emmy sat up. "We could use it for a spyglass—"

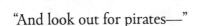

"And look out for pirates—"

"And buried treasure!"

"We'll make the pirates walk the plank, or"—Joe gripped his throat with both hands—"hang them from the yardarm."

Emmy rolled over to the edge, feeling for the ladder. "I'll get the spyglass."

"Get a bottle of ginger ale—no, grog—," Joe called, "and we can christen the ship!"

Emmy slammed the kitchen door behind her, sprinted up the stairs, and nearly collided with Maggie on the second-floor landing.

"Sorry," said Emmy, edging past the housemaid, who was emptying wastebaskets.

Maggie smiled broadly. "That's all right; I like to see a child run. It's better than watching you sit with your hands folded."

Emmy flushed. "I just did that when Miss Barmy made me act like a lady."

Maggie chuckled, pulling a section of the *Grayson Lake News* from one of the stacks. "Take a look; I saved this for you. Time enough to act like a lady when you're grown up and can wear these." She pointed to the society-column headline.

Emmy glanced at a picture of her parents, read "Addison Family Sapphires on Display at Grayson Lake Jewelers," and lost interest. She knew she was rich—Mr. and Mrs. Addison had inherited a lot of money a year ago, when her great-great-uncle William had died—but except for living in a house that looked like a castle, which *was* cool, she found the subject boring. "Maggie, please could I have a bottle of ginger ale? We want to christen the tree fort."

"That's a fine idea," said Maggie comfortably. "I'll check the pantry."

On a blue-painted windowsill in the northeast turret of the Addison mansion, a glossy black rat lay panting. He had never been in the best of shape, even when he was a human. Now that he was a rat, all the tunneling and gnawing and climbing that seemed to be expected of him was a bit much.

"You're getting too old for this, Cheswick," he muttered to himself.

But of course he was doing it for his darling Barmsie, whom he had adored for years. True, she was now quite a bit shorter than she had been—and hairier—with a prominent set of whiskers. And though her piebald blotches were interesting, and her long tail was certainly nice and pink, she was no longer the beauty queen of former days.

But she was still his precious tulip, and he was glad to do anything she asked. Just now he was on a daring mission into enemy territory. Cheswick grasped the window-blind cord, slid into Emmy's bedroom, and trotted into the playroom. He took a brown rucksack from his shoulders and waded manfully into a pile of doll clothes.

He was stuffing whatever he could reach into his sack—a green-and-gold track suit, a glittery evening gown, a white fluffy thing he couldn't identify—when a vibration in the floor sent a shiver through his claws.

The black rat lifted his head alertly. Someone was pounding up the stairs, someone gigantic. He dropped the rucksack at once. If he had learned one thing in his few weeks as a rat, it was to avoid anyone who was large and thumping. In a moment, all that could be seen of him was his tail, disappearing beneath a toy chest; and in one moment more, the only sign of his presence was a small sack half full of Barbie clothes.

Emmy skidded into the playroom, dropped the newspaper, and rummaged in her toy chest. No

9

telescope there . . . She checked in the science cupboard, and the art cabinet, and behind the carved Austrian dollhouse. It wasn't on any of the shelves lining the room from floor to ceiling; and it wasn't rolling among the balls and hockey sticks. Emmy peered inside all twenty-three Lego bins, and wished (not for the first time) that she didn't have so many toys. It was embarrassing when people came to visit; and when she tried to find something, it took forever.

Emmy turned in a circle. Now, if she were a telescope, where would she hide?

She gazed at her model train set with its miniature town, and then her eyes returned to the toy chest. Might it have rolled under there?

Emmy reached beneath. "Come on, spyglass," she muttered, and gave a cry of triumph as she grasped something long and skinny. She pulled it out, covered in dust, and sneezed.

It was not the telescope after all. It was Miss Barmy's old cane, the cane she had whittled herself. It was carved with little faces, their hair intertwined and their expressions pleading, and Emmy recoiled as she saw it.

Miss Barmy had told her that they were the faces of girls she had taken care of. She had said that she was saving a blank patch for Emmy's face, some-day . . .

Every grown-up who had seen the cane told Emmy she was lucky to have such a creative nanny. But something about the little faces had always both-ered Emmy; and, whatever might have happened to the other girls carved on the cane, Emmy was terri-bly glad it had not happened to her.

Emmy stalked to her window, lifted the screen, and hurled the cane over the lawn and straight at the trees. She watched with deep satisfaction as the awful thing speared into a bush at the edge of the woods.

Good. Let it stay there and rot.

A small grating sound drew Emmy's eyes back to the playroom as the telescope rolled slowly out from beneath the toy chest.

Emmy looked at it, startled. How——? Oh, it must have been dislodged by the cane that she'd just pulled out. She jammed the spyglass into an old backpack and ran down to the pantry with a light heart.

"Here you go," said Maggie, tucking a plastic bottle in Emmy's backpack. "Now, don't forget, Emmy—come in early tonight. There's company coming."

"Who is it, Maggie?"

"Peter Peebles. You do remember Mr. Peebles, don't you?"

Emmy grimaced. She remembered him, all right. He was the lawyer who had helped Miss Barmy draw up the papers she had tried to get Emmy's parents to sign—papers that would have sent Emmy to the Home for Troubled Girls and given Miss Barmy total control if Emmy's parents died.

"Now, child, don't make a face. You know that Mr. Peebles was tricked right along with your parents."

Emmy nodded politely. But deep down, she couldn't help feeling that anyone who would help a person like Miss Barmy had to have something wrong with him.

"And don't you worry about that horrible Miss Barmy, either," said Maggie. "She's long gone and far away, and she's not likely to bother you ever again."

Two stories up, Cheswick brushed off his paws (the spyglass had been dusty), pattered onto the newspaper

Emmy had left behind, and read slowly, swinging his dark furry head from side to side.

He bared his yellow incisors and clipped out the society column with small, neat bites. And a moment later he shouldered the rucksack and was on his way to his beloved Miss Barmy, who was not nearly so far away as Maggie believed.

"Mouse droppings," Emmy called, and the rope ladder came tumbling down. There was a rustle in the bushes, but Emmy was too busy climbing to pay attention.

She flopped over the edge. "Here. It won't break unless you really whack it."

Joe shook the bottle violently. "So what do you want to name the ship?"

Emmy looked around. The sun shone through layers of green, and the platform was tiled with a shifting mosaic of gold. "Let's call it Golden Fortress!"

Joe shook his head firmly. "Nah, too sappy. How about Good Fort?"

"Too boring." Emmy wrinkled her nose.

Joe shrugged. "Then let's call it G.F., and it can stand for both."

There was a sudden scurry in the branches overhead. "It could also stand for Gophers are Fabulous," said a voice, "except they're *not*."

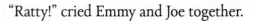

"Ratty!" cried Emmy and Joe together.

Raston Rat's pointed gray face grinned at them through a cluster of leaves. "Or maybe Gerbils Forever, except I can't stand gerbils. They're twitchy little rodents." The Rat gripped a green twig, swung through the air in a swashbuckling manner, and landed with a thump on the overhanging branch.

Emmy gazed at him with pleasure. She might not want to be seen with rodents, but the Rat was special. His gray fur was glossy, his whiskers neatly trimmed, and on his head, tilted jauntily to one side, was a little black beret. "You're looking good, Ratty!"

The Rat smoothed his whiskers, tipping his head in a modest manner. The beret slipped farther to one side, and he made an undignified lurch in an attempt to tip it back the other way.

"You might need a bobby pin, though," said Emmy, as the beret fell off entirely.

"Or some Super Glue." Joe picked up the small felt cap. "Where did you get this? Emmy's Barbie collection?"

"It is *not* Barbie's," said the Rat in a chilling tone. "It's G.I. Joe's, and it goes with his *paratrooper* uniform."

Joe nodded seriously. "So where's your 'chute, then? And your plane?"

The Rat's ears turned a faint pink. "Just because *you* have no style," he muttered, "no sartorial instinct—" He snatched the beret from Joe's hand with a scathing look.

"*Sartorial?*" said Joe, grinning.

"Why, Raston!" said Emmy, as she cast a warning look at Joe. "You're improving your vocabulary!"

"*I* do not wish to wallow in ignorance," said the Rat, settling the beret on his head with an airy flick. "Unlike some I could mention." He glowered at Joe.

"I'm *not*—"

"Be that as it may," the Rat interrupted, holding up a paw as Joe began to speak, "I have come for a Purpose." He reached into his satchel, pulled out a creamy-white envelope the size of a matchbook, and handed it to Emmy with a deep bow.

The envelope bore a small paw print in the upper left-hand corner, and the names "Emmaline Addison and Joseph Benson" were written in a cramped but even script. Emmy opened it cautiously and saw it was an invitation.

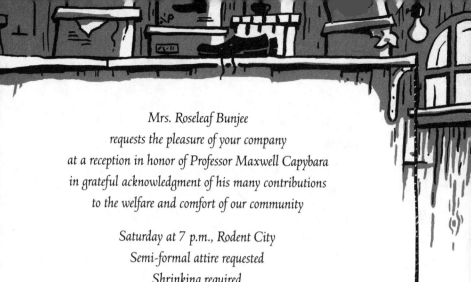

Mrs. Roseleaf Bunjee
requests the pleasure of your company
at a reception in honor of Professor Maxwell Capybara
in grateful acknowledgment of his many contributions
to the welfare and comfort of our community

Saturday at 7 p.m., Rodent City
Semi-formal attire requested
Shrinking required
Dinner music by the Swinging Gerbils
R.V.R.P.

Emmy tried to ignore the hollow feeling in her chest. Of course it was fine to honor the professor—after all, he'd helped many rodents escape from Cheswick Vole, and then helped them build Rodent City. "R.V.R.P.," she read aloud. "What does that mean?"

"Respond Via Rodent, Please," said the Rat. "That's me. So—are you coming?"

"Of course we're coming," said Joe, reading over Emmy's shoulder. "Only what's 'semi-formal'? No shorts?"

Emmy was amused. "It means we're supposed to dress up. You'll have to wear a suit—or at least a jacket and tie."

"What?" Joe's voice was high with alarm. "You're kidding, right?"

Emmy shook her head.

"But it says *semi*-formal. That means *partly* dressed up. Like good jeans and tennis shoes, right?"

"Wrong," Emmy said firmly. "Listen, I *know* about this stuff; my mom and dad are always dressing up. Formal means you wear a tux—"

"A *tuxedo*?" Joe's voice scaled up.

"And there are different degrees of formal—white tie, black tie—"

"No one," said Joe fervently, "is getting me into a tuxedo."

"Calm down—that's only if it's formal. Semi-formal is a suit and tie, or you can get away with a sports jacket sometimes."

"A sports jacket?" Joe sounded interested. "I've got a soccer jacket. It's pretty nice, has the team logo—"

"Not *that* kind of sports jacket. A sports jacket looks almost like a regular suit coat, only it doesn't have matching pants."

Joe stared at her in disbelief.

Emmy tried not to laugh.

"Wear something of Ken's," the Rat suggested helpfully. "You're going to have to shrink anyway.

Just go through the Barbie clothes and find something snappy."

The hollow sensation in Emmy's chest increased. "I don't know if I can come."

"But they're all *counting* on you," the Rat protested.

Emmy reached for the ginger ale and pretended to read the label. She could hardly say she didn't want to hang out with a bunch of rodents—not to the Rat's face.

Joe looked at her keenly. "Does the biting bother you?" He turned on the Rat. "Listen, when you bite to shrink us, you don't have to chomp so hard. A little nip is all it takes."

"I," said the Rat with dignity, "do not *chomp*. I bite with a minimum of fuss and near-perfect control."

Joe hooted. "*Near*-perfect is right, you carnivore—"

"It's not the bite I mind," Emmy muttered.

She had been bitten several times by the Rat; it hadn't hurt much. And although it had taken her (and Joe) a long time to figure it out, eventually they had realized what Raston's bites could do.

The first bite allowed a person to understand rodent speech. Emmy had discovered this last year, on the first day of school, when she'd reached into the Rat's cage to fill his water dish.

The second bite was not so pleasant, for it caused the person receiving it to shrink to rat size. Emmy still remembered how small and helpless she had felt at four inches tall, the terror of looking *up* at a cat's sharp teeth, and how she'd had to nerve herself to go through the crack in the steps that led to the underground Rodent City.

She had done it because she *had* to. And later, after a kiss from Raston's twin sister, Cecilia, had caused her to grow back to full size, Emmy had even told the Rat to shrink her again, when she needed to escape from Miss Barmy.

So Emmy was no stranger to shrinking. And some of it had even been fun. But she'd had time to think since then, and to realize how lucky she'd been.

For instance, she'd been fortunate that nothing had happened to Cecilia—or Sissy, as she was called. If the Rat's twin hadn't been there to reverse the effects of his bite, Emmy would have remained four inches tall forever.

She had been lucky, too, that Raston had not bitten her again, once she was already shrunken. That had happened to Miss Barmy, and *she* had turned into a rat. Worse yet, Sissy's kiss had failed to turn the nanny back into a human, the way the professor thought it should.

Which meant that Miss Barmy was still around somewhere—only now she had sharp claws and teeth.

Emmy sighed. She owed too much to Professor Capybara to skip his party. But even wearing one of Barbie's gowns wasn't going to make up for having to spend a whole evening with a bunch of rats.

The tree house dipped and creaked, almost like a real ship. Joe and the Rat were still arguing.

Emmy picked at a scab on her knee. "Listen, I'm *going* already. Stop fighting, will you?"

The Rat looked offended. "We weren't fighting."

"We were discussing," said Joe.

"If we were fighting, you'd see claws."

"You'd see punching."

"You'd see blood," said the Rat cheerfully.

Emmy rolled her eyes.

"Hey," said Joe, looking again at the invitation in Emmy's hands, "who are the Swinging Gerbils? Are they any good?"

The Rat snorted. "That depends on your standards."

"Well, I don't exactly know what kind of music gerbils play—"

"Squeaky," said the Rat. "Listen, are you going to christen this tree fort anytime soon?"

Joe shook the bottle once more and took a firm stance. "Okay, whether it's Golden Fortress or Good Fort—"

"Or Gophers are Fabulous, or Gerbils Forever," added Emmy—

"Or Glabrous Ferrets with Glandular Fistulas," suggested the Rat—

"I hereby christen thee—G.F.!" Joe struck the bottle against the thick edge of the platform, but the plastic bounced off. "One more time," he said, and bashed it hard against the cleat where the rope ladder was attached.

The soda sprayed. There was a yelp from below. Two chunky hands gripped the platform, and a round head with dripping blond hair popped up over the side.

"Mouse Droppings," said Joe's little brother.

Joe dropped the bottle and glared. "Get lost, Thomas. Go bother someone your own size."

"I know the password," Thomas said sturdily.

"So what? You were spying, and we don't want you!"

"But I know the *password*," Thomas repeated patiently. "You have to let somebody up if they know the *password*. That's the rule."

"Oh, for crying—" Joe gripped his hair in exasperation.

"He does know the password," said the Rat, enjoying the scene from his branch.

Thomas raised a damp face and fixed his round blue eyes on Raston. "Oh, hi, Rat."

"Hey, old buddy. Did you bring me any peanut butter?"

Thomas shook his head. "I didn't know you'd be here. Why are you wearing that funny hat?"

Joe and Emmy looked at each other in dismay. Thomas could understand the Rat!

"Don't," said Joe hollowly, "*don't* tell me you bit him, Ratty."

Thomas climbed over the edge and sat on the platform, listening with interest.

"Of course I did," the Rat answered, sounding aggrieved. "*Months* ago. When I was the class pet and it was your turn to take me home for the weekend."

Joe glared at Thomas. "I suppose *you* opened the cage and tried to pet him."

Thomas nodded. "He talked to me. And I talked back. And then I got him some peanut butter, like he wanted."

"Skippy," said the Rat with a dreamy look on his face. "Super Chunk."

Joe put his head in his hands.

"Thomas," said Emmy urgently, "did you *tell* anyone that the Rat could talk?"

Thomas nodded. "I told everyone. And they all said, 'There goes Thomas, making up stories again.' So I stopped telling."

"That's good, Thomas," said Emmy. "Just keep that up, okay? Don't say *anything* about the Rat."

Thomas looked at her solemnly. "Do I get to play with you guys? And come up in the tree fort and you won't yell at me?"

Joe picked moodily at his thumb.

"Yes," said Emmy recklessly. "But you have to promise, on your honor—"

"I'm a Cub Scout," said Thomas.

"Okay, *Scout's* honor, then—"

Thomas held up two fingers for the Scout pledge.

"Repeat after me," said Emmy sternly. "I, Thomas Benson, do solemnly swear—"

"I, Thomas Benson, do solemnly—I'm not supposed to swear, you know."

"Oh, for—" Emmy shut her eyes. "Okay, just

promise. If we let you play with us, you have to promise, Scout's honor, that you won't ever tell about the Rat."

Joe lifted his head. "And you have to do everything we say, no questions asked." He paced the deck. "You're the cabin boy, and if the captain gives an order, you obey."

"Who's the captain?"

"I'm the captain today," said Joe, "because I thought of it."

"And I'm the captain tomorrow," said Emmy, "because it's my tree fort."

"We will switch off," Joe announced, "but you will *always* be the cabin boy."

"Or the lookout," Emmy added.

"You have to do the rowing when we go ashore—"

"You have to bury any pirates that we kill—"

"And you only get a tenth of any treasure we find," Joe finished sternly. "Agreed?"

"Scout's honor," Thomas said, his round face shining. He undid a cord tied to his belt loop and began to steadily raise something from below. "I found a cool thing for the fort. I thought it could be like that lady thing they put in front of ships."

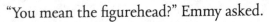

"You mean the figurehead?" Emmy asked.

Thomas nodded, pulling the cord hand over hand. "We could nail it to the front."

"Not the front, you landlubber," said Joe, "the *bow*. And you have to ask the captain's permission to bring something on deck."

"Can I?" Thomas asked, grunting a little as the thing he was towing caught.

"You don't say it like that. You say, 'Permission to bring cargo aboard,' and then you say 'captain' or 'sir.'"

"Permission to bring cargo aboard, sir?"

"Permission granted," said Joe, helping Thomas yank the object free. It came over the edge with a clatter of wood on wood, rolled to Emmy's feet, and stopped, its small carved faces staring sightlessly.

"Wow! Remember this, Emmy?" Joe untied the cord from Miss Barmy's cane. "It'll be a perfect figurehead!"

Emmy stared at the little faces. Up here in the tree fort, as the sun moved over the carved surfaces with light and shadow, the cane looked different, somehow. The entwined hair looked more elaborately carved than she had ever noticed—almost like some kind of curving script—

"Hey!" Emmy leaned closer, tracing the wooden

strands with her finger. "These are letters . . . There's a 'P,' and an 'R' . . ."

"I . . . S . . . C . . ." said Joe, moving along the wooden strands with his finger. "I . . . L . . . It's a name! *Priscilla*."

Emmy looked up. "That's old William Addison's daughter," she said slowly. "The one who died, or drowned, or something . . . "

Joe nodded soberly. "This one's Ana," he said, tracing the hair of another tiny face. "And . . . Berit. And Lisa."

"The one next to her is Lee," said Emmy, turning the cane gently. "And this one—the littlest—is Merry."

Thomas and the Rat moved in closer. There was a long silence.

"I wonder where they all are now," said Thomas.

3

THE AFTERNOON SUN SLANTED through the dusty air of the attic room. The window was dirty, but the rays stamped the wooden floor with gold, and a long trapezoid of light stretched out to touch a small girl with her back to the wall.

She was *very* small—about four inches high—with long brown hair and watchful eyes. Her name was Ana, and as the sun warmed her bare legs, she looked up and quickly pushed a bundle of knotted shoelaces under one of the long shelves that lined the room from floor to ceiling. "Almost time," she called, clapping her hands twice.

Light footfalls stirred the dust as three tiny girls, clothed like Ana in handkerchief dresses of ragged white, came running from various parts of the vast room. Ana reached up to unhook a shoelace ladder from the shelf above, and the girls began to climb.

"Into the box with you," said Ana, giving an encouraging smile to the youngest, who hung back. "Where's Berit?"

"I dunno." The child put a ragged piece of cloth to her cheek and smoothed it with her thumb. "Ana, I don't *like* the box."

"No one likes the box, Merry." Ana gave the child a boost up the knotted ladder. "But Miss Barmy moved into our old house, and you wouldn't want to live with her, would you?"

Merry shook her head vigorously.

"All right, then. You try to be brave, and I'll tell you a story tonight."

"We're *usually* brave," said a voice from within the box. "Right, Lee?"

"Right, Lisa," said another voice, sounding identical to the first.

The floor vibrated slightly. Ana turned, listening, and the voices fell silent.

There was another vibration, and another, as if a giant were stepping heavily somewhere outside the room. Ana cupped her hands around her mouth. "Berit!" she called, her voice anxious. "He's early!"

There was a flurry of activity in a dim, far corner, and a small white figure ducked out from beneath a pile of clutter.

"Run!" cried Ana as the floor shook again.

The tiny girl pelted across the floor. Her arms and

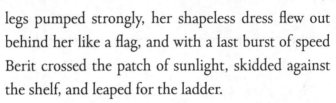

legs pumped strongly, her shapeless dress flew out behind her like a flag, and with a last burst of speed Berit crossed the patch of sunlight, skidded against the shelf, and leaped for the ladder.

There was a shuffling at the door and the metallic sound of a key scraping in a lock. Ana hastily climbed to the second shelf, hooked the shoestring ladder safely out of sight, and flung a leg over the side of a box marked "Wingtips, Black Leather, Size 11B."

The doorknob turned. The door to the attic room creaked open. Ana scrambled inside the cardboard box and pulled the lid over their heads with a paper-clip hook.

All was suddenly dark. There was a smell of shoes. Berit's gasps were loud in the space as she tried to catch her breath.

"All right, everyone," Ana said. "Time to be brave. And don't forget to act stupid."

The girls fell back as the box slid out with a jerk. There was a horrible swaying sensation as it was carried through the air, then downward in a series of bumps.

"Is h-he g-going to dr-drop us?" Merry clutched Ana's arm.

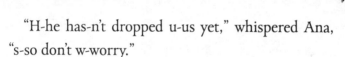

"H-he has-n't dropped u-us yet," whispered Ana, "s-so don't w-worry."

"I-I'm n-not wor-ried," said Lisa. "Are y-you w-worried, L-Lee?"

"Hush!" said Ana, as the bumping stopped.

The box slid onto a hard surface, and was still. One by one, the girls reached for one another's hands. A reedy, discontented voice from somewhere outside the box said, "Where are my dollies?"

The lid came off in a blaze of light. The girls, blinking, looked up at two watery eyes and a red-veined nose in a huge, chubby face. A thin white fuzz ringed the sides and top of the old man's head, giving him the appearance of a large and amiable powder puff.

"Here they are, my little daffodil," he said, giving the girls a gigantic wink. "All ready to play with Mrs. B."

"Bring them here," said the voice peevishly. "I want to play beauty parlor. Where's that one with the long hair?"

Ana suppressed a violent shudder as she was lifted out of the box and set before a scrawny woman with a neck like a chicken.

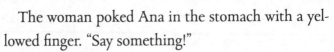

The woman poked Ana in the stomach with a yellowed finger. "Say something!"

Ana pasted a dim-witted expression on her face. "Hello-my-name-is-Ana," she said in a monotone.

"Hee-hee!" tittered the woman. "She's not very bright, is she?"

"But they like to play with you, Addie," said the old man, who had sat down under a bright lamp and taken out a bit of wood to whittle.

"You think so?" The woman pulled Ana's hair into a tight ponytail and let the rubber band snap.

Ana pretended she was someplace else. She gazed at the dollhouse that used to be their home, now sitting in splendid isolation on a table by the front window of Mr. and Mrs. B's walk-up apartment. She could see tiny rooms full of delicately carved furniture, and the grand curving staircase down which Merry had loved to slide. It had been a pretty place to live, in spite of the sign over the door that read "Home for Troubled Girls." Mr. B had created a little world for them on the table—a park with miniature trees, an edged mirror for skating in the winter, a slide and swings arranged on the green velvet "lawn" for summer—but it was still a prison, and on the whole Ana preferred the attic. In the attic, they had a lot more freedom.

"This one's *boring*," said the woman petulantly, slapping down the brush on the tray so that Ana jumped. "Where's that feisty one? She's more amusing. Or the little one. Sometimes she even cries."

"They're *all* boring, Mother," said a voice from the dollhouse. A piebald rat, white and brown and tan, stepped from the shadows, flicked on the tiny spotlight that shone on the central staircase, and paused a moment, her tail looped elegantly over one paw. "Why don't you get some use out of them for a change? Have them do your nails."

Ana stiffened and turned away. She didn't look at the piebald rat more than was absolutely necessary. Miss Barmy had been horrible when she'd been Ana's nanny, long ago and in another place entirely; her transformation into a rat hadn't improved her.

Mr. B fumbled with the knife in his hands, and set down his carving. "But nail polish might be dangerous. All those toxic chemicals—"

"Nonsense," said Miss Barmy. "Nail polish can't possibly hurt Mother; she's used it her whole life."

"I meant for the little girls," Mr. B said apologetically. "They're so small . . . and they'd have to breathe the stuff . . ."

"Oh, the *girls*," said Miss Barmy coldly. "Really, Father, I don't understand you at all. You're not thinking of *Mother*. She would so enjoy a pretty, new color . . ." She looked at Mrs. B consideringly. "The girls could dig out your earwax, too."

Mrs. B tilted her head to one side and consulted a pocket mirror. "I do have a few nose hairs that need clipping."

A low whimper came from the vicinity of the shoebox. Ana looked up at Mrs. B's dark and yawning nostrils in horror.

A sudden scuffling came from somewhere near Mr. B's feet. Ana peered over the edge of the tray and saw a hole in the baseboard.

It was a new hole; she could see fresh tooth marks all around the edges. It hadn't been there when the girls had lived in the dollhouse, or Ana would have noticed it.

"Paper!" bawled a voice from the hole, and a sleek striped rodent crawled out, stood up, and adjusted the sling on its shoulder.

"Well? Toss it up!" commanded Miss Barmy from the table.

"I'm collecting," the gopher said, flipping open a small notebook. "You owe me for one week's delivery of the *Rodent City Register*. Five seeds, please."

"Seeds? What kind of seeds?" Miss Barmy glanced at her father and jerked her head sharply. Mr. B got up and ambled to the kitchen.

The gopher shrugged. "Oh, pumpkin, apple, sunflower—the usual."

"We don't have any pumpkin," called Mr. B, peering into a cupboard. "Caraway we've got. Sesame, yes. Anise, dill—"

"Would any of those do?" Miss Barmy interrupted.

"Cumin, celery, mustard, poppyseed . . ."

The gopher looked startled. "Those are rare seeds, ma'am. Very valuable. Just plain pumpkin is good enough for me."

Miss Barmy's eyes widened. Then slowly, greedily, she smiled, her furry cheeks bunching until her eyes were squeezed almost shut. "Father," she called, "sesame seeds, please."

"But, ma'am," the gopher protested, wagging his head, "it's too much—really it is."

Miss Barmy, still smiling, looked down over the table edge. "Count out *six* seeds," she said as Mr. B returned with a jar. "Our gopher friend"—she glanced at his name badge—"Gomer works hard. He deserves a big tip."

"Oh, ma'am!" cried the gopher. "You're too kind!"

"Perhaps I *am* too softhearted," said Miss Barmy. "I'm told it's my only flaw."

Gomer's beady eyes were joyful. "Now I can rent my tuxedo for the party!"

"What party?" Miss Barmy's voice cooled ever so slightly.

"The big party at Rodent City. There's a notice on page three. I'm—I'm sure you'll be invited, ma'am . . ." Gomer trailed off, flushing, and dived back into the gnawed hole in the wall. "Thanks awfully!" His voice floated out, dwindling, and he was gone.

Miss Barmy leaned back in her chaise longue, crossed her hind legs at the ankles, and rustled the *Rodent City Register* discontentedly. "I don't know why I wasn't invited," she muttered, reading the notice. "It's a reception to honor Professor Capybara—I know Professor Capybara. They'll have music, and dancing—I'm a *marvelous* dancer. Now that I'm a rodent, I really can't think why I wasn't included."

"But, Janie," began Mr. B, "didn't you tell me you and Cheswick tried to get *rid* of Professor Capybara?"

"That was *long* ago!" said Miss Barmy, waving a dismissive paw. "I can't understand why people insist on holding a grudge forever."

"It wasn't *that* long ago," Mr. B said hesitantly. "Just a few weeks, if I remem—"

"Chessie!" cried Miss Barmy, sitting up with a jerk as a weary black rat shuffled into the room, dragging a rucksack by the strap. "Let me see *everything* you got!"

It was one of their lucky nights, Ana thought as Mr. B put her back in the shoebox. Miss Barmy and Mrs. B had no interest in anything but the outfits Cheswick had brought, so Mr. B carried the girls to the kitchen, where he fed them bread and milk in bottle caps. Then he filled a cereal bowl with warm water, chipped a corner off a bar of soap, and laid out bits of rag for washcloths and towels.

"I'll come back in a while to take you to the attic." He looked at them mournfully. "If only you had been more lively, Addie might have played with you longer."

"If only," Ana said politely.

"Yeah," said Berit. "If only."

Mr. B sighed. "You could try harder. You could sing, or dance, or . . . do somersaults?"

Silence greeted this suggestion.

"If you were more entertaining, she'd let me take you out of the box more often. You can't *like* staying cooped up all day in a shoebox."

Merry shook her head. "But we *don't*—"

"—really mind it," Ana interrupted, as Berit clapped a hand over Merry's mouth and pretended to tickle her.

Mr. B ran his hand through his wispy hair. "Of course, we have plenty of other boxes, since we live right above my shoe shop. I can put you in a new one, if you're tired of the old. How about a nice leather pump from 1965? We have lovely colors, electric blue and alligator green and a really striking mustard . . ." He trailed off, looking apologetic. "It's not as nice as the dollhouse, but we couldn't ask Jane to share. I mean, even if she *is* a little furry, she's still our daughter, whereas you're just—"

There was an awkward pause.

"The Troubled Girls?" said Ana.

The old man looked embarrassed. "I'd better be getting back," he said hurriedly, and shambled off.

"Me, I'm getting more troubled every day," said Berit through her teeth. "I'd like to put that old fool in a shoebox and see how *he* likes it."

"Well, it's nearly over for tonight," said Ana. "Merry, let me undo your belt—you always get the shoelace in a knot. There, hop into the bath. And, Merry, don't *ever* let them know we can get out of the box by ourselves. They'd only shut us up in something harder to escape."

"Oh," said Merry, splashing in the bowl. "I forgot."

Bathed and fed, Ana and the girls watched through the half-open door as they waited to be put back in the box. Miss Barmy had gotten to the point of trying things on, but she seemed to be having trouble with the fit.

"I don't know what kind of measurements these dolls have," she snarled, jamming her hindquarters into the skirt of a silvery dress, "but they can't be healthy! Any rat that could fit into this evening gown would have to be *anorexic*."

"*You're* certainly healthy," said Cheswick, struggling to zip the back.

"I'm big-boned," Miss Barmy gasped, writhing as she wedged her ample chest into the silver bodice. She popped three buttons and split each sleeve as she shoved in her furry arms, but at last the dress was on—in a manner of speaking.

"Lovely!" she said, breathing with difficulty as she looked in the mirror. "But I might just need a seamstress. Where's that girl? Yes, that's right—bring me the oldest one. Surely *someone* must have taught her to use a needle and thread."

Ana sat on the attic windowsill and leaned her head against the dirty glass. She liked climbing up here, to look at the sky and watch the sun sink behind the trees. And tonight, with her fingers sore and her palms pricked from trying (and failing) to sew with a needle as long as her arm, she needed a glimpse of the outside world more than ever.

She wasn't afraid of heights. She had learned not to be, after more than three years of visiting the attic. For although she and the girls used to live in the dollhouse most days, now and then Mrs. B had banished them to the attic. It was supposed to have been a punishment.

Ana grinned and swung her legs over empty space. It had actually been more like a reward. Although the attic was cold in winter, hot in summer, and gritty with dust, the girls had a freedom in the attic that they never had in the pretty dollhouse. With hundreds of shoes in boxes, the girls had been able to pull out as many laces and knot as many ladders as were needed to climb to the highest shelves. And it had been important to explore the attic room to the very top, for it was full of wonderful clutter.

As far as Ana could tell, Mr. B had never thrown anything away in his life. All the old-fashioned shoes he had never been able to sell; all the hooks and tiny nails and worn-out tools he had no further use for; broken watches, eyeglasses with one earpiece gone, faded ribbons, bits of pencils, assorted books, and almost empty bottles of glue—all of that and more the girls had found in their explorations, and much of it was useful.

Small hooks supported ladders and safety nets. Lenses from broken glasses focused the sun's rays for extra warmth on cold winter days. Ribbons were woven together over bits of rag to make soft, warm comforters; and pencil stubs, though as thick and long as Ana's arm, were used to help the younger ones remember their letters and numbers. And many more bits of clutter, outdated or left over or nearly used up, could be found somewhere in the vast attic room.

And it *was* vast. To a girl only four inches high, the attic was the size of three football fields together. For Ana, the windowsill was as high above the floor as if she were dangling her legs from the top of a six-story building.

A movement outside the window caught her eye. She pressed her nose to the glass and looked down as a white puppy romped on the grass, barking madly at a butterfly.

There were people below, too. She could see a lady locking the candy store for the night, and a teenage boy polishing the windows of a funny-looking shop with a gray animal painted on its sign. Ana wished, and not for the first time, that one of them would look up and see her. But even if someone did, how could that person know that the tiny bit of movement at an attic window was really a girl, shrunken and imprisoned? And how could anyone possibly hear her thin small voice through the window, even if she screamed for help?

Even in the same room, people might not understand what they were hearing. Ana had found that out the hard way not long ago, when she had been awakened suddenly by loud voices and stomping feet and then the quick unpleasant swooping that meant the box they slept in was being picked up.

At first the girls had clung to one another, terrified. But when Ana had tried to push open the box lid and failed, and when they had heard the nasty-sweet voice of Mrs. B saying, "Of course you can look, officers, but there are no little girls here," the children had begun to call for help.

It had been useless, of course. Mrs. B had just talked louder, shaking the box for emphasis. Finally, one of the men had told her to take her box of squeaky toys and get out so they could search.

"Scream like that again," Mrs. B had hissed after the police were gone, "and I'll call the exterminator."

No, shouting had not worked. But the whole episode had given Ana a kind of hope that she hadn't felt for a long time. Someone, somewhere, was looking for them.

Ana's eyes came into sharp focus as she looked

directly below. Her favorite person was coming out early from the building next door, an old blue house that had been fixed up as a law office. He must be going somewhere else for dinner; usually at this time of night he was in his kitchen on the second story, scrambling some eggs or pouring a bowl of cereal for his supper.

She felt as if she had gotten to know him over the years, although only in glimpses—the back of his head as he ate his lonely meals, a bit of his elbow as he worked at his hobbies. But sometimes on his way out the front door he would look up at the sky, and she would see his sad, kind face.

Today he stopped to pet the white puppy, which ran to him as if expecting a treat, and then he bent over the garden at the side of his house. Ana loved his flowers; sometimes a sweet, elusive scent would rise on the warm summer air, all the way to the third floor.

She watched the man pick a bouquet, pleased that he had someplace to go tonight—and then she stopped smiling, for all at once she had an idea.

It was more than an idea. It was a plan.

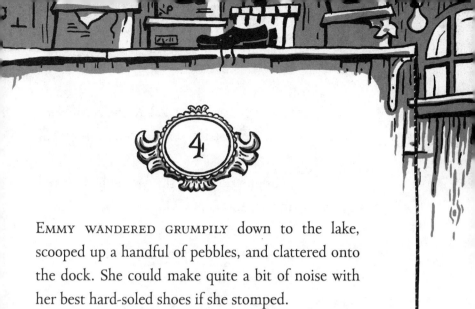

4

Emmy wandered grumpily down to the lake, scooped up a handful of pebbles, and clattered onto the dock. She could make quite a bit of noise with her best hard-soled shoes if she stomped.

She hated waiting around in her good clothes with nothing to do. If only she hadn't had to get cleaned up for their dinner guest, she would have had another hour in the tree fort with Joe. Now, because of the soccer tournament, they couldn't play for the rest of the weekend.

Thomas wasn't much of a substitute. He was only six and a half. And Ratty was in Rodent City, delivering their reply to Mrs. Bunjee's invitation.

Emmy shrugged, clicking the wet stones in her hand. That was just as well. She'd never make new friends this summer if she had a rodent hanging around.

The blue water of Grayson Lake slapped against the keel of the family sailboat, moored to the dock.

Emmy didn't know how to sail, but she wanted to learn. It was on her list for the summer, right after "Build a tree fort."

The lake, choppy now that the breeze had picked up, wasn't smooth enough for skipping rocks. Emmy tossed her pebbles into some rushes at the water's edge, and glanced back toward the empty driveway that curved at the side of the gray stone mansion. Wasn't Mr. Peebles ever going to show up? She was getting hungry.

"Blast that girl! She chased away my minnow! And you were going to make me a pie, Menna!"

The voice, low and oddly gravelly, came from somewhere near lake level. A sleek brown head poked out from the reeds and gave Emmy an intensely irritated look.

Emmy almost apologized—then clamped her lips shut and tried to look as if she hadn't understood. The last thing she needed was another rodent in her life.

"I'll make minnow pie tomorrow, Marshall," said a second muskrat, popping up. "Let's have a nice snack of cattails out at the point; it'll be healthier, anyway."

"I *hate* eating vegetarian," grumbled Marshall, but he pushed off after his wife and swam strongly toward the sandy point, the water streaming behind his head.

Emmy wandered out to the end of the dock, ignoring the muskrats. The waves slid in, great slabs of water that smacked the rocks to her left with a fine white spray.

"That's a pretty little sailboat." Menna's voice came faintly back from the cattails. "I do so like a white sail."

Emmy turned as a small boat glided into view around the point. Two figures with ponytails, silhouetted by the dipping sun, suddenly ducked their heads and shifted sides.

"They don't know how to handle it, though," said Marshall gruffly. "There, what did I tell you?"

"Oh dear," said Menna. "They'll be on the rocks in a minute."

Emmy, watching, could see that the girls were in trouble. They had been trying to change direction, but something had gone wrong. The sail was flopping uselessly, and they were being pushed by the wind straight at the rocky shore.

"They'll smash," said Marshall furiously, "and serves them right. Put your tiller to starboard, sailors!"

The girls didn't seem to understand the squeaking coming from the cattails.

"Put your tiller to starboard!" Emmy called, clear and strong.

"But that will put us on the rocks!" cried a panicked voice from the boat.

"No, you lubbers!" spluttered Marshall. "The wind's pushing you backward, so the rudder works backward, too!"

Emmy looked at Marshall, then away. "The wind's pushing you backward," she shouted through cupped hands. "So the rudder works backward, too." She grinned privately. They didn't have to know she was taking directions from a muskrat.

"Huh!" grunted Marshall, turning his furry face toward Emmy.

"Now what do I do?" cried the girl at the tiller. The sailboat was still moving toward the rocks, but it had begun to turn.

Emmy glanced at the muskrats.

"She needs to loosen that sheet a bit," Marshall muttered. "When she feels the wind take hold of the sail, she'll have to straighten out the tiller quick."

"Loosen that sheet a bit!" Emmy said confidently. "When you feel the wind take hold of the sail, straighten the tiller right away!"

There was a flurry of action on the sailboat. And then, hesitatingly, the white sail puffed lightly out, the boat began to move away from the shore, and the girls on the boat cheered in relief.

The one steering leaned toward her companion. "Isn't that the new kid?"

Sound carried surprisingly well across the water, Emmy realized as she recognized her former classmates. At the tiller was Kate, who always had a crowd around her at recess. Meg, near the mast, had sat in front of Emmy the whole year.

"Her name's Emmy," Meg murmured.

"She sure knows how to sail. Hey, Emmy!" Kate called. "Want to crew for me at the race tomorrow?"

As the sailboat angled past the dock, Meg clasped her hands. "Please?" she implored. "Then I won't have to. I'm a terrible sailor!"

Emmy was dumbstruck. This was what she had been waiting for! If she became friends with Kate and Meg, she'd be invited to parties and sleepovers and go horseback-riding and biking and swimming and—

"With an expert like you," Kate added persuasively, "I might even win!"

Emmy's dream crashed like water on rock. She was no expert. Without a certain muskrat along for the ride, she would be so hopeless that Kate would hate her forever.

The sailboat was slipping away from the dock. Emmy took in a breath. "I'm sorry," she said wretchedly. "I can't."

Peter Peebles came at last, but dinner was boring. The adults spoke about the sapphires that were on display at Grayson Lake Jewelers—"And why on earth they bothered to print that in the paper, I'll never understand," said Emmy's mother—and the spicy scent of the small flowers called "pinks" that Mr. Peebles had brought in a vase. Then, more interestingly, they talked about the Home for Troubled Girls, which Peter said he had investigated with the police after Jane Barmy had tried to send Emmy there. "It was only a shoe shop," he said. "Old Mr. B—I've known him for years, he's actually Jane's father—made this dollhouse he likes to call 'The Home for Troubled Girls,' and he thought it would be cute to put up a sign outside. It's nothing, really."

"I wonder if the police will catch up with Miss Barmy," mused Kathy Addison.

Emmy thought they probably wouldn't, unless the police had a description of Miss Barmy that included fur and a long tail.

"It's strange to think," said Emmy's father, "that Jane Barmy grew up in the caretaker's cottage on this estate. Didn't you know her, Peter?"

"She was a friend," said Peter, a little grimly. "That's why I trusted her. We used to go sailing together—Jane and Cheswick and Priscilla—" He stopped abruptly.

Emmy fidgeted in her seat and twisted a strand of hair around her finger.

Mrs. Benson changed the subject smoothly. "And do you still sail, Peter? Emmy wants to learn someday, don't you, dear?"

Emmy nodded.

Mr. Peebles smiled at her, the strained look leaving his face. "There's a youth race tomorrow, and I'll be on the signal boat. I invited my cousin's oldest boy to come along, but he's busy with a soccer tournament."

Emmy sat up alertly.

"Would you be interested, Emmy? I could explain the race, and maybe you'll see some kids you know."

"What a good idea!" said Emmy's father.

"Make sure you wear a life jacket," said Emmy's mother.

There was a scurrying sort of noise, and something furry brushed against Emmy's ankle beneath the table. She suppressed a shriek and lifted a corner of the tablecloth.

"I'm coming, too," said Raston Rat, grinning up at her. "I've always wanted to be a pirate."

Emmy swirled her fork in the raspberry sauce on her plate. It was hard to have much of an appetite when the warm, furry body of a rat was draped across her foot and a slender tail kept tickling her ankles.

"Psst!"

Emmy sighed inwardly, dropped her napkin, and ducked beneath the tablecloth. "What is it *now*?" she whispered, under cover of the clinking of silverware and the hum of grown-up conversation, which had gone back to boring.

"Does G.I. Joe have a pirate hat?" the Rat asked.

"I doubt it," Emmy said coldly. "Now, will you please stop bothering me? I can't keep on dropping things—they'll get suspicious."

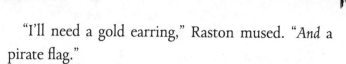

"I'll need a gold earring," Raston mused. "*And* a pirate flag."

Emmy sat rigidly upright. If she ignored him, maybe he would go away . . . A moment later, she nearly yelped aloud.

"Are you all right, Emmy?" asked her father with concern.

Emmy wanted to tell him the truth—that a rat had just run up her leg—but she gave up the idea as too complicated to explain.

"I'm fine," she said. "Really." As the adults began to talk again, she glowered down at the rodent.

"Can you draw me a skull and crossbones?" Raston begged.

At last the adults pushed back their chairs. At a nod from her mother, Emmy left the room to get Mr. Peebles's coat. But, as was usual with grown-ups, they couldn't seem to stop talking. Emmy sat on a bench against the wall and waited with her eyes half closed, listening to the voices in the next room.

"I heard it from the detective. She did the same thing over and over again in different states. She'd get a position as a nanny in a wealthy household, and get some kind of influence over the parents."

"I still don't understand how she did that with us," said Kathy Addison, very low, as they moved into the hall.

"Some kind of drug, maybe; but not one we're familiar with. Anyway, in the end the story was always the same. The children would be sent off to some place that sounded all right—but they would never be heard from again."

Emmy sat very still. No one seemed to notice her on the bench.

"Their parents must have been frantic, once the drug wore off," Emmy's father said.

"They may have been," said Peter Peebles quietly. "But they're all dead now. And, one way or another, Miss Barmy ended up with a great deal of their money."

Emmy stood up and moved from the shadows against the wall. "What were their names?" she asked, holding out Mr. Peebles's coat.

The grown-ups looked at her in sudden silence. "Whose names?" asked Peter Peebles at last.

"The little girls. What were their names?"

Mr. Peebles took a long time getting on his coat. "Strangely enough, they *were* all girls." The lawyer

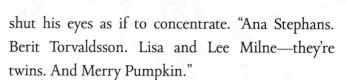

shut his eyes as if to concentrate. "Ana Stephans. Berit Torvaldsson. Lisa and Lee Milne—they're twins. And Merry Pumpkin."

"Merry *Pumpkin*?"

"Her last name was really Pumke, but she was only four, and apparently everyone called her Pumpkin . . ."

Jim Addison cleared his throat. "Doesn't *anyone* have an idea where they are now?"

"No," said Peter Peebles.

"No," said Emmy firmly the next morning, pulling her swimsuit out of a drawer. "I know you want to be a pirate, but you can't come with me."

Raston, who had found a plastic cutlass, tied a red kerchief around his head, and put on a black eye-patch with a rubber band, was aghast. "But that's not *fair!*" he cried.

"Listen, Ratty, I can't. I won't be able to hide you on the boat."

The Rat flipped up his eyepatch to glare at her. "Why not? Just put me in a pocket, like you always do."

Emmy held up her bathing suit. "Look. Do you see any pockets?"

The Rat pursed his furred lips. "So wear a sweat-shirt over it or something."

"They get clammy when they're wet. All I've got is a windbreaker, and it's too thin to disguise you . . . Here, leave my life jacket alone and listen to me. Why don't you go back to Rodent City and spend time with Sissy?"

"Maybe tomorrow," said the Rat, jumping on the life jacket that Maggie had brought up that morning. "Are you sure you need all this padding? This jacket could float an elk."

Emmy sighed and went into her bathroom to put on her suit. Then she pulled her hair back and snapped an elastic band around it, making a ponytail just like Kate and Meg had worn the evening before. "Why don't you play in the tree fort?" she called through the half-open door. "You and Sissy could be pirates together . . ."

The Rat's reply was indistinct. Emmy followed his voice into the playroom, where he was sniffing at a pile of Barbie clothes. "Who's been in here?" he asked. "There's a scent I can't place."

Emmy shrugged. "No one, as far as I know. So—why don't you play with your sister?"

"She's busy today. They're training her as a messenger rat."

"Really?" Emmy was pleased. Cecilia, Raston's twin, had been caged as long as he had, but while the Rat had been in a classroom where he had learned science, math, history, and more, Sissy had been stuck in a back room at the Antique Rat.

At first glance, the Antique Rat had seemed to be just an old furniture store with an apartment on the upper story. But the back room had once held cage upon cage of rodents, each with its own special power, and each one extremely valuable. Cheswick Vole (formerly an assistant to the famous Professor of Rodentology, Dr. Maxwell Capybara) had shrunk the professor, stolen the rats, and used them to try to get rich. And now that Cheswick had turned into a rat himself and run away with Miss Barmy, Professor Capybara ran the shop and lived in the apartment above it.

The professor was a brilliant rodentologist, and since he was full-sized again, he had gone back to his research. But even he couldn't change the years Sissy had spent in a cage, with no opportunity to learn much of anything.

"I didn't know Sissy could read and write," said Emmy.

Raston straightened. "She can't," he admitted. "But she can repeat short messages, and . . . well, she deserves a chance just like anybody else, don't you think?"

"Of course," Emmy said.

"It's not her fault that she's uneducated. It's not her fault that she hasn't had my advantages. She'd *like* to be smooth and sophisticated, like me . . ."

Emmy rolled her eyes.

"I have an idea! Take me sailing! I'll tell her about it and expand her horizons!"

"You're not coming," Emmy said flatly, and went to brush her teeth. By the time she had clattered downstairs for breakfast, put on sunscreen, found her sandals, and run back up to get the life jacket she'd forgotten, the Rat had disappeared.

Emmy shrugged. So maybe he'd taken her advice; or maybe he was hiding somewhere, sulking. Either way, she had one less rodent to worry about.

To Emmy's surprise, Thomas was sitting on the back step.

"My mom said I could come here if I promised not

to go up in the tree fort alone." He lifted a hopeful face. "Would you play pirates with me?"

Emmy shook her head with regret, wishing she didn't have to go with Mr. Peebles. It would be bad enough to watch the other girls having fun sailing— but now that she had disappointed both Ratty and Thomas, she would feel guilty the whole time.

Thomas trailed after her and sat on the wooden dock, swinging his pudgy legs. Emmy explained about the race, and was relieved to see that Thomas didn't seem to mind too much.

"This isn't as boring as Joe's soccer game," he said, peering into the water beneath the dock. "There are minnows down there, and snails, and everything! I'll just play here till you come back."

"Can you swim?"

"I'm in Guppies," Thomas said proudly. "Last week I ducked my head underwater before anyone else in the class."

Emmy sighed. Guppies was only the second class after Tadpoles, and four classes below Dolphins, which she had just passed. There was no way she could leave Thomas to play by the lakeshore with a clear conscience.

Emmy trudged across the lawn to her back door. "Mrs. Brecksniff? Oh, Maggie. Would you please tell Mrs. Brecksniff that Joe's little brother is here playing on the dock? I'm leaving when Mr. Peebles comes, so could someone watch him?"

A blue-and-white boat was motoring up past the point. Emmy trotted back to the shore where she had left her life jacket and stopped to watch Thomas as he squatted by the rushes, collecting pebbles and snails. He looked up happily. "Did you know that every time you throw a rock in the water the minnows all swim away? And then they come back, and you can do it all over again?"

"There goes my minnow pie for the second day in a row!" roared a hoarse voice, and a blunt, furry face popped out from between the cattails and snarled.

"Now, Marshall," came a placating voice from the rushes, "he's just a child."

"He's old enough to learn some manners!" bellowed Marshall, swimming at Thomas with his whiskers bristling.

Everything seemed to happen at once. Thomas, delighted to find more rodents that he could understand, surged toward the muskrat. At the dock's end,

Peter Peebles was tying his boat to the cleats. And out of the corner of her eye, Emmy could see the sturdy figure of Mrs. Brecksniff hurrying toward them.

Emmy grabbed Thomas by the collar and hauled him back onto the lawn. "Thank you, Mrs. Brecksniff!" she called, giving Thomas a shove in the right direction. She snatched up her life jacket and threw it on, struggling with the buckles. It seemed strangely lopsided, but she was in too big a hurry to adjust it. She sprinted to the end of the dock, jumped in the boat, and helped Mr. Peebles cast off. She waved at Thomas and Mrs. Brecksniff as the boat accelerated, and fell back in her seat with a gusty sigh. She had managed pretty well, considering everything.

There was a squirming sensation in the front of her life jacket. Startled, Emmy looked down. A familiar gray head poked out from the armpit hole, and grinned.

"See? I told you this life jacket didn't need all that padding."

Emmy suppressed the urge to throw the Rat overboard and be done with it. "I suppose you think you're clever," she said through gritted teeth.

"Well, yes, actually." Raston turned back a flap of the life jacket's outer covering to display neatly snipped stitches and a gnawed-out section of the buoyant padding. "See? I fit right inside. And if you ever want to take another rat with you—say, Sissy— I can just chew out a spot on the other side."

"And what if I fall in the lake?" Emmy said under cover of the boat's motor. "With a life jacket full of holes?"

"Oh, *that*," said the Rat, waving a dismissive paw. "If worse comes to worst, you can always swim. And there's certainly enough left to float Sissy and me."

"Oh well, if you and Sissy would be all right," Emmy said gloomily, staring out at the lake whizzing by.

It was true that the Rat had come up with the perfect camouflage. And Mr. Peebles was too busy driving the boat to notice anything happening behind his back. But as they approached the yacht club, and Emmy saw the bright sails gliding smoothly past, she had a feeling of doom. It was a hopeless sort of feeling, as if everything that had already gone wrong would just keep on getting worse, no matter what she did.

As it turned out, she was right.

When Mr. Peebles tried to show her how to put up the signal flags, she ended up losing one overboard in the breeze.

She blew the whistle at the wrong moment, and the whole fleet got confused.

And when Kate and Meg came sailing past, they were so startled to see her that they bumped into another boat and had to turn three circles as a penalty. The breeze carried their comments over the water. "She could have crewed for me," Kate said, and Meg added, "It's not like she's really *needed* on the signal boat."

To top it all off, Emmy was so distracted by Ratty (who kept saying "Arrr, me hearties," and popping out to feel the breeze in his whiskers) that she missed half of Peter Peebles's explanations; and then the other half didn't make any sense.

But the worst moment came at the race's finish, when Ratty lost his head completely and leaped from his hiding place in her life jacket to the glossy white deck.

"Put your backs into it, maties!" he cried, waving his cutlass as the boats passed the final buoy. "Shiver me timbers! Yo ho ho and a bottle of ru—"

His voice cut off suddenly as the boat rocked on a wave. Emmy, who had already caught up her towel to muffle him, watched as if in slow motion as the Rat lost his balance and fell backward over the gunwale, his mouth open in a soundless shriek.

There was a very small splash. Peter Peebles, absorbed in watching the end of the race, hadn't noticed. The racers had eyes for nothing but the goal ahead. No one seemed to have seen the Rat go overboard—no one but Emmy.

Emmy leaned over the gunwale. The Rat, his paws thrashing, looked up at her with panic in his eyes. He tried to speak, got a mouthful of water, and went under.

Emmy sighed. Bleakly, resigned to her fate, she got up on the deck, leaned past the balance point with a convincing sort of lurch, and dropped in. She realized, one moment too late, that she was still holding her towel.

The water was cold, with the chill of a very large lake that iced over every winter and never really warmed up until August, and Emmy sneezed violently as she bobbed to the surface. She grabbed for the Rat and stuffed him in her life vest without any particular tenderness. She swam around to the ladder at the boat's stern and climbed up, dripping and miserable, to meet the white and frightened face of Peter Peebles and the scornful glance of Kate, who was crossing the finish line in last place.

Emmy sneezed all the way to the yacht-club restroom. She was just making the discovery that a fistful of paper and a hand blower were a poor substitute for a dry towel when Meg came through the swinging door.

She looked at Emmy curiously. "Why did you fall in?"

Emmy rubbed her goose-pimpled arms. "My towel," she said vaguely, waving at the soggy mass of terry cloth on the counter.

"You went in after a *towel*? Why didn't you just use the boathook?"

"Because I was stupid," Emmy said bitterly. She wished she could disappear and be done with it, but no—she was going to have to answer questions. She sneezed again.

Meg pulled a duffel bag from a locker. "I always pack extra dry things. Most sailors do."

"I'm not much of a sailor," Emmy confessed.

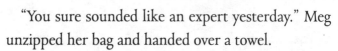

"You sure sounded like an expert yesterday." Meg unzipped her bag and handed over a towel.

Emmy received it gratefully. "Um—I heard something once from a real expert about what to do if a boat went backward, and it just happened to work."

"Lucky for us. Listen, here's a dry set of clothes—we're about the same size." She hesitated. "I could pick them up after I help Kate put the sails away and tidy up the boat."

"Thanks!" Emmy said, startled.

"That's okay. I bike right past your street on the way home." Meg grinned, a little shyly. "Besides, I've always wanted to see the inside of a castle."

Emmy waved good-bye to Peter Peebles as the blue-and-white boat roared away from her dock.

All right—this was her chance. She was about to make a normal, regular friend, only this time no rodents were going to interfere.

"Can I get out of the life jacket *now*?" Raston pleaded. "I'm wet, and cold—"

"And whose fault is that?" Emmy asked severely as she walked into the boathouse, a stone building at the water's edge that they used for storage. She hung the jacket on a hook, found a dry rag for the sodden Rat, and turned as Thomas trotted in.

"Oh, good, you're back," he said, panting. "Mrs. Brecksniff was no fun. She made me wash my snails off in the sink and then wait while she scrubbed the floor. *Now* can we go up in the tree fort?"

"Cabin boy," Emmy commanded, "come to attention when your captain is speaking."

Thomas straightened instantly, two fingers to his forehead in a salute.

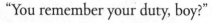

"You remember your duty, boy?"

"Yes, sir! To obey orders, sir!"

Emmy considered telling him to address her as "ma'am," but she let it pass. "All right. This pirate"— here she indicated the damp Rat—"was—um— forced to walk the plank. I rescued him from a watery death—"

"From sharks, too!" put in the Rat. "And a giant squid!"

"—from a watery death," repeated Emmy sternly, "and now he's giving up the pirate life. Take him to Rodent City, where Mrs. Bunjee can dry him off and put him to bed with a cup of hot cocoa."

"Hot cocoa," said the Rat dreamily, shutting his eyes. "Arrr."

"Rodent City, captain?" Thomas looked puzzled. "Where's that?"

Of course Thomas didn't know where Rodent City was, Emmy realized. He had never been bitten a second time by Raston, had never shrunk to rat size; so he'd never gone through the hole in the art-gallery steps to the lively, colorful, bustling city beneath.

"Just bring him to the steps in front of the art gallery on Main Street, and he'll take it from there.

And, Thomas, I'm trusting you to keep him hidden the whole way. This is a secret mission."

"Aye-aye, captain!" said Thomas, his round face beaming. "Do I report back here when I'm done?"

"No." Emmy made the syllable emphatic—she didn't want to be playing with a little kid when Meg came over. "But we can meet at the ball fields. Where the natives play a game called soccer."

"Yes, sir." Thomas sighed. "*Then* can I play in the tree fort—I mean the ship?"

Emmy clapped a captainly hand on Thomas's shoulder. "Just do your duty, cabin boy, and you'll soon be back on the good ship G.F."

Emmy stood in front of the mirror and redid her ponytail. She had already sent Meg's clothes down with Maggie to be laundered; now she had to decide which of her new tops looked the coolest.

Oh, what did it matter? She flung herself out of her blue-tiled bathroom and went to the window in the turret. If she looked closely, she could see where Chippy had clipped a corner of the screen free from its frame.

Chippy was Mrs. Bunjee's son, and the most

inventive chipmunk Emmy knew. He and his brother, Buck, had created a catapult that threw cockleburs—it worked very well on cats, as Emmy knew from experience—and Chippy loved to tinker with the pulleys and levers and wiring of Rodent City. He sometimes came to play on her electric train, and occasionally brought a friend—so she wasn't bothered that the Rat had picked up an unfamiliar scent. He didn't know how *everyone* in Rodent City smelled.

Still, Emmy decided, if she wanted fewer rodents in her life, she should probably close her window more often.

She gazed through the screen. High in the trees, bits of the fort showed between leafy branches. Would Meg like to play in the tree fort? Or would she be the kind who was afraid of heights?

Oh well, there was plenty to do in the playroom. Emmy wandered over to the door that connected her bedroom to the room stuffed with toys. Let's see, what would Meg like? A board game? The electric train? Maybe she liked to play Barbies. If she did, Emmy had a pile of clothes . . .

The clothes were moving. Emmy leaned forward intently. Yes, there was something behind the pile of doll clothes, rummaging about and muttering. Emmy held very still. The words faded in and out, like a radio on a weak frequency.

". . . Accessories, she said . . . Gold beads? . . . A purple purse? . . . Something shiny . . ."

Emmy edged closer, sock-footed, making no sound.

". . . maybe that tiara . . . It might fit between her ears . . ."

Emmy lowered herself quietly to her knees. Behind the mound of doll clothes, a black rat was busy cramming a rucksack full.

"I wish she'd just come herself, but no," grumbled the rat to himself. "I don't know what she wants." He looked at the mountain of clothes with an air of desperation, grabbed a last armful at random (Emmy recognized a balaclava, a pair of bright-pink tights, and a tutu), and wedged it all in the rucksack.

"What do you think you're doing?" Emmy demanded.

The black rat jumped four inches and whirled.

"No offense or anything," said Emmy coldly, "but you do realize that if you take that sack out of this room, you're stealing?"

The rat's paws, which had gone up in a defensive

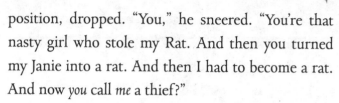

position, dropped. "You," he sneered. "You're that nasty girl who stole my Rat. And then you turned my Janie into a rat. And then I had to become a rat. And now *you* call *me* a thief?"

"Only because you are one, Cheswick Vole," said Emmy, recognizing his glossy black coat. "You stole the Rat in the first place—from his own nest, and then from Professor Capybara—remember?"

The black rat shuffled his hind paws and blinked rapidly.

"Besides," Emmy said with disdain, "I didn't turn Miss Barmy into a rat. Ratty bit her because she was choking his sister—and you *asked* to become a rat, to be like Miss Barmy. Though why," she added as an afterthought, "anyone in his right mind—"

"You *never* understood her," Cheswick said passionately. "She had a difficult childhood."

"I know how that feels," said Emmy darkly.

"She's a victim. She didn't get her rights. This house should have been hers when old William died . . . so this room and these doll clothes really all belong to *her*."

Emmy shrugged. "Sorry, but they don't. Get over it." She glanced at the rucksack. "Dump that out, and then go. I'm keeping my window closed from now on."

Cheswick lifted a scornful lip. "That isn't the only way into your house, you know."

Emmy suppressed a shudder. "Why would you want to come back, anyway? Those clothes will never fit Miss Barmy."

Cheswick sniffed. "Of course they will. With a little ripping and a little sewing, my darling Barmsie will outshine them all."

Emmy tried to envision Miss Barmy, industrious with a needle and thread, and failed. Was *Cheswick* going to sew for her? And, more important, where was Miss Barmy now?

"She'll show them," Cheswick gloated. "She's got big plans, clever plans. She's going to—" He glanced over his shoulder, swiveling his dark head.

Emmy followed his gaze automatically, whereupon Cheswick snatched up the bulging rucksack and darted to a shadowy corner.

Exasperated, Emmy scrambled to her feet. She had some idea of trapping him and putting him in a box until he told her what he knew, but the rat skittered away, shoved the rucksack into a gnawed hole in the baseboard, and backed inside, his beady eyes glowing in the darkness. "You'll regret crossing Jane Barmy—you and Professor Capybara and Mrs. Bunjee and all the rest."

Emmy listened with dismay. "Leave them alone!"

"You'll never know what we're doing until it's too late . . ." The yellow eyes blinked into darkness.

Emmy dropped to her hands and knees. "Stay away," she yelled into the shadowy hole, "or I'll call the exterminator!"

There was a mocking echo of a ratty laugh, and a sound of pattering feet fading away into the distance. Emmy smacked the wall in her frustration. "You dirty rat!"

There was a shuffling sound on the floor behind her. Emmy jumped.

"Um," said Meg, "is this a bad time to pick up the clothes?"

Emmy slumped on the window seat, her forehead pressed against the glass. Of course Meg hadn't stayed. She'd made some excuse to leave right away, and Emmy didn't blame her. Who would want to be friends with someone who shouted at the wall?

Once again, everything was wrecked because of a

rat. Emmy gazed hopelessly at squirrels in the oak trees, chipmunks on the ground, at all the small furry forms darting here and there in the underbrush; and as she turned her head to the lake, she knew that there, among the rushes, a couple of muskrats were probably eating minnow pie.

There was no way to escape them. Rodents were *everywhere*. Worse yet, according to Cheswick, there were lots of ways they could get into her house.

Emmy rubbed her hand, sore from hitting the wall, and brooded. It wasn't so much that she missed a few Barbie clothes; it was the idea that Cheswick had come into her room and stolen them. What would he take next, she wondered—her stuffed animals? Her paints? And what exactly were he and Miss Barmy planning?

Something nasty, that was certain. The Bunjee family and Professor Capybara had to be warned.

Emmy's thoughts were interrupted by a snuffling sound coming from outside the window. Resignedly, she watched as two small paws appeared over the windowsill's edge, and then a familiar gray head. "You're supposed to be in bed with a cup of hot cocoa, Ratty."

"It's only me," gasped an apologetic voice, and

75

Raston's twin crawled through the flap in the screen, stood up, and adjusted the name badge on her smart blue blazer. "I'm sorry, were you expecting Rasty?"

"Not at all," Emmy said politely, thinking that it was easy to mix up the two rats. Cecilia looked exactly like her brother except for the triangular patch of white fur behind her right ear. On him, it was behind the left.

The gray rodent cleared her throat, clasped her paws together over her jacket, and fixed her gaze somewhere past Emmy's head. "A message for you," she began in a high singsong, "from the Speedy Rodent Messenger Service. Testing. Testing. Testing."

There was a pause. "Is that all?" asked Emmy.

"It's just a test," said Sissy, looking worried. "Should there be more?"

"No, no, that's fine," Emmy said quickly.

"I could quote the Messenger Service Slogan," Sissy offered. She twisted her paws together and shut her eyes. "If for a message you are needy, then call us anytime— No, that's not it." She flushed beneath her fur and tried again. "If you want a rodent speedy, just call us because we're greedy— No, that's not it, either." She hung her head.

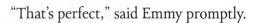

"That's perfect," said Emmy promptly.

"No, no—I got it all wrong—"

"But you hadn't practiced the slogan. You said the real message perfectly."

"I did, didn't I?" Sissy regained a little confidence. "And I tried to speak clearly, and—and distinctly—"

"I have *never* heard a rat speak so clearly and distinctly," Emmy said with great firmness. "Never in my life. Now, why don't you sit down and tell me about yourself. What made you want to be a messenger?"

Emmy smiled encouragingly at Cecilia. She knew what Raston's sister could do—that is, reverse the effects of her brother's bites. But she didn't know very much about Sissy herself, and the rat did look tired.

Cecilia shook her head. "I can't sit down on the job. I have to get right back for the next message. You see," she added humbly, "I don't have much of an education, so I have to work twice as hard as the other rats."

"But," said Emmy, thinking fast, "I want to send a message back with you."

Cecilia's eyes opened wide. "You do?" Her voice scaled up with joy.

"Only I need some time to think of how I want to say it. And then you'll need time to practice it. So sit down."

Emmy filled a cup with water, and looked in a drawer for her stash of peanut-butter cups. They were Raston's favorite, and she always kept a few around.

"Here you go." She unwrapped the candy, set the water on the windowsill, and thought about her message. In the meantime, Sissy, after one cautious bite, settled down to an ecstatic munching.

"Okay," Emmy said as Cecilia licked up the last crumbs. "This message goes to Mrs. Bunjee, of Rodent City. Tell her, 'Do not—repeat, do *not*—trust Miss Barmy or Cheswick Vole. More information later.'"

Sissy clapped her somewhat chocolaty paws. "Oh, good, it goes to Rodent City! I'm not sure of all the field addresses yet," she added confidentially. "There are *so* many tunnels outside." She dipped her paws in the cup of water and rubbed hard. "My, what a wonderful treat. All right, now I'll repeat back to you."

Emmy had a sudden thought. "Wait—can you carry a peanut-butter cup to Raston? And why don't I just write a note for you to deliver?"

Sissy shook her head. "I'll carry the candy, but I'm not allowed to carry dispatches."

"Really? It seems like it would be easier—"

"'A messenger must be able to transmit the message,'" Sissy quoted stiffly. "'If the recipient is unable to read for any reason, the messenger must be able, upon request, to open and read aloud the message. Rodent messengers who have not passed their reading test will not be certified to carry dispatches.'"

Emmy shrugged, tucked a peanut-butter cup into Sissy's satchel, and went over the message with Cecilia until the rat had it word-perfect. With a quick salute, the small gray body slipped over the windowsill and down the latticed vines.

Emmy's smile faded. She yanked the window down tight and pulled the shade. Sissy was a nice little rat, but Emmy had had enough of rodents. Besides, she had to go warn the professor. He could help her figure out how to stop Miss Barmy and Cheswick—whatever they might be planning.

6

EMMY WAS CUTTING ACROSS the schoolyard when she heard the jackhammer, a spurting percussion that rose above the cheers from the soccer field. She glanced across the playground to the shops that lined Main Street on the other side, and saw yellow tape and orange cones amid a cloud of dust in front of the art gallery.

She paused for a single heartbeat and then began to run.

"Emmy! Wait up!"

A small stocky boy was jogging toward her. Emmy slowed to a walk, but she couldn't bear to stop entirely—she had to find out what was happening to Rodent City. She thought anxiously of Mrs. Bunjee's cozy loft being broken up by the deafening violence of a jackhammer, and her pace quickened.

"Captain, sir!" Puffing, Thomas tugged at her elbow. "Permission to report?"

"Permission granted," said Emmy, her eyes on the

art-gallery steps. The workman wasn't as close to the steps as she had thought—but he was near enough. The noise and vibration must be scaring all the residents of Rodent City to death.

"I couldn't get the pirate into the city," said Thomas, panting at her side. "The crack in the steps was all blocked off."

"The—pirate?"

"Ratty."

"Oh, right." Emmy stopped at the street and looked across. The yellow tape went to the art-gallery steps, but the workman was breaking up the sidewalk in front of the jewelry shop next door. She relaxed. "So where did you take him, then?"

"My house." Thomas spoke directly into her ear, cupping his hands around his mouth. "My parents are at Joe's game, so it's safe."

"Let's get away from here." Emmy grabbed his hand, and they ran across the street and through the alley, past jackhammer dust and garbage cans smelling of sour milk and rotting fruit, until they emerged into light again. They were in the quiet backstreets, with a grassy triangle in the center and interesting shops on all three sides.

"Hey, cool!" Thomas said. "My ears are still ringing!"

Emmy glanced past the bakery, the tattoo parlor, the candy store, to the grand blue house on the corner and its sign: "Peter Peebles, Attorney at Law." She winced, wishing she could forget her humiliating plunge off his boat.

But it was the narrow building next door to the Peebles place that worried her most. Weeks ago, Emmy had discovered that the odd people who lived above the ground-floor shoe shop were actually Miss Barmy's parents. And though Mr. Peebles had said the "Home for Troubled Girls" sign was a joke, it was toward this building that Miss Barmy and Cheswick had run when they had been turned into rats.

Emmy shuddered lightly and turned away, steering Thomas toward a shop of vine-covered brick with a painted sign swinging over the doorway. "So Raston is at your house—alone?"

Thomas looked up at the sign. "The Ant—" he began, sounding out the tall spidery letters beneath the painted gray rat.

"The Antique Rat," Emmy finished, impatient. "So what did you do with Ratty?"

Thomas looked at her calmly. "I made him chocolate milk—I'm not allowed to use the stove for hot cocoa—and turned on the TV. Then I came to meet you for my next mission." He paused, waiting.

"Emmy!" cried a big, jovial, white-bearded man, throwing open the door with a jangling of bells. "And you've brought a friend—what a very pleasant surprise!"

Professor Capybara leaned back in his swivel chair, placed his fingertips together, and smiled kindly over his glasses. "But, my dear Emmy, I don't think any of this needs to worry you. After all, how much harm can Miss Barmy do now? She's only a rat."

"Well, yes," said Emmy. "But she's a very *mean* rat."

"Still, I can't see that there's anything to be done. You've heard no real plans, I take it? Just some rambling talk of revenge." The professor's face took on an austere expression. "Cheswick Vole was never very reliable, not even when he was my laboratory assistant back in Schenectady."

"But—"

"What do you want me to do? I have my research—I can't just run about after rodents, trying to catch them doing something wrong. It's beneath *anyone's* dignity."

Emmy gazed around the room, wishing she could put her feelings into words. The afternoon sun streamed in through polished windows, highlighting the tables and chairs, each with its carved or painted decoration of rats, which gave the store its name. "But don't you think," she said slowly, "that if someone says she wants to harm you, you should pay attention?"

"Certainly, certainly." The professor's glance strayed to the other end of the shop, where the antiques had been moved to one side to make room for a laboratory. "But just now, I'd like to check on an experiment, if you don't mind. I'm still trying to find a cure for the Snoozer virus." He pushed back his chair. "If only I hadn't taken that trip to Palm Desert! The Bushy-Tailed Snoozer Rats were everywhere, and I didn't take proper precautions . . ."

Emmy sighed inwardly, and wandered after him to the cluttered counter where a bubbling retort competed for space with rows of vials, trays of glass slides, and innumerable pieces of paper covered with calculations and handwritten notes.

Over to one side was an odd-looking microscope that Emmy had used before. It was Professor Capybara's own invention, and although it was no good at showing ordinary things like red blood cells and bacteria, it was surprisingly good at showing other things.

"Brian!" called the professor as he hunched over a petri dish. "He was supposed to check on this regularly," he muttered. "Where did the boy go?"

"Here, Professor!" A tall, slightly stooped teenage boy emerged from the back room with Thomas in tow. "I was just showing Thomas the little apartments you fixed up for the rodents that wanted to stay."

"But you were supposed to check this every fifteen minutes," said the professor irritably.

"I am. The next check is due in"—Brian checked his watch—"two minutes seven seconds. Try not to get upset, Professor—you know it puts you right to sleep. The Snoozer virus, you know."

"Yes, yes, my boy." Professor Capybara pulled at his white beard. "I'm sorry I snapped at you. I'm just a little nervous about something . . ."

Emmy stopped listening as Thomas appeared at her elbow.

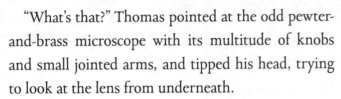

"What's that?" Thomas pointed at the odd pewter-and-brass microscope with its multitude of knobs and small jointed arms, and tipped his head, trying to look at the lens from underneath.

"It's called a charascope."

"What does it do?"

"You can see for yourself." Emmy pulled out a slide labeled "Barmy," and slid it under the charascope. It was old, and the blood had dried; instead of a moving, living sample, with the tumble of changing bright and dark shapes that Emmy remembered, this was like a snapshot. But Emmy could still see the dark-green ball made of massed wormlike shapes that had so appalled her before.

"What's that?" Thomas looked through the eyepiece. "It looks nasty."

"That's a drop of Miss Barmy's blood, from about a month ago. What you're seeing is probably hatred, with some fear mixed in."

"Hatred?" Thomas raised round blue eyes to Emmy's. "You can't see hatred through a microscope."

"You can through a charascope. Here, I'll show you. Give me your finger."

Thomas held out his finger trustingly. Emmy dipped it in rubbing alcohol and poked the fleshy pad of his forefinger with a lancet, squeezing out one bright-red drop.

"You're pretty brave for six and a half." She smeared the blood on a glass slide, replaced Miss Barmy's sample with Thomas's, and looked through the eyepiece. Yes, it was just like before—small glowing shapes of every color, swimming and twirling in a kind of bright liquid dance. She moved aside so Thomas could see.

"Wow!" he breathed. "This doesn't look like the other one at all!"

"I doubt you have much hatred in your blood. The shapes you see are probably more like— Here, just a minute." Emmy took up a colored chart lying nearby and read down the list. "Love, happiness, curiosity, wonder, courage, hope—"

"Hey! One just split into two!"

"Yes, they multiply if you let them—"

"And two different ones just stuck together, and now there's a whole new shape! How come?"

"It's got something to do with character," said Emmy. "I don't know how it works; ask the

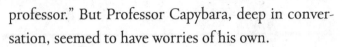

professor." But Professor Capybara, deep in conversation, seemed to have worries of his own.

"I'm not nervous about making a speech," he said. "I'm used to that. But there's a dance afterward, and I'm supposed to lead with Mrs. Bunjee . . ." He looked at Brian helplessly.

Brian grinned. "What's so bad about dancing with chipmunks? They're pretty light on their feet." He arranged a petri dish, an eyedropper, and a small box of colored paper on the counter.

The professor looked at him sideways. "Just because you don't have to go—"

"Someone has to mind the experiments," said Brian cheerfully, picking up the eyedropper.

Emmy's shoulders slumped. She'd forgotten all about the party tonight. What did it matter if she shut her window or stopped up holes to keep out rodents? She was going to have to go underground tonight with hundreds of them. She would be forced to listen to the Swinging Gerbils, too, which didn't exactly help.

"What's wrong?" asked the professor, glancing at her. "Don't you want to go?"

"That's not it," Emmy said quickly. The party was

in the professor's honor, after all. "But I have to give some excuse to my parents, or they'll wonder where I am."

"Not a problem—not a problem at all!" The professor was beaming. "I'll just tell your parents that you're invited to a supper party, and that Brian will pick you up in the truck and bring you back again . . ." He trailed off, looking at Thomas. "Are you coming to Rodent City, too?" he asked kindly.

"Um—he wasn't invited to the party," Emmy said hesitantly. "I don't think Mrs. Bunjee knows him."

"That's all right," said Brian. "He can stay here with me; I could use a helper. Do you like pizza, Thomas?"

Professor Capybara walked back to the soccer fields with Emmy and Thomas to ask Mr. and Mrs. Benson's permission. On the way, they stopped to look at the sidewalk, where the workman was taking a break. Behind him, the sign in the jewelry store window read "Closed During Construction," and the window blinds were shuttered.

"What's going in under the sidewalk?" asked the professor genially.

The workman looked up from his sandwich, took off his ear protectors, and pulled a small foam plug from his left ear. "Eh?"

"Why are you breaking up the sidewalk?"

"They're replacing the old pipe with new. Musta had a leak somewhere."

"Are you putting in the new pipe today?" Thomas asked. "Can I watch you put it through the wall?"

"I'm just breaking up the sidewalk and pulling out the old pipe, sonny. New pipe'll be laid by somebody else, come Monday afternoon. Or maybe Tuesday, I dunno. Plumbers, they kind of take their time."

The workman screwed in his earplug and went back to his sandwich, clearly finished with the conversation.

"But—" said Thomas as Emmy dragged him off.

"You can go back on Monday," said Professor Capybara, "and get all your questions answered."

Thomas was silent. As they neared the soccer fields, he began to lag behind.

There was a sound of wild cheering. Joe's team was celebrating with high fives, and Mr. and Mrs. Benson were grinning widely as they received congratulations from the spectators. Apparently Joe had scored another goal.

Emmy patted Mrs. Benson's sleeve.

"Why, Emmy!" Mrs. Benson turned around. "How nice that you could make it!"

"Looks like we play for the championship tomorrow," said Mr. Benson, exultant. "Our son is a powerhouse! Whoops," he added as his cell phone rang. He walked away from the crowd to take the call.

"Actually, Mrs. Benson," said the professor in his courteous way, "I was wondering if both your boys would like to join Emmy and Brian and myself tonight for a supper party."

"That's very kind of you, Professor," said Mrs. Benson. "Are you sure they won't be in the way? I know you're busy with your research."

"Not at all, my dear Mrs. Benson; the children are very good with the rodents, after all. Shall I have Brian drive them home a little after nine?"

Emmy wandered back to where Thomas was poking at something on the ground. "Hey, Thomas." She looked down at his smooth blond head.

He lifted the caterpillar onto his finger. "Look— it's so nice and fat and green!"

"And with yellow spots," Emmy added politely.

Two sharp whistle blasts sounded behind them, and the game was over. Emmy turned to see the

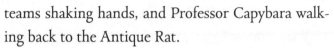

teams shaking hands, and Professor Capybara walking back to the Antique Rat.

"Did my mom say I could go?" Thomas asked.

Emmy nodded. "You'd better make sure Ratty's hidden before they get home, though."

Thomas tipped his finger, inducing the caterpillar to walk up and onto his other hand, and shrugged. "Dad always talks to the coach after a game. He talks, and then the coach talks, and then Mom tries to keep them from getting mad. It takes a long time."

But Joe's father was still speaking into his cell phone when Joe left his teammates and wandered over, sweaty, grass-stained, and happy.

"Good game!" said Emmy.

Joe grinned. "You faker. Did you even see any of it?"

"Not really," Emmy admitted. "But I *heard* it was a good game. Listen, though. Cheswick Vole and Miss Barmy are planning some kind of revenge."

"How do you know?"

Emmy told him.

Joe looked serious. "At least I've only got one soccer game left. Once that's over, I can help figure out what's going on."

"I saw Miss Barmy's blood in the charascope," Thomas said suddenly. "There was something in it that looked like a big ball of caterpillars. Only not so nice." He held out his caterpillar for Joe's inspection.

"That's a big one," said Joe. "How many do you have in your collection now?"

"Twenty-three," said Thomas. "I've drawn pictures of every one—"

"Joe! Great news!" Joe's father came striding toward them, snapping his cell phone shut. "You'll never believe it!"

Joe looked suddenly wary.

"Remember that exclusive soccer camp we were trying to get you into? The month-long one, in California?"

Joe nodded slowly.

"There's been a cancellation, and you were next on the list! I just called the airlines and managed to get us seats on the next flight out. We're going to California, Joe—tomorrow, right after the championship game!"

7

EMMY SAT on the slippery vinyl seat of Brian's
ancient truck, bouncing with every bump in the
road, and hung on to the bag of doll clothes in
her lap.

"Where's the turnoff for Joe's street?" Brian's voice
was pitched to be heard above the roar of the engine.

Emmy leaned out of the window to point. "Two
more blocks, on the right."

The car door was warm from the summer sun,
and the rushing air cooled her cheeks. And in spite
of the fact that Joe had to go away tomorrow, Emmy
felt almost happy. Maybe she was looking forward to
this party after all.

Sure, she would have to shrink, but there was no
fear of cats, because Brian was going to carry them
straight to the Rodent City entrance. Then, too, the
party was underground, so at least she wouldn't be
seen hanging around with rodents.

Besides, it would be a good opportunity to tell the

Bunjees about Cheswick's threats. Buck and Chippy would see the danger, even if the professor hadn't. And practical, no-nonsense Mrs. Bunjee could never be fooled by Miss Barmy.

Emmy smiled, thinking of the chipmunks. It would be fun to see them again, even though they weren't real, human friends . . .

Up ahead, on the sidewalk, three girls walked arm in arm. Two of them looked all too familiar, and they were laughing.

In a panic, Emmy pulled her head in and slid down on the vinyl seat just as the truck passed the girls. She was almost sure that she had ducked in time.

"What's the matter, Emmy? Did you drop something?" Brian asked.

Emmy pretended to search for something on the floor mat, hoping that Meg and Kate hadn't seen her. It had been embarrassing enough to have to fall off Mr. Peebles's boat right in front of them. But by now, Meg must have told the other girls how she'd caught Emmy talking to herself and pounding the wall. No wonder they had been laughing, Emmy thought gloomily as Brian's truck screeched to a stop in front of Joe's house.

It was a nice house, though small, built of cream-colored brick with a peaked roof and windows set in gables. It looked like a happy sort of place. But as Emmy neared the door, the voices from within didn't sound happy at all.

"Well, of course I said yes!" Joe's father sounded exasperated. "If I hadn't, someone else would have gotten his spot. We discussed it months ago; he said he wanted to go—"

"He doesn't want to go now. And I should think you would have asked him, Jack. People change, you know."

"But this is about his future! He could have a big career in sports! And I've laid out a lot of money already—the airline tickets, and the camp fees—"

Emmy didn't want to knock and interrupt, and she didn't want to stand there listening. She backed away and stood on the walk, irresolute.

"I don't want him to go out tonight." Mr. Benson's voice carried clearly through the screen door. "He needs to pack for his trip and rest up for tomorrow's game."

Mrs. Benson murmured something Emmy couldn't hear.

"But it's the *championship*!" Mr. Benson said, his voice rising in anguish. "You don't seem to understand how important that is to him!"

A toot from Brian's horn made Emmy jump. The voices stopped, and Emmy rushed forward and rang the bell before the argument could start up again.

"We're here to pick up Joe and Thomas," she said brightly. "Are they ready?"

"I am," said Thomas, squeezing past his mother. He wore a sweatshirt in spite of the heat, and he walked hunched over, his arms folded across his stomach.

"Joe will be just a minute," said Mrs. Benson with a slight worried frown, and in the background Emmy heard Mr. Benson muttering, "We've got to hide the cookies again, Caroline—I swear that kid's gained five pounds since yesterday."

Emmy leaped off the doorstep and followed Thomas with a sense of relief. She caught up to him at the elm near the street, where he was squatting with his back to her.

"All clear, Ratty." Thomas opened his sweatshirt.

The Rat skidded out and landed on his feet, lurching. He brushed the sweatshirt lint off his paws,

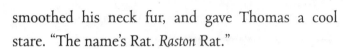

smoothed his neck fur, and gave Thomas a cool stare. "The name's Rat. *Raston* Rat."

There was a little pause.

"Agent 86," clarified the Rat, shading his eyes as he scanned the lawn. "Hold your position; I'm going to secure the perimeter." He flattened himself against the elm tree, blending in with the gray bark, and edged, claw by claw, around to the opposite side.

Emmy looked at Thomas. "*What* did you let him watch?"

"Just *Sesame Street*," said Thomas, shrugging.

"I put in *Get Smart* instead." The Rat poked his head out briefly. "I'm not a kindergartner, in case you hadn't noticed. Besides, Big Bird gives me a headache. Too much yellow."

"Oh, for—"

The Rat narrowed his eyes and held up a paw. "Enemy agents sighted!" he hissed. "Lurk! Lurk!"

Emmy made an exasperated noise and turned around. Standing in the street were three girls.

"Hi," said Meg.

"Hi," said Kate.

"Um—" said Emmy, startled and cautious. Had they seen the Rat?

The third girl jingled some coins in her pocket.

"This is Sara," said Kate politely. "We're going to the candy store. Do you want to come, too?"

Emmy looked at Kate in hopeless frustration. Of *course* she couldn't go with them. *Naturally.* She was going to a party with a bunch of *rats*.

She found her voice at last. "I'm sorry, I can't," she said with an effort. Her gaze fell on Thomas, and she had an inspired excuse. "I'm babysitting."

"You are *not!*" said Thomas indignantly, and the three girls exchanged glances.

"Well, have fun—*whatever* you're doing," said Kate in a bright, false voice, and the girls walked off, giggling.

Emmy wanted to kick something. It was so unfair! Every time—every single time she had a chance to do something normal, something ordinary, something that regular kids did *all the time* . . .

The front door slammed. Joe skimmed down the sidewalk and vaulted into the back of the truck. "Let's go!" he called, hanging over the side. "Next stop, the Antique Rat!"

The children sat in the cargo bed of the truck with their legs stretched out straight. The Rat, who had

found a pair of G.I. Joe field glasses in Emmy's bag, took a position on the ledge behind the window and swept the horizon with a professional air.

"Ah, the old 'enemy agents pretending to go to the candy store' trick," he said out of the corner of his mouth. "I'll keep my eye on them for you, Chief."

"Which one of us is 'Chief'?" murmured Joe.

"I'll be Chief," Thomas volunteered, raising his hand.

Raston frowned. "You can't be the chief. You're Special Agent 99."

"Oh," said Thomas.

"It's Emmy's turn to be captain today," said Joe. "Remember Good Fort?"

"Golden Fortress, said Emmy automatically.

"Gophers with Flugelhorns? I certainly do," said the Rat.

"Right. So, since she's captain of the good ship G.F., I can be chief of . . . whatever it is you're doing."

"Making the world safe for rodents," said the Rat promptly. "But if you want details, I'm spying on three enemy agents who are pretending to be innocent schoolgirls."

Emmy slid onto her back as the truck passed the girls, and stared at the sky. Its pure blue was deepening to cobalt, and high in the east she could see the pale disk of the moon, like a coin rubbed thin.

She was going to be awfully lonely in the next few weeks without Joe. "What did your dad say?" she asked as the truck rumbled on down the street.

"He's going to call the airlines and the camp and try to get a refund."

"Really?" Emmy watched some birds soaring overhead, trying to feel hopeful but wishing Joe hadn't said "try."

"He was picking up the phone when I left." Joe leaned forward, seemingly unworried. "What's in the bag?"

"Doll clothes." Emmy sat up. "We've got to have something to wear to the party, remember?"

Joe scowled. "I'll go as I am, thanks."

Emmy shook her head firmly. "You can't. But you can go in uniform."

"Seriously?" Joe brightened.

"Yup. If you're in the military, that's what you're *supposed* to wear." Emmy grabbed for the side of the truck as Brian barreled around a corner.

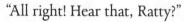

"All right! Hear that, Ratty?"

Raston looked fixedly through his binoculars, ignoring Joe, and Emmy rose to her knees. They had entered the backstreets, and the Rat's binoculars were aimed directly at the shoe shop. No, the sign out front, for he read the words aloud:

"The Home for Troubled Girls." Raston lowered the binoculars. "Now, *that* sounds suspicious."

Joe glanced at Emmy. "Miss Barmy was going to send you there, right? Remember Mrs. B and her flowerpots."

"Maybe that's where the girls are!" Thomas bounced up excitedly.

"What girls?" Joe grabbed the back of Thomas's shirt. "Sit down, or you'll fall out of the truck."

"You know, the girls on the cane—with the carved faces?"

"They're dead." Emmy looked at Thomas's stricken face and amended, "Well, Priscilla's dead, anyway. And Mr. Peebles said the girls' parents were all dead. So it stands to reason—"

"They *can't* be dead." Thomas gripped the side of the truck with dimpled fists. "Maybe they're just prisoners in that house."

"They're not," said Emmy flatly. "The police even searched it. Mr. Peebles said Mr. B only put up that sign outside because they had a dollhouse inside with that same 'Troubled Girls' sign on it. He thought it was cute or something."

"Stupid, more like," said Joe in disgust.

"I want them to be alive," said Thomas stubbornly, his blue eyes troubled.

"Better pray for a miracle, then," said Joe. "You're going to need one. What were their names again? Ana, and—and Carrot—"

"Berit," corrected Thomas, counting on his fingers. "Lisa. Lee. And—who was the last one, again?"

"Merry Pumpkin," said Emmy with a sigh.

Thomas was fascinated with the shrinking process. He sat on a swivel chair at the Antique Rat and watched as the Rat bit the others one by one.

"Do it again!" he said, round-eyed, as Professor Capybara shrank down, down, until he was doll-sized, perfectly attired in the gray pin-striped suit that shrank with him.

"The lad is strangely bloodthirsty," said the Rat.

Joe grinned and held out his finger for a bite. "I'm

melting . . . melting!" he cried, writhing as he shrank. "Oh, what a world, what a world . . ." He collapsed in a tiny heap on the desk blotter.

Emmy sat on the broad desk that abutted the window of the Antique Rat, and braced herself as the Rat's teeth grazed her finger. Her stomach contracted, as if she were on an elevator dropping fast, and her arms and legs prickled intensely. When at last it was over, she opened her eyes to see a gigantic and beaming Thomas overhead.

"*I* want to do it!" he cried, twirling in the swivel chair. "I want to shrink, too!"

"Not tonight," said the professor firmly, stretching high to pull the chain of the desk lamp. "You'd need Cecilia's kiss to grow again, and she's in Rodent City."

"But I could go *with* them!" Thomas was near tears.

"Only then you couldn't help me with the experiments," Brian pointed out.

"And you get to order pizza," Joe added, using the stapler for a springboard. "Hey, Brian, want anything stapled? I can jump on the end, like this—"

Thomas wiped the back of his chubby hand across his eyes. "Can I look through the charascope again?"

"Of course," said Brian kindly. "Now, what would you like? Pepperoni?"

"Sausage and onion," said Thomas, sniffing a little as Brian led him away. "And would you call me Agent 99, please?"

It took some time to find doll clothes that fit. And although Emmy was tempted by a pair of Barbie's high-heeled shoes, she couldn't walk in them without tripping. At last she took an armful of clothes behind an open book and grimly tried on the lot.

She ended up with something blue and shimmery, with enough stretch so she could get it on and still be able to breathe, and a pair of flat silver slippers. Relieved, she came out from behind the book to see Joe looking handsome in a dress uniform of blue and gold, and the professor looking anxiously at his watch. "Brian!" he called.

Emmy walked across the desktop to gaze through the window. Across the way, jars in the window of the candy shop glowed with colors of lemon, cherry, and sour apple, and girls' shadows moved. She felt a small dull pain in her chest.

"Here I am, Professor. Will this do?" Brian set a cat carrier down on the desk, complete with airholes and a side door.

"Admirably, my boy, admirably," said the professor. "We won't be in it long. But where is Raston?"

Emmy, still gazing out the window, caught sight of a small gray form creeping across the street and up to the Antique Rat. "He's coming to the door," she said, surprised. "How did he get outside?"

Brian opened the door. But it was Sissy who came in, tired, dusty, and footsore.

"I'm sorry," she gasped. "I've tried and *tried* to find him." She limped across the floor, her satchel dragging, and gazed up as Emmy looked down over the edge of the desk. "I'm having trouble following his scent—I think I'm getting a cold—but that's no excuse, of course," she added hastily, wiping her nose. "At the Speedy Rodent Messenger Service, we *never* make excuses." She looked anxiously around the room. "I don't suppose you've seen him anywhere?" she asked faintly.

"Seen who?" said Raston, leaping from behind a stack of books and skidding across the desktop in a belted trenchcoat and dark glasses.

"Rasty!" Sissy fumbled with the straps of her satchel, pulled out a battered peanut-butter cup, and held it up with pride. "Delivery accomplished!" she said, and collapsed.

The carrying case was clean, dry, and large enough for the five of them. Cecilia, more or less recovered, went inside, followed by Raston, Joe, and the professor. Emmy stepped in last of all, and Brian shut the door with a snap.

Suddenly they were plunged into a deep-brown gloom. Thin pencils of light came in through the air-holes, crisscrossing above, but they didn't illumine much. Emmy was glad of the dark; she couldn't see the Rat's accusing eyes.

She had only meant to make Sissy happy by giving her a delivery to make. It was hardly an urgent delivery—nobody ever died for lack of a peanut-butter cup—but Cecilia had spent the afternoon dragging herself from place to place, searching for her brother, and getting sick in the process.

She tried too hard; that was the whole problem. It wasn't Emmy's fault that Sissy was the anxious type.

Brian cleared his throat high above them, and the steady joggle of his long strides turned to an uneven sliding as he stopped and set the carrier down. There was a scraping sound, as of shoes on cement, and the creak of a large body settling on a wooden bench.

"We must be at the tunnel entrance," whispered the professor. "What's he waiting for?"

A slight vibration trembled through the bottom of the case, and Emmy turned her head. A sound of voices, high and giggling, came in faintly and grew steadily louder.

". . . but don't you think she's stuck-up?"

"She's rich enough, that's for sure."

"I don't think she's stuck-up, exactly," protested a third. "Just . . . different."

Emmy recognized Meg's voice with a rush of silent gratitude. But Kate cut across the others.

"Well, *I* think she's stuck-up. Every time I invite her to do something, she makes up a stupid excuse . . ." The voices faded, became indistinguishable, as the girls passed the place where Brian sat. A last fragment of conversation wafted back: ". . . never going to ask her to do *anything* again . . ."

Silence. A fumbling sound at the latch of the pet carrier, and a click as the side door was opened. Five small figures pressed toward the opening, formal clothes rustling.

Emmy looked dully past Brian's ankles, large and hairy, to a sweep of grass beyond. She could see the girls in the distance, walking away. She winced.

Joe turned to the professor. "But why are we on the green?"

"Keep your voice down, lad . . . They haven't cleared the front entrance yet of the mess from that infernal jackhammer. Follow me, everyone."

The small man in gray pinstripes ducked his head and entered a hole, cleverly hidden beneath the low, spreading branches of a yew and angling down beneath the bench's concrete slab.

Sissy muffled another sneeze in her paw, and turned to whisper to Emmy as she passed. "I'm sorry—truly, I am. I'll do better with the next message."

"It's okay," Emmy protested, but Sissy had already disappeared after the others.

Emmy looked at the gaping mouth of the tunnel.

"Go!" said Brian urgently, as a slobbering, snuffling sound came to Emmy's ears, along with a bounding vibration of the earth and a smell of damp dog. Emmy glanced up to see a gigantic white puppy approaching faster than she could have believed possible.

The puppy's high-pitched yapping brought her to her senses. With a shimmer of blue, she caught up her long dress and scampered into the hole.

8

THE TUNNEL WENT ON and on, dimly lit by a long string of twinkle lights. Some of the bulbs were out, and in those patches the tunnel was dark indeed, and smelled strongly of worms.

"Criminy," said Joe over his shoulder, "what if we *met* a worm?"

Emmy gripped the professor's coattails and tried not to think about the size a worm would be, or its moist pink-and-brown squishiness. And then she tried not to think about screaming. And just as she was deciding she could not possibly think about the tunnel collapsing all around her and burying her alive, they came to a section where track was laid, and the walls were rough timbers instead of packed dirt, and a handcart stood ready. The lighting was better, too, and when they all got on the cart and Joe and Ratty pumped the handle and they began to roll smoothly down the track, Emmy breathed a little easier. In a minute the rough timbers changed to smooth paneling, and the twinkle lights changed to sconces of gleaming brass, and then the track stopped abruptly and they were standing on a polished parquet floor with padded benches on either side. Just before them was a carved wooden archway hung with velvet curtains of a deep forest green.

From behind the curtains came the vague muffled noise of many voices talking all at once, combined with the clink of bottles and an occasional shriek of laughter. Professor Capybara pulled back the heavy curtains and the sound spilled out in a burst of light and color and a vaguely familiar scent.

"Oh, here you are at last, Professor! And Raston and Joe—my, don't you two look handsome—and Emmy dear! I'm *so* glad to see you again!" Mrs. Bunjee, swathed in violet silk, flung her furry arms wide and clasped Emmy to her chest.

Emmy tried not to breathe in. Chipmunk fur up her nose always made her sneeze, and she wasn't sure that her dress could stand the strain.

"And, Cecilia, how lovely that you're here! You'll want to run up and put on your party dress; it's laid out and pressed."

Emmy looked up, but she couldn't pinpoint the

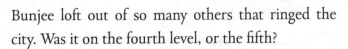

Bunjee loft out of so many others that ringed the city. Was it on the fourth level, or the fifth?

Rodent City had been built in the crawl space of the art gallery. Its walls were of red brick, and rough wooden uprights supported the floor above. But the massive pillars were connected by carved trusses, and twiggy lofts, and swinging ladders, all hung with garlands of twinkling Christmas lights like stars on a rope. And tonight, for the party, the central area on the ground floor had been covered with tables and lit with candles, creating a festive look.

"I have to deliver my message first." Sissy straightened the badge on her jacket and stood proudly, her eyes bright and her voice pitched above the noise of the crowd. "A message for Mrs. Bunjee, of Rodent City, from Emmy Addison. Do not—repeat—do *not* trust Miss Barmy or Cheswick Vole. More information later."

The hum of conversation near them died down, and Emmy winced. That message should have been given in private. Still, Sissy had remembered it word for word . . .

Emmy looked around. What was wrong? Sissy had blurted out her message at an awkward time, but that shouldn't have caused Mrs. Bunjee to look so annoyed, or stopped all conversation nearby.

"Didn't I say it right?" Sissy whispered to Emmy, wiping her nose on her paw.

A light, tinkling laugh broke the silence, and an amused voice spoke clearly from the outer edges of the group. "Emmaline always did like to make jokes . . ."

Emmy's breath stopped. She felt as if she'd been hit in the chest.

The crowd parted to reveal a piebald rat, elegant in a rose-and-silver gown, with curled whiskers and a sparkling tiara between her ears. ". . . but perhaps she's still too young to realize there is a time and place for everything, even her delightful sense of humor."

A black rat with a sleek coat and a red bow tie murmured something in her ear.

"Of course I forgive her, Cheswick. She's a lovely, dear child, and then she's an Addison, too. I'm sure that someday her manners will reflect her training." Miss Barmy smiled at the rodents around her, dimpled charmingly, and waved at Emmy. "Have a wonderful time at the party, little Emmaline, and don't forget to thank your hostess."

The rodents crowded around her again, not without a few disparaging looks at Emmy, and the conversation rose to its previous hum. Emmy took a step backward—she hardly knew what she was doing—and bumped into Joe.

"Wow," he said, very low.

"You almost have to admire her," said Professor Capybara. "Such a splendid example of manipulation! A textbook case!"

Emmy didn't trust herself to speak as she watched the piebald rat move gracefully away. With growing outrage she saw that the rat's dress was made of several Barbie gowns, re-cut and stitched together in a striking pattern.

"Did I do it wrong?" Sissy sneezed again and turned to her brother, bewildered. "Maybe I'm not cut out to be a messenger."

Mrs. Bunjee turned, paws on her hips. "The problem isn't with the messenger; it's with the message. Cecilia, dear, go get your dress on, and don't forget a handkerchief—your nose is running. Raston, bring her to table three afterward—you're sitting with the Gopnichiks and the Grebblers. Don't forget to congratulate Mr. and Mrs. Grebbler on their new litter— they had four boys and two girls."

"Gophers," muttered the Rat, taking Sissy by the elbow. "Oh, joy."

"Now, Emmy," said Mrs. Bunjee firmly. "No matter what Miss Barmy has done in the past, she deserves our support and help."

"Deserves?" said Joe, with a rising inflection.

"Everyone deserves a second chance." The chipmunk looked from Joe to Emmy to the professor, her face calm and certain. "Miss Barmy wants to turn over a new leaf. She told me while we were sewing her dress."

"*My* dress," Emmy said in a choked voice. "And I'll bet she watched while you did all the work."

Mrs. Bunjee shrugged. "It's true that she didn't know how to sew, but she did pay me—very well, I might add."

"She didn't pay *me*," said Emmy coldly. "She sent Cheswick to steal doll clothes from my own room."

Mrs. Bunjee blinked. "Perhaps there was a misunderstanding," she suggested. "If you look carefully, you may find that Cheswick left a nice pile of seeds to pay for the things he took. Of course," she added quickly, "he shouldn't have taken them without your permission. But people can't switch from bad to

115

good all at once, without a few false steps along the way. It's our job to help and guide, not to criticize."

"B-but," Emmy sputtered, "Cheswick said Miss Barmy had plans—she was going to do something behind our backs, to show us—"

Mrs. Bunjee made a chirking sound of disapproval. "And why do you assume Miss Barmy's plans must necessarily be bad? Perhaps she has *good* plans. Perhaps she wants to surprise us."

Emmy was speechless.

"For instance," said Mrs. Bunjee, beaming, "we had so much dust from that awful jackhammer, I couldn't think how I would ever get ready for the party. But Miss Barmy paid the Finicky Field Mice Cleaning Service to take care of everything. And then she had flowers delivered, enough to fill the city! Look around you, breathe in that lovely fragrance, and tell me she's not trying to become a better person!"

Emmy looked at the flowers in tall floor vases everywhere—huge pink blooms with ragged edges and a spicy-sweet smell. Now she knew why she recognized the scent. The flowers were just like the ones Mr. Peebles had picked and brought to their table last night; only now, the tiny pinks were as big as her head.

"My dear Mrs. Bunjee," said the professor, patting her furry shoulder, "you're an optimist, and I certainly hope that you're right."

"After all," said the chipmunk, looking up with a pleased smile, "you said Jane had to learn to love, if she wanted Cecilia's kiss to work and turn her back to a human again. She's taking your advice very well, I do believe!"

"Perhaps so," said Professor Capybara kindly. "Now, where should I sit, and when do I give my speech?"

"Oh, the head table, of course." They moved off together, Mrs. Bunjee chattering away. ". . . and Chippy rigged up a microphone just for you . . ."

Joe looked at Emmy, his face somber. "This is *terrible*."

Emmy nodded emphatically. "We'd better talk to her again after the party."

Joe shook his head. "Mrs. Bunjee won't listen. She's made up her mind. But what about the professor? He doesn't believe Miss Barmy's changed, does he?"

Emmy threw up her hands. "No, but he doesn't

take her seriously. He says she can't do much harm—she's only a rat."

"Yeah, well, show me another rat who could have everybody against her one day and then turn it all around the next. That lady has talent, and she *scares* me."

"Appetizers? Sparkling pear cider?"

Two mice were at their elbow with silver trays. The speaker, a kangaroo mouse, held out a tray with slender glasses of something pale and fizzy. Emmy reached out and then stopped, hand in midair, as she caught sight of the other mouse, dwarfed by its tray.

"Endear? Is that you?" She peeked under the silver tray of hot appetizers. The mouse, balancing the tray above its head, gave her a shy, pleased smile.

"Joe! Look who's here!" Emmy touched the Endear Mouse lightly, and the two exchanged delighted greetings without needing to say a word.

The Endear Mouse had the power to transfer thoughts, just through touch. This had been very useful a few weeks ago, now it was just an easy way to say hi—especially since the mouse had never been known to speak. And though Endear was still very young, and didn't always understand big words, it was quick to sense feelings.

118

Unfortunately, Emmy remembered this too late to hide her own.

"Bad lady—bad," came the thought from the small mouse, and Emmy realized that it had taken in all her fear and anger about Miss Barmy.

"Don't worry," Emmy said hastily, withdrawing her hand. "She's gone now. The bad lady won't bother me again."

The Endear Mouse's big eyes looked solemnly at Emmy from beneath the tray.

"Don't you have a job to do?" Emmy asked, smiling, and the Endear Mouse nodded happily, easily distracted. Its tail curled around Emmy's wrist just long enough to send a quick good-bye, and then the mouse moved off into the crowd, offering appetizers to anyone who stopped.

"I'll bet anything the bad lady *will* bother you again," said Joe at her elbow.

"Of course she will," said Emmy absently. Her rage had faded, but in its place was a cold determination. "Let's see if we can figure out what she's up to."

9

EMMY AND JOE SLIPPED through the crowd of chattering rodents, unnoticed in the dim light, and mounted steps that wound around a central pillar. There was a gap in the string of lights—three bulbs in a row had burned out—and Emmy and Joe stood in shadow, observing the scene below.

Rodents moved about, breaking and re-forming in swirling groups of fur. Masses of wide, pink blossoms stood in vases everywhere, filling the room with a strong, sweet scent of cloves.

"I bet Miss Barmy stole these flowers." Emmy yanked a pink petal off the nearest bloom and methodically shredded it. "I'll bet she told her father to steal them from Mr. Peebles's garden. And Mrs. Bunjee says she's generous! Ha!"

Joe leaned on the railing, looking down. "Where did she go?"

Emmy glanced over the crowd, and suddenly put her finger to her lips. She pointed straight downward.

"And then I had to connect the positive

terminals—but of course I had to go into the conduit first, there was no possibility of shutting off the circuit-breaker—"

"But wasn't that very dangerous?" asked Miss Barmy in melting tones.

Emmy, dismayed, stared down at the top of a black-and-tan-striped head. It was leaning close to Miss Barmy's sparkling tiara.

Joe's eyes were wide and unbelieving. "Chippy?" he mouthed.

Emmy nodded grimly. Apparently Miss Barmy wasn't going to rest until she got *all* the rodents on her side. And the way to Chippy's heart, as everyone knew, was to show an interest in electricity, or motors, or anything with gears . . .

"—but I just used an insulation displacement connector. Then, puncturing the black wire first—of course that's safest, you understand, it has a neutral charge—"

"This is *terribly* fascinating," said Miss Barmy, placing a paw on Chippy's forearm. "And you explain it all so *well*."

Chippy gave a foolish sort of giggle.

"But I just wondered if you could assist with a little project of mine . . ."

"A project?" Chippy's ears pricked forward.

"No, I shouldn't ask you. It's too much . . . You couldn't possibly . . ." The tiara glittered as Miss Barmy's head drooped. She withdrew her paw.

"Oh, please!" Chippy fumbled for her paw. "If there's *any* way I can help you—"

"Well," said Miss Barmy briskly, "since you insist. Can you cut glass?"

"I-I haven't lately," stammered Chippy, "but I *could*."

"Could you cut holes in glass? I mean, circles?"

"Why, sure . . ." Chippy seemed to be thinking. "I could use a hole saw . . . one of those with grit instead of teeth. They'd cut glass, all right, if I could apply enough pressure. Let's see, I could rig up a crosspiece and a frame—"

A piercing electronic squeal filled the crawl space, and Emmy put her hands to her ears. Down below, on the low platform that held the head table and a lectern, Mrs. Bunjee was trying to adjust a microphone to Professor Capybara's height.

"I have to go help them with the amplifier," said Chippy breathlessly, "but maybe later we can discuss—"

"I don't know." Miss Barmy's tone was suddenly

cool. "I didn't realize you would be jumping from one project to another like this."

"But—but I'm *not*—"

The piebald shoulders, swathed in rose and silver, shrugged elegantly. "We were talking about *my* project. Then, all of a sudden, you lose interest and make excuses."

"I'm not making excuses, they need me up there—"

"I'm *sure* they do."

"No, really! I'd rather talk about your project, I truly would!"

"Perhaps your brother, Buck, could help me." The piebald rat pulled away, turning to look over the crowd. "He's quite intelligent, you know, and so *steady* . . ."

Chippy glanced nervously over his shoulder at the rodents on the platform. "They might not need me so very much," he said in a low, anguished tone. "Now, Miss Barmy, what were you saying about your project?"

"Call me Jane," said the piebald rat, patting his cheek with her white-gloved paw. "Dear Chipster, what would I do without you?"

The dessert course had been served, the professor had made his speech, and the assembled rodents had all applauded wildly, their furry paws making an oddly muffled clapping. The Swinging Gerbils ambled onto the stage and took out their instruments, playing short riffs of disconnected melody as they tuned up.

Joe swallowed his last bite of Prairie Pudding Pie and leaned back in his chair. "Almost time for the professor to lead the first dance. Ten to one he doesn't make it without falling asleep."

Emmy, slumped glumly at the end of the table, didn't respond. This whole night had been a misery beyond compare. She hadn't wanted to shrink in the first place, but she had at least thought she'd have fun with her friends. Instead, she had to watch all evening as Miss Barmy swished and smiled and flirted her way into everyone's hearts.

"How does she do it?" Emmy glared at the head table where Miss Barmy, squeezed in between the professor and Mrs. Bunjee, was laughing and batting her eyelashes at a handsome brown rat who was leaning over her shoulder.

"Do what? Get seated at the head table?"

"Well, that, too," Emmy said. "But what I mean is, how does she get everyone to think she's so great? I lived with her a year, and I can tell you—she's deep-down nasty."

"I don't know how she gets everyone on her side," said Joe, "but I know how she got to sit at the head table. She bribed the headwaiter."

"Seriously?"

"Yup. I saw her slip a few seeds into his pocket, and right away he went and rearranged everything. That's why our name tags were down here. He moved them."

Emmy felt a flush of resentment on her cheeks. "Why didn't you say anything?"

Joe stretched his legs. "I didn't want to sit at the head table anyway." He grinned. "If the professor gets a sudden attack of Snoozeritis because he's upset about having to dance, I didn't want Mrs. Bunjee to grab me instead!"

Emmy glanced at Professor Capybara, who was eyeing the band with a look of pale unease, but any further comments were made impossible by the drummer, who suddenly decided to try out his cymbals.

The microphone squealed, and a spotlight swung

around to the podium. Mrs. Bunjee's furry, smiling face poked above the lectern. "Ladies and gentle-rats," she began, "while the Swinging Gerbils are getting ready, I need to thank each and every rodent who helped with tonight's party . . ."

"This is boring," muttered the Rat, coming up behind them. "When does the action start? I've been sitting with those gophers for *ages*."

"That must have been exciting," said Joe.

"Don't get me started," said the Rat in tones of deep disgust. "I made the mistake of congratulating the Grebblers on their new litter, and I couldn't shut them up. Did they seriously think that I'd be fascinated by the burping habits of Gloria, or the cute way little Dribble spits up, or the incredible genius of Baby Grubby? Grubby Grebbler, what a name. I hope the kid learns to use his paws, that's all." He thumped down on a chair, poured himself a tumbler of berry juice, and drank deeply.

Emmy swallowed a laugh. "Where's Sissy?"

Raston scowled. "She's sitting at the Grebblers' table, giving Grubby his bottle and practicing her Speedy Rodent Messenger Service rules. She forgot the one about delivering a message in private—"

Joe glanced at Emmy.

"—and now she feels terrible. She keeps worrying about being fired."

"I won't complain to the Messenger Service," said Emmy quickly.

The Rat shrugged. "She could be a secret agent with me. I could use another assistant."

"Speaking of secret agents," said Joe, "you can help us figure out what Miss Barmy is up to. She's got Chippy doing something with cutting glass in circles—"

The Rat whipped out his dark glasses and put them on. "I'm on the job, Chief. So Chippy's a double agent, eh?"

"Well, not exactly," Emmy began, but suddenly the microphone crackled and one of the Swinging Gerbils was speaking.

"And now, starting off the dance to the sweet strains of "Ain't She Fuzzy," is our guest of honor, Professor Maxwell Capybara, and our hostess, Mrs. Roseleaf Bunjee! A one! A two! A one, two, three, four!"

The band swung into the opening bars, the spotlight arced around to Mrs. Bunjee in her violet silk, a panicked-looking professor beside her—and then, suddenly, the professor dropped to the floor, taking Mrs. Bunjee with him.

"Told you," said Joe, chuckling.

There was a moment's confusion as the professor was dragged away to sleep it off, and Mrs. Bunjee, looking dazed, was helped to a chair.

The band leader raised his eyebrows at Chippy, who stood at once and offered his paw to the piebald rat at the head table. Miss Barmy rose amid cheers, and blew kisses as Chippy whirled her off in the spotlight for the first dance.

Emmy, so furious that her stomach hurt, ignored the discussion Joe and the Rat were having about the band's singer ("Too squeaky," said the Rat. "Right, like you could do better," said Joe. "Watch me!" said the Rat), and didn't even notice the rodent who had come to stand beside her, until he tapped her arm.

"Want to dance?"

Taken by surprise, Emmy hadn't had the wit to say no. And now, gripped firmly by two hairy paws, she was jigged and jogged all over the dance floor by an enthusiastic gopher. His name, he had shouted, was Gus.

His name didn't matter to Emmy, who planned to forget him as soon as possible. She wasn't a big fan of gophers anyway, and to be bounced around by one whose idea of dancing was limited, to say the least, was like living a nightmare that had no end.

"I *have* to sit down," Emmy gasped, groping past a thicket of chairs to Sissy's table, where she collapsed. Baby Grubby, who had just finished his bottle, chose that moment to screw up his tiny face and cry.

Sissy looked helplessly around for the parents. "They said they'd be right back. What do I do now?"

Emmy, sighing, picked up the baby gopher, laid him against her shoulder, and patted the fuzzy back briskly until he burped. Little Grubby, instantly happier, began to play with her buttons.

"Oh," said Sissy. She twisted her paws together. "I guess there are a lot of things I still don't know."

Emmy tucked the baby gopher into Sissy's awkward arms. "There. Rock him a little, maybe."

"I keep *trying*," said Sissy, anxiously rocking the baby a shade too fast. "I can't read, I don't know anything, but I listen as hard as I can . . ."

"You're doing fine. Just"—Emmy searched her brain for something inspirational to say—"hang in there."

"Hang in there." Sissy raised brown eyes to Emmy's. "What does that mean?"

"Well, you know, keep doing what you're doing. Don't give up, even when you're discouraged. Believe that things are going to get better soooo—"

"Hi-oh!" cried Gus happily, pulling Emmy to her feet before she knew it. "The next one's a slow dance!"

Emmy caught a glimpse of Raston in his dark glasses, walking the lead singer off the podium—how had he managed that?—as she was towed onto the dance floor. The next thing she knew, Raston was crooning "Bye Bye Ratbird," as the smooth brass of the Swinging Gerbils filled the room.

Clutched in a hairy embrace, Emmy suddenly rebelled. She didn't care if Gus thought she was rude—she was *not* going to slow-dance with a gopher.

She twisted sideways, yanked hard, and broke free. "Thanks for the dance!" she cried, waving as she ran. She dodged around couples all the way across the room, until at last she slid into her place beside Joe. "Let's go," she panted.

"And miss Ratty's song?" Joe turned to Emmy.

"Besides, don't you want to dance anymore with—what was his name?—Hoppy? Jumpy?"

"Stinky," said Emmy. "I don't think gophers believe in deodorant. Seriously, let's get out of here."

But before they could push back their chairs, the music died down, and Mrs. Bunjee was at the microphone again. "Dear friends—I have a wonderful announcement to make! I've just been speaking with the lovely Miss Jane Barmy—"

Emmy choked.

"—and she has graciously offered to sponsor a beauty contest for our female rodents!"

Chippy leaned in toward the microphone. "She's commissioned me to cut a number of small round mirrors out of her large one, so there'll be a mirror for everyone that enters the contest."

"There will be prizes, of course," said Mrs. Bunjee. "The third-place winner will receive slivered almonds. Second place, macadamia nuts. And first place wins three bottle caps of poppyseeds!"

There was a gasp. And then, "What about Miss Congeniality?" said a voice from the crowd.

"Seventeen Southern pecans," called Miss Barmy, to general laughter. She made her way to the microphone and stood there gracefully in the spotlight, her tiara glinting, her white-gloved paw waving. Then she raised her paws to her head, lifted the tiara off, and held it out.

"Two days from now, the winner will be crowned. And her title will be—"

"What? What?" cried the crowd.

Miss Barmy's smile gleamed. "Princess Pretty of Rodent City!"

10

"THAT'S RIGHT, MERRY—make a 'y' with a nice long tail. Now give me the pencil, and I'll sign my name."

Four tiny girls crouched on the dusty floor of an attic room, each one holding down a corner of a wrinkled piece of paper. Ana grasped a pencil stub as thick and long as her arm and carefully printed her name at the bottom. "There." She looked at the smudged paper with satisfaction. "Now help me roll it around the stick."

It was a good thing for Ana's plan that the attic was full of so many bits and pieces. It hadn't been hard to find string and a pencil and even a stick of wood, smooth and rounded and not too heavy for the girls to lift. And every shoebox contained crumpled packing paper; they had only to smooth it out, and Ana could write the message she had been planning all day long.

"Is this tight enough?" Berit tied a third knot and tugged, with her feet braced on either side.

"Yes, but do two more," said Ana, looking critically at the result of the day's labor. The letter, rolled around the wooden dowel, was already tied like a sausage around both ends and the middle, but it wouldn't hurt to be safe. She didn't want it to fall off and blow away.

Lee tilted back her head to look at the windowsill, high above. "How do we get it up there?"

"Yes, how?" echoed Lisa. "Do we all climb up and pull?"

"I'm scared to climb that high," said Merry, putting her thumb in her mouth.

"You won't have to. I've figured it out. Where's that really long piece of string?"

Berit brought it and helped Ana tie one more knot around the middle of the stick. "We'll do the rest in the morning," said Ana as they rolled it out of sight behind a pair of green rubber boots.

They trudged back to the shoebox, their feet making tiny tracks in the dust. Shelves loomed high above them, reaching up to the dim and distant rafters, and the attic turned gray and shadowy as the sun went down.

"Do you think it will work?" asked Berit in a low voice.

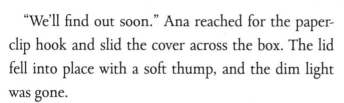

"We'll find out soon." Ana reached for the paper-clip hook and slid the cover across the box. The lid fell into place with a soft thump, and the dim light was gone.

"I *hate* the dark," said Lisa.

"Me, too," said Lee.

"Ana," said Merry suddenly, "why can't we have a window in the box?"

"Because the big people would see it. And if they saw we could make a hole in the box, they'd just lock us up in another box that was harder to get out of."

"I don't mean a big window," said Merry in a small voice. "Just a little one."

Berit tapped the paper clip against the cardboard. "We could poke a tiny hole with the straight end of our hook. They wouldn't notice that."

"But the box is cardboard," said Lisa.

"It's way too thick and hard," said Lee.

There was a little silence. "We could do it together, maybe," Ana said thoughtfully.

"I can help, too." Merry pulled her thumb out of her mouth.

"All right. Everybody grab on to the paper clip and push. Twist it back and forth—don't bend it—hey, it's working!"

With a last twist and a pop, the paper clip poked through the cardboard, and the girls fell down. A pinhole of light, like a tiny star, appeared in the side of the box.

"Wow!" Berit put her eye to the hole. "I can see right through!"

A key rattled in the lock of the attic door. "Everybody sit down," Ana ordered. "Now, all together, just like we practiced—yell!"

"Mr. B!" they all cried together. *"Mr. Beeeeee!"*

Footsteps creaked on the attic floor. "Now, girls, quiet down." The box lid tipped up to reveal a large, roughened thumb and a pair of watery blue eyes over a red-veined nose. "What's the matter?"

"Please, Mr. B," said Ana, clasping her hands, "it was *so* hot in the attic today. Would you open the window just an inch or two?"

"Well . . ." Mr. B's other thumb came up to rub the side of his nose. "I don't suppose I'd get in trouble over something that small." He bent closer and gave an enormous wink. "Just don't tell on me."

There was a scraping sound as the window was levered up, and then came the usual sickening swoop as the box was lifted and carried down the stairs. The girls hugged each other in silent glee, sliding in a mass from corner to corner.

Berit's mouth found Ana's ear. "Phase Two complete!"

Ana nodded. Phase One had been to create the message; Phase Two, to get the window open. Now all that remained was Phase Three. Tomorrow morning, when the nice man from next door came down the walk to get his morning paper, she would push out the stick at just the right time to catch his eye as it fell. With that hope ahead of her, Ana thought she could even bear Mrs. B tonight.

But Mrs. B was not interested in playing with the girls. "Take them back," she said pettishly, waving the box away.

"Why, my little squash blossom, what's wrong?" Mr. B put the girls' supper inside the box—five pieces of macaroni and cheese, each piece as long as the girls' forearms—set the box on the floor, and sat beside his wife.

"Why hasn't Jane come back? I don't care for her associating with those lower classes. *Field* rats go to those parties. And now she's late—never a thought for *me*."

Ana nibbled halfheartedly on her macaroni. It was slippery, and the cheese smelled strong. She peered out of the pinhole they had made. She could see nothing but a table leg, and beyond it the baseboard and a few inches of wall.

Mrs. B was still talking in a thin, discontented drone, but between the words Ana thought she heard a scrabbling behind the plaster. She moved her head slightly, and suddenly she was looking straight at the new hole in the baseboard that the paper boy—or, rather, paper gopher—had used.

Where did it lead? Maybe to the field rats Mrs. B had talked about?

Ana had often thought about escape, and here was a hole just their size. If only they weren't watched so closely! But escaping was one thing, and finding some way to live afterward was another. They would need food and a safe place to stay. There were cats and dogs out there (Mr. B had once brought in a stray kitten to play with them, and Ana had never gotten over the fright), and owls, and hawks, all of which might pounce on very small girls.

If they could make it to wherever the field rats lived, perhaps the rodents would take them in. Ana didn't think she would mind living in a burrow in a field—not *very* much—and almost anything would be better than living with Miss Barmy and her mother.

Ana watched the hole as the rustling sound grew louder. All at once she saw a flurry of skirts as a piebald rat in a tiara crawled through, stood, and dusted herself off with soiled white gloves.

A chipmunk, handsome in a tuxedo, emerged behind her. He didn't look about the room, Ana noticed. He only had eyes for Miss Barmy.

"I'll bring it to you tomorrow," he said earnestly. "If I work all night, I might be able to bring it over sometime in the morning."

"*First* thing in the morning, Chippy dear," said Miss Barmy with a melting look. "I'm sure you understand how important this is to *all* the rodents."

"Yes, of course," said Chippy uncertainly. He bent low over Miss Barmy's paw. "Dearest Jane, allow me to express my deepest—"

"Just bring it to me tomorrow by sunrise," Miss Barmy said impatiently. "Then you can express whatever you want."

Chippy swallowed hard and kissed Miss Barmy's paw. "Of course, Jane dear. I'll do anything you say."

Ana scowled as the chipmunk backed through the

hole, his black eyes misty with longing. So there was another rodent on Miss Barmy's side—maybe they *all* were. Ana slid down, her back to the cardboard wall. Escaping through the hole wouldn't do them any good if the rodents on the other end just brought them back to Miss Barmy.

After a while, Mr. B took them up to the attic. The girls stuck out their tongues at his back—a nightly ritual—and climbed out of the box.

They had made comfortable beds on a low shelf, but Ana went first to the stick and tied the loose end of the long string around her waist. Then she climbed up a series of shoelace ladders, shelf by shelf, until she reached the windowsill; hooked the string around a nail in the sill; and climbed back down, pulling the loose end with her.

She tied the end to a low brace and looked at her handiwork with satisfaction. "See, Merry? You won't have to climb. If you four grab the end of the string and pull, you'll raise the stick right up to the windowsill."

"This message was a very good idea," said Berit.

"I hope it works," Ana said. "Off to bed, everyone. We have to wake up early."

It took Ana a long time to fall asleep. But even so, she was the first one up the next morning. And once she had climbed to the windowsill, and the stick had been raised by four small girls pulling heartily on the string, saying "Heave! Heave ho!" (that had been Berit's idea), Ana felt as if she had been waiting forever for this chance.

The sun rose and tipped the eaves with pinky gold. A dog barked on the green, the birds raised their small voices in a trilling clamor, and then came the ting-ting of the paper boy's bell and a rubbing sound of bike tires on asphalt. He pulled a paper out of his bag and tossed it. As usual, he failed to hit the front porch, and the paper landed halfway up the sidewalk. Ana nodded. Perfect.

Nervously she rolled the stick into position. Somewhere in town, church bells rang, and Ana found herself praying—"Please. Oh, *please*, let it work."

The front door of the blue house creaked open, and the nice man padded out in his slippers.

Ana took a breath and shoved, hard. The stick fell, end over end, the white paper making a fine flash in the sun as it dropped. The man looked up, then at the stick, now lying in the grass. He stepped off the path.

And then Ana saw a pale blur streaking across the road from the green. There was a sudden pounce, and the blur became a white puppy with a madly wagging tail and a paper-wrapped stick in its mouth. The puppy looked up expectantly.

The man chuckled and took Ana's stick. With one smooth motion, he pulled back and tossed it in a high, turning arc. The puppy tore after it with short, delighted barks.

"At least you didn't get my newspaper this time, you scamp." The man grinned, picked up the Sunday edition, and went inside. His door shut behind him with a click.

Ana stared down in disbelief.

Footsteps sounded on the attic stairs. "Someone is coming!" cried the little girls as they raced for the box.

The attic door was opening. It was too late to climb down the ladder. Ana lay flat on her stomach and rested her head on her arms with the calm of desperation.

"In here," said Miss Barmy's voice, and rat toenails clicked across the wooden floor.

Ana shivered as a cool breeze from the window touched her shoulders. Miss Barmy had never come up to the attic before.

"Careful, Father! Lay it flat. Now, Cheswick, set up the pieces just like Chippy showed you."

Ana looked hard between the rows of shelves. She could see something vast and shiny on the floor, and the feet of a piebald rat.

"Chippy," grumbled Cheswick, coming into Ana's field of view as he dragged a sack behind him. "*He's* not such a genius." The black rat pulled out something that clanked.

"Now, Father, get the little girls."

Ana's muscles tensed. There was a tremor of heavy footsteps, and a sliding sound as of a box being moved, and then no sound at all for what seemed to be a long time.

"Only four girls," said Miss Barmy pleasantly. "I wonder why?"

"There were five when I put them away last night," said Mr. B, sounding perplexed. "Don't blame me, Jane. I counted 'em, I know I did."

Miss Barmy didn't bother to answer. Ana watched with growing dread as the piebald rat's feet passed back and forth. Then the rat stopped, its tail alert.

A sniffing nose, a patchy face of pink and white and brown, thin veiny ears perked to catch the slightest sound—Miss Barmy's furry body slowly emerged from behind a shelf and turned, her eyes following the line of tiny footprints that showed plainly in the dust and stopped at the wall.

Miss Barmy raised her eyes to the windowsill, where the small bump of Ana's body showed dark against the window's light, and smirked. "Bring me the girl on the windowsill," she ordered Mr. B. "The rest of you, stand on the mirror. Cheswick will show you what to do."

Mr. B gave Ana a reproachful look as he picked her up in his callused hand. "Now you've gone and gotten me in trouble!"

Ana didn't really care. She was listening to an odd grating noise that had suddenly started up.

"Here she is, Jane," said Mr. B as he set Ana down on the floor. "She's very sorry. Right, little girl?"

Ana ignored him. She was watching Lisa and Lee walk in circles, pushing around something that looked like a cross between a turnstile and a miniature merry-go-round. The push-bars were pencils stuck into holes in the side of a thick metal ring about two inches high. The grating noise came from the metal ring, coated with grit on its bottom and pressed against the surface of a large mirror. Berit and Merry stood on a platform that fit on top of the metal ring, and held on to a central pole as they were turned slowly around. It was their weight that pressed the metal ring down, and Ana could see that, given enough time, the metal ring would cut a hole right through the mirror.

"Faster! Faster!" said Miss Barmy, looking at a watch that had been laid on the floor. "You have lots to cut, and not much time!"

"I could do it, precious," said Mr. B humbly. "I could do it for you faster."

"No, I want them to learn," snapped Miss Barmy. "Besides, they need the exercise."

Merry looked as if she were getting dizzy. "I'll help," said Ana suddenly. "Let Merry get off for a while."

Miss Barmy ignored her. "Bring me the archery set, Cheswick."

Ana stiffened as Cheswick pulled a bow and arrows out of his sack. Was he going to shoot her? But no. Miss Barmy put the bow in Ana's hands, and notched an arrow to the string. Ana flinched slightly at the touch of her claws.

"There you are, dear. While the other girls are cutting glass, I want you to practice archery. Shoot this arrow as high as you can, over and over. When you can shoot it over the third shelf up, I'll let your little friends rest."

Ana glanced at the girls' faces, already weary, and felt a slow, cold anger. Somewhere in the distance, church bells rang faintly once more, but this time she didn't bother to pray. "Why are you making us do this?"

Miss Barmy smiled with all her pointed teeth. "Why, for your health, of course. And that reminds me. Father, shut that window, and don't open it again. Too much fresh air is bad for little girls."

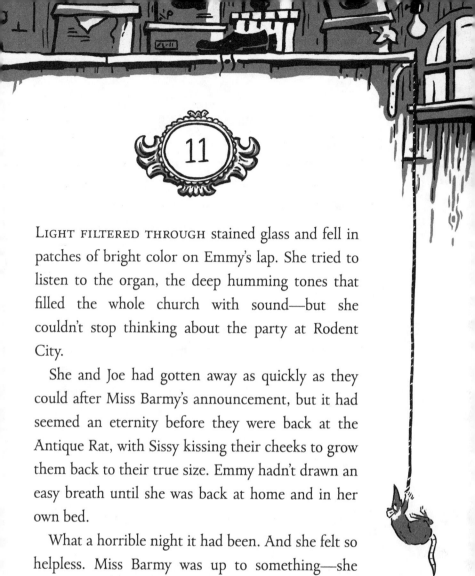

11

Light filtered through stained glass and fell in patches of bright color on Emmy's lap. She tried to listen to the organ, the deep humming tones that filled the whole church with sound—but she couldn't stop thinking about the party at Rodent City.

She and Joe had gotten away as quickly as they could after Miss Barmy's announcement, but it had seemed an eternity before they were back at the Antique Rat, with Sissy kissing their cheeks to grow them back to their true size. Emmy hadn't drawn an easy breath until she was back at home and in her own bed.

What a horrible night it had been. And she felt so helpless. Miss Barmy was up to something—she knew that in her bones. But she had no proof.

The congregation shuffled to its feet for the first hymn, and Emmy looked over her shoulder as latecomers filed in. A familiar pudgy figure trudged down the aisle, stopping to put a piece of paper in the box marked "Prayers."

What was Thomas so worried about that he had to put it in the prayer box?

The hymn was over. Emmy sat down and tried to listen, but it was just announcements.

All right, so maybe Miss Barmy was planning something. Why should Emmy care what happened in Rodent City, anyway? She had plans for this summer, and they didn't include her rodent friends. Her friends—ha! Mrs. Bunjee had turned against her, and Chippy had gone crazy for Miss Barmy. Sissy tried too hard, and as for Gus—if only to avoid Gus the gopher, Emmy would happily never set foot in Rodent City again. And Ratty? He was probably rehearsing with the Swinging Gerbils, and good luck to him.

Everyone stood up again, this time for prayers. Emmy shifted her weight as an usher brought up the request box . . . The pastor was reading them now. Most of the names Emmy didn't recognize. Her mind drifted off . . .

"Ana. Berit."

Emmy's head snapped up.

"Lisa. Lee."

Emmy turned her head to look for Thomas. He was sitting with his head bowed.

"Merry Pumpkin."

Emmy shrugged uneasily. Thomas could pray for a miracle if he liked, but she, for one, planned to forget about the girls. If the police couldn't find them, there was certainly nothing *she* could do.

Emmy sat alone on the sidelines of the soccer field. Joe's team seemed to be winning, but she didn't want to ask the score. The only people she knew (besides Thomas, who was chasing grasshoppers) were Joe's parents, Peter Peebles, and the girls who were sitting on a small grassy knoll beneath a shade tree.

Joe's father yelled too much. She had embarrassed herself in front of Mr. Peebles. And as for the girls, Emmy knew what they thought of her. "Stuck-up," Kate had said to Meg and Sara, and "I'm never going to ask her to do *anything* again."

Emmy felt the heat rise to her cheeks. If only she *were* stuck-up, it would be easy. She wouldn't care whether they liked her or not.

But she did care. She cared more than anything.

"Hey!"

Emmy looked around, then down. Of course; she should have known it would be another rodent. This one was small, round, and bouncy. Had it been at the party?

"Why are you crying?" The mouse jumped on her knee. Its fur was a soft tan, with a white star-shaped patch on the back of its head, and its tail was a long and delicate question mark.

"I'm *not* crying," Emmy said stiffly.

"Close enough." The mouse scanned her critically. "Listen, sad-eyes. What is it you want?"

"Nothing," mumbled Emmy. She wasn't going to tell her problems to a mouse, no matter how cute.

"Don't give me that." The mouse put a paw on its hip. "Make a wish. Pick one thing you really want, and tell me."

Emmy sighed. "That you would go away?"

The mouse blinked up at her, and Emmy felt suddenly ashamed. "Sorry, I didn't mean that. Let's see." She hesitated, looking around for inspiration.

"Do you want a new bike? More toys? World peace?"

"Sure. I'll take world peace."

"Just kidding. World peace is for everyone. Pick something for *you*."

Emmy smiled. She was starting to like this little mouse. She looked across at the group of girls—larger now, more had joined them—and pointed at them with her chin. "Okay, then, I wish I could go to a pool party with those girls. Or a sleepover."

"Is that all?"

"That's a lot," said Emmy. "Because it will never happen."

"I don't know," said the mouse. "Why don't you go over there and say hi?"

Emmy shook her head.

"Just do it," urged the mouse. "What's the worst that could happen?"

"They could laugh at me," said Emmy promptly, "or ignore me, or say something mean, or trip me and pretend it was an accident, or—"

"They don't look *that* mean," said the mouse, squinting. "Go on. You won't get your wish if you don't take the first step."

Emmy watched the mouse bounding away—it jumped an amazing distance for such a little thing—and thought about what it had said. It was true that the girls weren't really mean. They just had gotten the wrong idea about her.

Well, maybe it was worth a shot. Her heart beating lightly in her throat, Emmy walked along the sidelines. She would speak to Joe's parents after all, and on the way . . .

"Hi!" said Emmy, as she walked by Meg and Kate. Then she was past, and breathing again. At least she had shown them she wasn't as stuck-up as they'd thought—

"Hey, Emmy!" Meg ran up behind her and fell into step. "Listen, my mom said I could have a sleepover tonight. Do you want to come?"

Stunned, Emmy tried to act normal. "Sure—I'll just have to ask my parents." She thought of something else to say. "Should I bring anything? Chips?"

"Just your swimsuit. It's going to be a pool party, and we're having pizza, too."

Feeling as if she were in a dream, Emmy asked to borrow Mrs. Benson's cell phone. As she punched in her number, she dimly heard Mr. Peebles tell the Bensons that he couldn't stay but hadn't been able to resist stopping by to see how Joe was doing.

"After all, he's my—let's see—not a nephew, exactly . . ."

"You're my cousin, Peter," said Mrs. Benson promptly. "So that makes him—"

"Hello, Mom?" said Emmy into the phone. "Oh, Maggie. Could you get Mom, please?"

"—first cousin once removed," finished Mrs. Benson.

"Close enough," said Mr. Benson. "Look at that boy go!"

At last Emmy's mother got on the phone and gave permission. Mr. Peebles walked back to his office, and Emmy shyly joined Meg and her friends on their blanket.

Of course it was just a coincidence that she'd been invited, Emmy thought as she sat with the girls. The tan-and-white mouse had just given the advice grown-ups always gave—to smile, be friendly, say hi. And for once it had happened to work. There was nothing mysterious about it at all. And the fact that it was a sleepover *and* a pool party—well, that was coincidence, too. Kids had parties like that all the time.

There was a sudden commotion near the tree trunk behind Emmy. "Oh, he's so cute!" squealed one of the girls.

"Good doggie," coaxed Meg. "Do you want to play?"

Emmy turned to see a white puppy frisking at the edge of the blanket. He had dropped a stick, curiously wrapped with paper and twine, right in front of Kate.

"Ugh, dog slobber," said Kate. "*I'm* not throwing that thing."

"Why is it all tied up like that?" wondered Sara aloud.

"Hey, there's writing on it. Cut the string, somebody. Who's got a nail clipper?"

Meg had a jackknife in her pocket, and worked the blade under the tight strings, wet with dog drool.

"Read it, Meg."

"What does it say?"

"Not much—it's all chewed and wet. See?"

"It says, 'help us,'" said Kate, looking closely at the paper, "and here's another word—might be 'up'—up something. 'Upsies'?"

"'Upstairs,'" said Meg, looking over Kate's shoulder. "And 'prison'—no, it's 'prisoners.' Here, unfold it—there's another line. 'We are only four inches tall' . . ."

The girls all laughed.

"It's just some kids pretending," said Meg. "Here,

154

puppy, go fetch!" She tossed the stick, and the puppy shot off, barking happily.

"Does anybody know these kids?" asked Kate. "Ana, Berit, Lee something—I can't read the rest . . ."

Emmy caught her breath. "Could I see that?"

She looked at the paper in her hand, and the pieces suddenly fit together. Of course the police hadn't found the girls when they'd searched. They would have been looking for full-sized children, not girls that could fit inside a teacup.

Emmy got up, unable to sit still any longer. "Just stretching my legs," she said vaguely. She walked off and looked at the paper in the sun. Yes, there they were: five signatures, faint and wet, but still legible if you knew what to look for. She could see the long tail of Merry's "y" curving past a chewed part.

Prisoners . . . upstairs . . . at the Home for Troubled Girls. Five girls, smart and brave enough to send a message the only way they knew how. Hoping that whoever got it would figure out how to find them.

Emmy walked slowly back to the shade tree. She could report this to the police and ask them to search again, but what good would that do? They'd just laugh, and tell her to stop playing.

The professor would believe her. He would know what to do next.

Emmy folded the paper carefully and put it in her pocket. Out on the field, someone blew a whistle. And at her feet, there was a tiny sneeze.

Emmy glanced down to see a rat's face poking from a hole in the ground, and flinched. Not Sissy, not now . . . She walked on, hoping Sissy would get the hint.

"Pssst! Emmy!" said Cecilia, trotting after.

Emmy turned, irate. Hadn't anyone at the Speedy Rodent Messenger Service told her to stay far from crowds? Hadn't anyone taught her the first rule of rodent safety?

"A message for Emmy Addison, from Raston Rat . . ." Sissy's nose was running again, but her words were clear.

Emmy squatted down and pretended to watch the game. Whoops—it was halftime already. All right, she would pretend to adjust her sandal strap. "Go away, Sissy," she said, very low. "Go back down the tunnel. It's not safe here."

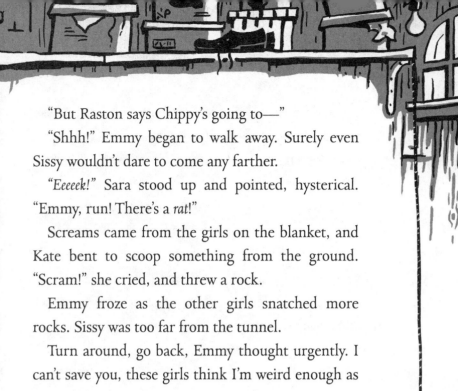

"But Raston says Chippy's going to—"

"Shhh!" Emmy began to walk away. Surely even Sissy wouldn't dare to come any farther.

"*Eeeeek!*" Sara stood up and pointed, hysterical. "Emmy, run! There's a *rat*!"

Screams came from the girls on the blanket, and Kate bent to scoop something from the ground. "Scram!" she cried, and threw a rock.

Emmy froze as the other girls snatched more rocks. Sissy was too far from the tunnel.

Turn around, go back, Emmy thought urgently. I can't save you, these girls think I'm weird enough as it is . . .

Stones rattled on either side of the rat. Sissy shot one terrified look up at Emmy, then whirled in desperation and ran the wrong way. Someone threw a rock that hit her hard, flipping her onto her side with a high-pitched squeal that pierced Emmy's heart.

"No!" Emmy cried, too late to do any good. She ran toward the girls with her hands outstretched. "It's okay, I'm okay, don't throw any more—look!" she said with false brightness. "It's halftime!"

Somehow she convinced them all that it was only

a ground squirrel, that it was no threat, that Joe had waved to one of them to come over—no, she didn't know which one—yes, he was the cutest boy in class, she thought so, too . . .

Emmy chattered on until their attention was solidly on something else, and then she sneaked a backward look. Sissy, trailing a thin line of blood, was dragging herself along the ground. As Emmy watched, the slender gray rat inched into a tunnel and slowly disappeared.

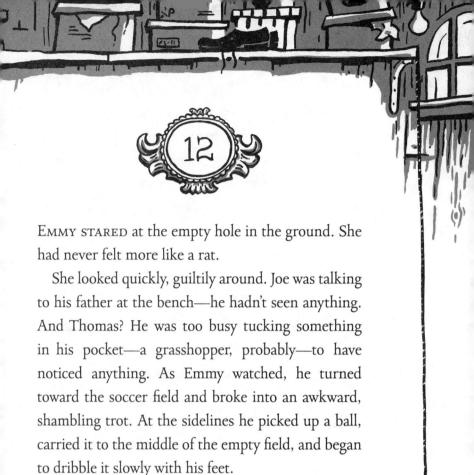

12

EMMY STARED at the empty hole in the ground. She had never felt more like a rat.

She looked quickly, guiltily around. Joe was talking to his father at the bench—he hadn't seen anything. And Thomas? He was too busy tucking something in his pocket—a grasshopper, probably—to have noticed anything. As Emmy watched, he turned toward the soccer field and broke into an awkward, shambling trot. At the sidelines he picked up a ball, carried it to the middle of the empty field, and began to dribble it slowly with his feet.

He couldn't dribble at all. It was almost painful to watch him, but he shuffled along and kicked it at last, right into the goal. Of course, Emmy thought, he could hardly have missed, he was standing ten feet in front of it—but the ball was solidly kicked and it hit the net with a satisfying *thwap*.

Thomas looked to the sidelines, where his father was talking with the coach.

"Good job, honey!" called his mother, waving.

Thomas waved briefly, then retrieved the ball and put it down on the field again, a few yards farther from the goal this time. Emmy was surprised that he was showing such an interest in soccer, when there were grasshoppers to catch and rodents to talk to.

She glanced over her shoulder again at the tunnel into which Sissy had crawled. Still empty. Or wait— *was* that the same hole?

Emmy felt irritable. She couldn't keep track of all the little burrows in the schoolyard—there must be a zillion. And how the rodents themselves kept their bearings underground, she didn't know. Maybe they had little signposts.

The girls around her were giggling over something or other. Emmy tried to laugh along, but she couldn't stop thinking about Cecilia.

What had the rat expected, popping up like that in broad daylight? It was her own fault if she got hurt. And why hadn't the Messenger Service trained her better? For that matter, Ratty should have known that his sister was too inexperienced to be let out alone.

Emmy shifted her weight uncomfortably. Maybe all that was true, but she was the one who had stood by while a friend got rocks thrown at her. Emmy couldn't forget the look of helpless panic in Sissy's eyes.

Emmy lifted her shoulders and dropped them, as if trying to get a weight to slide off. It wasn't really her fault. *She* hadn't thrown the rock that hit Sissy. Anyway, Sissy was going to be okay. She must be nearly back to Rodent City by now. It was only across Main Street, and even if the tunnel had a few twists and turns, it wouldn't be long before she would be tucked up in bed, with a bandage on her leg and a mug of hot chocolate on a tray. Mrs. Bunjee would see to that.

Emmy cheered up at the thought of Mrs. Bunjee. Cecilia would be in good hands. Still, it would be a nice gesture to check in at Rodent City and see how she was doing. If Emmy walked over to the art gallery, she could quietly speak into the crack in the steps that was the front entrance, and some rodent might come up and give her the news.

The sun was high overhead, and warm on Emmy's neck. There was a pleasant buzz of conversation going on all around her, and bits and pieces came through the general murmur: "Whose puppy is that?" "And so I said to Jenna—" "Hey, that kid can kick!" None of it was about a rat, and none of it was about Emmy.

Relaxing, Emmy put her hands in her pockets. At least no one seemed to think she was any weirder than before. Her fingers rubbed against a damp piece of paper, and she stiffened. She couldn't forget the little girls. She had to show the letter to Joe.

She found him standing a little way off from his team, his shoulders hunched. "What's up?" He lifted his head.

Emmy had a sudden urge to confess what had happened to Sissy, but she didn't do it. "Look," she said, and told him about the note.

Joe studied the signatures. "Wow . . . you're right. There's the dot from the 'i' in Lisa, and part of the '-ry' in 'Merry' . . ." He looked up. "They're *alive*! We've got to find them. The minute this game is over, let's—" He stopped abruptly.

"What?" Emmy asked, startled at the black look of anger on his face.

"I forgot. I won't be here. I'm going to stupid *California*."

Thomas came up, flushed and happy, holding the soccer ball. Joe handed him the note and turned away, a muscle working in his cheek.

"But I thought your dad was going to get a refund!" protested Emmy.

Joe didn't answer.

Thomas looked up. "The soccer camp doesn't give refunds. Dad said they'd only give our money back if Joe had a letter from the doctor that said he couldn't play. Like if he broke his ankle or something."

"I wish I *would* break my ankle," said Joe bitterly. A whistle blew, and he stalked off to take his place on the field.

Thomas bent over the note, his lips moving as he read. A small tan-and-white mouse popped its head out of Thomas's pocket and turned an alert gaze on Emmy. "So—are you going to the sleepover?"

Emmy was startled. How had it known she'd been invited?

The whistle blew again, and the ball was kicked. Then, suddenly, there was a snap and a sharp cry. A blue-jerseyed player was down, his pale hair spread on the grass.

The coach ran on the field with a first-aid kit. Mr. and Mrs. Benson followed as the players milled around.

Emmy stared at all the commotion. "What happened?" she asked one of the players as he passed.

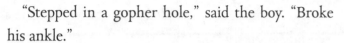

"Stepped in a gopher hole," said the boy. "Broke his ankle."

The mouse in Thomas's pocket nodded briskly and dusted its paws with a satisfied air. "That's three," it said, and leaped to the ground. It bounded off toward the field where Emmy had first seen it, jumping a foot at a time.

"Wait!" Emmy ran after it, but she didn't dare call out in more than a whisper, and the mouse didn't stop. It popped into the ground right before her eyes. Emmy sat down beside its burrow, breathing hard.

"Come out," she begged. *"Please."* She looked up to see her new friends glancing curiously her way.

"What is it now?" The bouncy rodent poked its nose out.

"Did you . . ." Emmy hesitated. "Did *you* break Joe's ankle?"

"Of course not!" The mouse was chagrined.

"But he wished, and then it happened, just like me getting invited to the party."

The mouse lifted one shoulder expressively, ruffling the star on its back. "I merely allowed his wish to take physical form."

"Well, then—could you take it back? What if I wished that Joe's ankle wasn't broken, after all? I don't think he really meant it."

"Sorry," said the mouse firmly. "Three wishes only, and no changing your mind."

"What do you mean? Three wishes per day? I know it's not three per person, because I only had one, and Joe only had one . . ."

The mouse scrubbed at its ears in frustration. "Leave me in peace, will you? You humans are never satisfied. You think you'd be happy to get your heart's desire, but noooo . . ."

The small annoyed voice dwindled as the mouse disappeared into the tunnel. Too late, Emmy realized that she had forgotten to ask what the third wish had been.

Thomas came up, puffing slightly.

"It was a *wishing* rodent," said Emmy. "Did you know?"

Thomas beamed over the soccer ball in his arms. "I thought it might be. Do you suppose it will give more wishes?"

"*No!*" cried a voice from the tunnel, and somewhere below a door banged shut.

165

"I guess not," said Emmy. She led the way back to the sidelines, where the spectators were clustered. Mrs. Benson had brought the car right up over the grass, and Mr. Benson, looking very anxious, was carrying Joe off the field.

Joe's face was tense with pain, but as he passed, Emmy thought he looked more mystified than upset. She gave him a small, private wave, and he attempted a grin.

"That's my brave boy," said Mrs. Benson, tucking him into the back seat. "Oh, Thomas. You'll have to come with us—we're going to the doctor's to get an X-ray."

"Can't I stay with Emmy? She'll babysit me." Thomas slipped his hand into Emmy's and looked up with wide, trusting eyes.

Emmy managed to keep from laughing. "I sure will, Mrs. Benson, if that's okay with you."

"All right—but you two stay together, and don't go swimming in the lake!"

"What did you run off for?" asked Meg curiously, as the Benson car drove away.

"Maybe she was playing cops and robbers," said Sara, to general laughter.

166

Emmy tried to think fast. She wasn't about to say that she ran after a wishing mouse—but she couldn't think of an excuse that sounded good.

"She was trying to catch something for me," said Thomas. "She's babysitting me, you know." He gave them the same blue-eyed, innocent look he had used on his mother, and it worked just as well on the girls.

"Cool," said Sara enviously. "I'm not allowed to babysit yet."

"Emmy, Emmy!" Thomas tugged at her sleeve in a babyish way. "Take me to see the professor, okay? You said I could show him my soccer kick. You promised!"

Emmy looked at him in admiration. For six, he was awfully quick. "Sorry, girls—I'll see you tonight." And just that easily, they were on their way to the Antique Rat.

"I should really make you hold my hand, crossing the street," said Emmy as they came to the road.

"Don't push it," said Thomas calmly. "Anyway, I'm carrying a ball."

Emmy grinned and steered him toward the art-gallery steps. "Do me a favor, will you? Pretend you're catching bugs or something, and call down

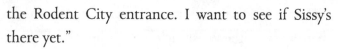

the Rodent City entrance. I want to see if Sissy's there yet."

Emmy sat on the brick steps while Thomas knelt by the crack, clearing away chunks of rubble. "Anyone there?" he called quietly.

No one answered. Thomas crawled around a large concrete planter in order to look at the broken sidewalk that the jackhammer had left in front of the jewelry store. The workman had pulled out the pipes and left them lying, and covered the pipe hole in the wall with a temporary flap. Thomas picked up a small copper pipe and fit it into a larger one, moving it back and forth like a slide trombone.

There was a sudden protesting squeak, and a black rat slid out the far end of the pipe, landing on the rubble. He had a cloth measuring tape in his paws. As soon as he saw daylight, he skittered past Thomas's knee and up the side of the planter. He dived in among a mass of pink petunias, the tape measure unrolling behind him.

Emmy parted the foliage and peered in. Cheswick Vole and Miss Barmy glared back with enraged expressions on their whiskered faces.

Emmy jerked away, her heart beating fast. Feeling

foolish, she remembered that she was now full-sized, and Miss Barmy was only a rat. Still, she was a mean rat with teeth and claws, and Emmy picked up a small piece of pipe just in case.

She felt much stronger holding the pipe. She looked closely at Miss Barmy, who had a clipboard in her paw, filled with small, neatly penciled numbers.

"What are you doing?" Emmy demanded.

Miss Barmy slid the clipboard behind a petunia stem and straightened, smoothing the front of her gold-and-green track suit. "Still no friends your own age, Emmy?" She turned to Cheswick, who was hiding the tape measure behind a thicket of leaves. "She was never very popular. She never brought anyone home to play."

"Only because you *drugged* them," Emmy said hotly. "You came to my class at school and used a rodent potion to make sure the kids didn't even know I existed!"

"Still pretending, I see." Miss Barmy's laughter tinkled. "Have you gotten any help yet, Emmaline? A psychiatrist could assist with your delusions . . . and perhaps help you make a few friends, too."

"I'm her friend," said Thomas stoutly.

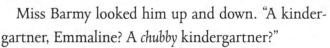

Miss Barmy looked him up and down. "A kinder-gartner, Emmaline? A *chubby* kindergartner?"

A wave of scarlet washed up into Thomas's round face, turning his scalp pink beneath his blond hair. "I'm not a kindergartner," he said, scrambling awkwardly to his feet. "My name's Thomas Benson, and I'm almost a second-grader."

"But you're fat, Thomas," said Miss Barmy pleasantly. "And clumsy, too, I see. Isn't your brother Joe Benson, the athlete? Why can't you be more like him?"

Emmy, rigid with anger, opened her mouth. But Thomas was already stumbling into the alley, the soccer ball clutched to his chest.

There was nothing Emmy could say that would make the slightest difference. She contented herself with banging the side of the planter with one of the pipes—a fine, ringing blow; she hoped it hurt their eardrums—and then ran after Thomas.

He said nothing until they got to the Antique Rat. "I'm not coming in." Thomas looked away.

"But don't you want to see Brian? And the charas-cope? And say hi to the professor?"

"I want to practice my kicks." Thomas dropped

the ball at his feet and bumped it slowly toward the green.

Emmy sighed deeply and rang the bell. She had a strong desire to go back to the planter and strangle Miss Barmy with her own two hands. She didn't think she could quite manage to murder her in cold blood, but it was tempting.

"They had a clipboard? And a tape measure?" Professor Capybara leaned back in his swivel chair, gazing absently at the vials lined up on the laboratory counter. "Buck, do you have any idea what they might be up to?"

A chipmunk, looking much like Chippy but a little bulkier in build, lifted his head from the eyepiece of the charascope. "They're up to no good, I can tell you that much."

"Now, now," said the professor, "let's not be extreme. Your mother and Chippy don't think so—"

Buck snorted. "Mother and Chippy have gone nutso."

Relief flooded Emmy. "So you don't think Miss Barmy's changed?"

"If that lady's changed, then I'm a marmot," said

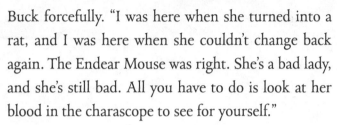

Buck forcefully. "I was here when she turned into a rat, and I was here when she couldn't change back again. The Endear Mouse was right. She's a bad lady, and she's still bad. All you have to do is look at her blood in the charascope to see for yourself."

Emmy felt a sudden twinge of conscience. What would her own blood look like now? She had stood by while a friend was pelted with rocks, just so she wouldn't look weird. Was her blood now gummed up with . . . with whatever cowardice looked like?

She picked up a pink marble paperweight—a rat, of course—and balanced it in her hand. It had a cool, heavy feel, and somehow it calmed her. Sissy was going to be fine. Emmy would ask Buck to go down the back tunnel to Rodent City and check. If only she could think of a good way to explain what had happened . . . Emmy opened her mouth and found herself telling about the wishing mouse instead.

Professor Capybara looked thoughtful. "I don't remember a wishing mouse. Did you say it could jump?"

Emmy nodded. "It practically *bounced*. I've never seen a mouse leap like that."

"It must have been some kind of field mouse," said Buck. "Not all rodents of power live in the city. Some prefer the wild."

"The playground isn't exactly the *wild*," said Emmy doubtfully.

Buck's chipmunk teeth gleamed. "They're surrounded by wild rodents, though. Most of them can barely understand us. They dig tunnels every which way—no sense of direction or signage."

The professor ran his fingers through his hair distractedly. "When Cheswick stole the rats and trucked them here, and I unlocked as many cages as I could, most of the escaped rodents helped me establish Rodent City. But others just scattered. I didn't know all their powers yet, anyway, and then Cheswick disarranged all my notes . . ."

"But I'm helping you now, Professor," said Brian, laying two folders on the desk. "Here's the data you wanted on Buck and the Bushy-Tailed Snoozer Rat."

"Do you think you're close to finding a cure?" asked Emmy. The Snoozer virus had the unfortunate effect of making a person fall asleep whenever there was a little too much excitement, and the professor was infected.

"Possibly," said Professor Capybara. "Buckram, here, has an interesting ability that may just help."

There was a pause as the professor opened Buck's folder and flipped through it. Emmy put a hand in her pocket and smoothed the crumpled paper, chewed by the puppy.

"Professor, I have something else to tell you."

"Yes, yes, just a moment—"

There was a muffled thud from outside, and the delicately balanced vials quivered. Emmy glanced out the window to see the soccer ball spinning back to Thomas.

"Well, Buck, are you ready to put Brian to sleep again?" The professor smiled at Emmy. "Buckram, we've discovered, has a rather unusual power. He can give a full night's sleep to anyone in just fifteen minutes."

Brian nodded. "I was up all night organizing the professor's folders, and I'm not even sleepy!"

The thud came again. The windows rattled slightly.

"I'm sure you're wondering how this can help with the Snoozer virus," said the professor, beaming.

"Uh—sure." Emmy fingered the note from the little girls.

"Well, we hypothesize that a reverse effect may occur when—" The professor stopped as the outside wall shook with a steady, rhythmic pounding.

"What's that noise?" Professor Capybara put his hands to his head. "I can't think!"

"It's just Thomas—I'll tell him to stop," said Emmy hurriedly. She stepped outside to see the pudgy boy, a look of fierce concentration on his face, kicking the soccer ball hard against the brick. Surprised, Emmy watched as his foot snapped out to catch the ball on the rebound with the precision of a machine.

"Um—Thomas? Would you please do that somewhere else?"

Thomas grabbed for the ball, fumbled, and fell down. "Okay," he said from the ground. "Where should I kick it?"

"Anywhere—just not against the wall. The professor can't think with all the noise."

Thomas nodded. Emmy went inside, where Brian was already stretched out on the couch, snoring. Buck, eyes shut, was curled up under his chin.

"I wouldn't mind getting a full night's sleep in fifteen minutes," said Emmy. "Especially before a sleepover."

"Perhaps we can let you try it sometime." Professor Capybara glanced out the window. "Now, what was it you wanted to tell me?"

Emmy opened her mouth—but in that instant, the Sunday-afternoon quiet was split by the violent sound of breaking glass.

Emmy ran to the door. Thomas stood in the middle of the green, open-mouthed, staring across to the shoe shop. From its shattered second-story window came a loud and piercing screech.

"UNBELIEVABLE!" The professor's beard wagged in his enthusiasm. "I didn't know Thomas could kick like that! Brian, did you *see*?"

"Brian's still asleep," said Emmy nervously as the screeching intensified. "Professor, we'd better go help Thomas. Mrs. B is coming out."

"Certainly, certainly." Professor Capybara hurried out the door and across the green to the park bench against which Thomas had backed in stunned silence.

Emmy followed more slowly. She was beginning to get an idea of what the third wish had been. And she was not eager to meet Mrs. B, who had a reputation for throwing flowerpots.

The scrawny figure of Mrs. B came stamping out of her front door. She was still screaming hoarsely, but now it was possible to distinguish a few words: "vandals," "damages," "the law." She was followed by an apologetic Mr. B, wringing his hands.

"You seem to be upset, dear lady," began Professor

Capybara in a tone apparently meant to be calming. Unfortunately, it seemed to infuriate Mrs. B even more.

"UPSET? I'LL SHOW YOU UPSET!!!" Mrs. B raised her purse and began whacking the professor about the head.

"Hey!" he shouted, trying to fend her off. "Get away, you—you crazy person—"

Emmy saw with horror that his eyes were closing. "Stay calm, Professor!" she cried, but it was too late. Professor Capybara rocked on his feet and suddenly slumped onto the park bench, sound asleep.

"Got him!" crowed Mrs. B in triumph. Then she tucked her purse under her arm, gripped Thomas by one ear, and towed the boy to the shoe shop, protesting and crying.

Emmy spared one look for the professor, snoring happily under the influence of the Snoozer virus. No help there. And Brian wasn't due to wake up for another ten minutes at least.

But she *couldn't* leave Thomas with that awful woman. Feeling as if events were moving too fast, Emmy ran after them, unsure of what to do. And then she had an idea.

"Mr. Peebles! Mr. Peebles!" she cried, running up the steps to his law office and pounding on the front door. "Come quick!"

Inside the shoe shop, Peter Peebles gazed gravely at the broken glass strewn on the floor of the second-story sitting room. Then he gave Mrs. B a long, measuring look. "And *this* is the reason you assaulted Mr. Capybara?"

"He broke it! He kicked that ball right through my window!"

"Who? Professor Capybara?"

"No, that little fat boy!" Mrs. B pointed a long, red-lacquered nail at Thomas, who had taken refuge behind the door.

Peter Peebles's face grew stern. "No personal attacks, *if* you please. Emmy and Thomas, step out of the room for a moment, will you?"

Emmy grabbed Thomas's hand and scooted out onto the second-floor landing. "Did you see it?" whispered Emmy.

"What? The crate of flowerpots?"

"The dollhouse on the table—it had a sign. 'The Home for Troubled Girls.'"

Thomas put his eye to the crack by the door hinges. "I see it! What did the professor say when you showed him the note?"

Emmy stood up, startled. In all the excitement over the broken window, she had neglected to tell the professor about the message from the girls. And now, of course, he was asleep. She put her hand in her pocket and felt the note, no longer damp. Were they in the dollhouse this very minute?

Mr. Peebles's courtroom voice, deep and authoritative, carried past the half-closed door. "You have already acted very foolishly over this incident. It is altogether possible that Professor Capybara will want to press charges. Furthermore," he added loudly as Mrs. B began to protest, "I am now going to see if the professor was badly hurt by your assault with a"—he coughed—"well, let us say with a leather weapon."

"It was a *purse*!"

"Deadly indeed, in the right hands," intoned Mr. Peebles. "And if you don't want him to call the police and charge you with assault, I'd suggest you come with me and beg him to accept your apology."

"Me? *Apologize?*" Mrs. B sounded outraged. "What about my *window*? What about that delinquent *boy*?"

Emmy took her turn at the crack between the door and the jamb. Mrs. B's yellow face had turned a furious tomato red. Mr. B, looking somewhat desperate, was trying to soothe her and placate Mr. Peebles at the same time. Emmy caught apologetic fragments— "Now, honey bunny . . . Now, my dear sir, don't be hasty . . . Precious lambkin, maybe we *should* . . ."

Emmy and Thomas backed quietly into the shadows as Mr. Peebles strode out of the room. He was closely followed by Mrs. B, who was clawing at his arm, and Mr. B, who was holding her around the waist. The whole heaving group went down the stairs as one mass and out the door.

Emmy darted into the room and peered inside the dollhouse. "Anybody home?" she called softly.

The dollhouse was empty. Thomas got on his knees to search below the table while Emmy picked her way through the glassy shards to the window. Mr. Peebles and Mr. and Mrs. B were on their way across the green. The professor was still stretched out on the park bench. This was going to take a while.

"They aren't *anywhere*," said Thomas.

Emmy was silent. The sound of angry voices came

faintly through the broken window like the distant buzzing of bees. Sunshine, warm and golden, stretched across the room. Tiny particles of dust swam through the bright rays, silently swirling. One shaft of light extended a long finger past the door to the square landing, illuminating the first two treads on the battered staircase leading to the attic.

Emmy felt shivery inside. She lifted one foot—

"Emmy!" Thomas pounded past her up the steps. "Come on, hurry!"

At the top there was a small landing and a thick oaken door with a brass keyhole.

"It's locked," said Emmy, trying the door. Thomas pointed silently at a key hanging on a nail just beyond his reach.

It was heavy in Emmy's hand. She fit it in the lock and heard the latch click.

"Come *on*, Emmy!" Thomas was hopping in his impatience.

Emmy took a breath and pushed at the door. It creaked open, and they slipped inside.

The attic was huge, dusty, hot, and lined with endless rows of shelves. It looked like some old, forgotten shoe warehouse, holding box upon box marked with sizes and colors and price tags. But there was more than just shoes. There was old furniture, and stacks of magazines and books, and piles of junk everywhere.

Emmy looked around in hopeless desperation. They didn't have much time. How were they supposed to find the tiny girls in all this mess—if they were even here?

"Little girls?" Thomas called softly, squatting to look under a shelf.

"No, Thomas." Emmy grabbed him by the shoulder. "Not you—me."

"But I want to find them!" he protested.

Emmy shook her head. "I'm older. I can look faster. You be the lookout."

"But—"

"Cabin boy! Obey orders!"

Thomas saluted reluctantly. "Aye-aye, captain." He went to stand by the open door as Emmy padded down an aisle, her head turning from side to side.

Light streamed in through a filthy window, shut tight. Emmy frowned. The window was awfully high off the floor. If the girls had been here—and if the window had been open before—they would still

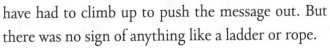

have had to climb up to push the message out. But there was no sign of anything like a ladder or rope.

She pushed aside an umbrella, a rubber boot, and a stack of boxes; she called softly, feeling like a fool. If the girls were too afraid to answer—and she wouldn't blame them if they were, she must seem like a giant—she wouldn't be able to locate them in a year, much less a few minutes. Or maybe they weren't here at all.

Emmy glanced nervously over her shoulder. Was Thomas still watching the stairs? She walked down another aisle, and another. Mr. and Mrs. B wouldn't stay away forever. She poked her head around a bin of old kitchen tools and gasped. Thomas was squatting down, gazing at the floor.

"Thomas!" she hissed. "Get back to the door!"

Thomas's smooth blond head didn't turn. "Emmy, look at this."

Upset and anxious, Emmy moved swiftly. "I don't care how interesting that bug is! When you're lookout, you can't just *leave*—"

Thomas pointed a chubby finger. Emmy bent over, staring. There, plain in the dust, was a trail of tiny footprints.

So it was true. They were really here—or had been recently.

Emmy got down on her hands and knees to follow the tracks. Behind her, Thomas made a small noise in his throat. All at once Emmy's head jerked back as a bony hand gripped her ear.

"Snooping, are you?" whispered Mrs. B, kicking dust over the tiny tracks. She hauled Emmy and Thomas out to the landing and shook them viciously as a startled Mr. B looked on.

"As if breaking—my window—wasn't enough," Mrs. B snarled between shakes, "now you *break*—into my *attic*! You're going to *jail*, you little sneaks!"

"I think *not*," said an authoritative voice.

Abruptly Mrs. B was pulled away, and the familiar form of Mr. Peebles took her place. He dusted off the children and looked at them grimly. "Let's get out of here. We'll deal with this in my office."

The attic door shut with a bang. Mrs. B turned the key in the lock with a *snick*. "We've been careless and trusting, Mr. B," she said, dropping the brass key into her pocket. "We won't make *that* mistake again."

"No, dear," said Mr. B. "Certainly not."

Mr. Peebles's grip on Emmy's shoulder was firm as

185

he hustled the children down the stairs and out onto the sidewalk. Suddenly the hair on Emmy's head lifted as something swooshed past. There was a shattering sound of crockery and she spun, startled, to see the smashed remains of a flowerpot on the sidewalk.

"Oops!" said Mrs. B, leaning out of the window over their heads. "Must have slipped. How *clumsy* of me."

Peter Peebles's face was grim. "Do that again and I'll sue."

"For what?"

"Reckless endangerment," he said coldly. "Illegal discharge of a flowerpot in a residential area. Come along, children."

He marched them up the steps to his wide front porch. "Sit," he commanded, pointing to the porch swing. "Whatever possessed you to go into that attic? Don't you know better than to poke around in people's houses without permission?"

"Yes, sir," said Emmy, nodding fervently. If she was polite enough, maybe he wouldn't tell her parents.

"It was my fault," said Thomas, clutching the soccer ball he had snatched up on their way out. "I ran upstairs, and then Emmy had to come after me." He opened his blue eyes wide, his round face angelic. "I always *wanted* to play in an attic."

Peter Peebles snorted. "If you want to play in an attic, you're welcome to visit mine—but stay out of other people's!" He fished a phone out of his pocket.

Emmy stiffened. Was he going to call her parents after all?

"Hello, Jack? Listen, I've got Thomas here—"

Emmy's shoulders slumped in relief.

There was a pause. "No, no problems—well, just one. He kicked a soccer ball through a neighbor's window, and they're upset. But I've talked to them, and—"

This time the pause was longer. "Yes, a soccer ball—yes, quite a long way. He's got a powerful kick, you know."

Mr. Benson's excited voice could be heard over the cell phone. Thomas swung his legs placidly.

Out on the green, the professor was sitting up groggily on the park bench, and Brian was bending over him. Emmy glanced at Mr. Peebles. He was still on the phone—now he was asking about Joe's ankle. She stood up, walked casually to the top of the porch steps, and looked back. Mr. Peebles frowned and shook his head.

Emmy sighed. She would have to wait to tell the professor about the tiny girls, but she hoped she didn't have to wait too long.

"He *did* break his ankle? I see . . . So what about the California soccer camp?"

Mr. Peebles's voice faded into a background drone as Emmy edged over to the railing and looked up at the house next door. She couldn't see much of the attic window from this angle.

The afternoon sun slanted over the tops of the trees. It was hours before sunset, on this longest day of the year. Emmy remembered that she had a pool party to go to, and Meg had said they were planning pizza. At the thought, her stomach growled lightly.

There was another growl, and then a series of noises that sounded like the clash of small cymbals mixed with the high-pitched squeal of an amplifier. The sounds were coming from somewhere beneath Emmy's feet. Improbably, she heard a familiar voice singing something that sounded like "a hunk, a hunka rodent love."

"Will you *stop* with the Elvis tunes?" shouted an enraged voice.

"But that's a *great* song!" pleaded another. "One of

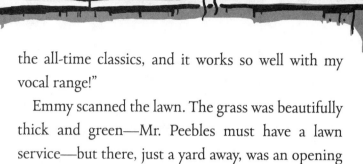

the all-time classics, and it works so well with my vocal range!"

Emmy scanned the lawn. The grass was beautifully thick and green—Mr. Peebles must have a lawn service—but there, just a yard away, was an opening in the ground the size of a large cookie.

As she watched, there was another shriek, and a confused scrabbling at the mouth of the tunnel. In a flurry of gray, a small rodent-shaped body flew out as if forcibly propelled from behind, and landed, tumbling, on the lawn.

"And stay out!" A rodent in a black T-shirt poked his head out from the tunnel's mouth and shook his fist. "We're a *swing* band, not a burnt-out Vegas act!"

"You're just jealous because I know all the words to 'You Ain't Nothin' but a Rodent'!" shouted Raston Rat, picking himself up from the grass.

Mocking laughter came from farther down the tunnel, and dwindled into silence.

Emmy leaned over the railing. "What was that all about?"

"Artistic differences," said the Rat. His whiskers bristled with indignation. "I had *vision*! I had *theme*! I could have taken them in a whole new direction!"

Emmy took a quick look over her shoulder.

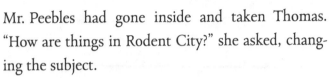

Mr. Peebles had gone inside and taken Thomas. "How are things in Rodent City?" she asked, changing the subject.

"Terrible." The Rat scampered onto the porch and up Emmy's leg into her pocket.

"*Ow!*" said Emmy, wincing.

"Beauty-contest this, beauty-contest that," said Raston, his voice muffled, "and Miss Barmy everywhere you look. She's even got Mrs. Bunjee and Chippy on her side now. Sissy gave you my message, so you know all about Chippy—"

Emmy caught her breath. If Ratty knew that Sissy had delivered the message, she must have gotten back then, and not been too badly hurt, or Ratty would have mentioned it. And she must not have told how Emmy had failed to protect her.

A feeling of warm gratitude seeped through Emmy. It came to her that she had never properly appreciated Sissy's tactful, loving heart.

But what *had* the message been about Chippy? Cecilia had never finished it. Emmy didn't want to ask straight out, or Ratty would want to know why the full message hadn't been delivered.

Emmy avoided looking down into her pocket at

the Rat. She glanced out at the green and saw the professor and Brian walking slowly toward her. At last. Now she could tell them about the little girls. The professor would figure out some way to rescue them, and she could go to her pool party tonight with a clear conscience.

The Rat was still talking. "—and so I said to Chippy, 'If you believe that piebald princess, then I've got some land in Rabbitville I'd like to sell you—'"

Beep! Beep-beep!

A jaunty yellow car pulled up to the curb. Mr. Benson waved from the driver's seat, and as Mrs. Benson opened her door, the rear window rolled down and Joe's thatch of pale hair poked out.

Thomas slammed the screen door and pounded down the steps of the porch, followed by Mr. Peebles and Emmy. Professor Capybara and Brian angled toward the car, beaming.

"We can't stay long," called Mr. Benson. "We've got packing to do."

"Are you and Joe still going to California?" panted Thomas, running up with the soccer ball clasped to his chest.

"Half right," said Mr. Benson. "I'm going to California, and I'm taking your mother."

Thomas stared. "Mom's going to *soccer camp?*"

There were chuckles all around from the grown-ups. Emmy thought this was not fair, because it was a perfectly reasonable question.

"No, the soccer camp let us cancel because of Joe's ankle. But the airlines didn't." Mr. Benson ruffled Thomas's smooth blond hair. "They did let us switch the tickets, though—"

"So we decided, why not take a couple of days off?" Mrs. Benson finished happily.

"But who's going to take care of us?" Thomas looked at Joe.

The Rat moved restlessly in Emmy's pocket. She stepped back behind the professor, where the bulge on the side of her shorts couldn't be seen.

"You'll stay with Cousin Peter," answered Mrs. Benson. "It's all arranged."

Cousin Peter? thought Emmy, confused, and then she remembered. Of course. Peter Peebles was Mrs. Benson's cousin. Sometimes Emmy thought that half the people in Grayson Lake must be related.

"The attic room has the spare bed," said Peter Peebles. "They can make as much noise as they want up there—it's two floors above my office. Besides," he added with the ghost of a wink, "I understand Thomas has *always* wanted to play in an attic."

"Can I see it now?" Thomas begged.

Emmy edged closer to the open car window. Joe's ankle, elevated on a folded blanket, was thickly wrapped with some kind of cloth around wide metal strips. On the floor lay two padded crutches.

"It's not that bad," said Joe, shrugging. "It turned out to be the smallest bone in the ankle. See, he didn't even put a cast on it—just a splint."

"How long will it take to heal?"

"The doctor said six weeks or so. But I can't play soccer—not hard, anyway—for the rest of the summer." Joe gave Emmy a small grin.

Emmy wanted to tell him about the wishing mouse and the tiny girls, but there were too many people around. She didn't mind not telling about Sissy. Even though all had turned out well, Emmy still felt terrible every time she thought of what had happened.

She looked up at Mr. Peebles's house, and then at the shoe shop next door. Suddenly she saw that the attic windows faced each other. She stared, a thought forming.

There was a sudden whirring of bike pedals and a skid of brakes. Five girls stopped on the other side of the car. "Come on, Emmy! We're going to order pizza!"

Emmy glanced at the sun, appalled. Was it that late already? She hadn't even gone home to pack an overnight bag.

"Did I hear someone say 'pizza'?" The Rat poked his nose out.

Emmy covered his head with her hand and shoved him down into her pocket again. He made an awfully big bulge. She had to get rid of him.

"Thomas!" called Mrs. Benson, shading her eyes as she looked up to the attic window. "Come down, we have to go home and pack!"

Emmy grabbed her chance. "I'll get him!" she cried, and ran into the house and up the narrow stairs.

The attic room had a double bed and a bathroom, books in a bookshelf, and fishing rods stacked in a corner. The Rat leaped joyfully from Emmy's pocket to join Thomas, who was playing with bobbers in a tackle box.

"Hurry down, Thomas," Emmy said. "Your parents

have to pack and catch their plane. Ratty will be here when you get back."

Thomas thundered down the stairs. Emmy paused at the window.

Outside, the roof stuck out in a little ledge, ending in a gutter. From one corner of the house, an insulated phone line was stretched to a telephone pole in the alley, and another phone line stretched to the house next door.

Emmy stared. Through the glass she could see across the alley to the shoe shop, right into its third-floor attic room. And there, on the windowsill, stood a tiny girl.

"Rat! ratty! come and look!" Emmy said in a low voice.

No answer. There was a scratching sound somewhere behind the far wall—the Rat must have found a hole to investigate.

Emmy wrestled with the window sash and dragged it half open with a screech. She put her head out.

"I see you!" she shouted impulsively, hoping the little girl could hear her through the glass. "I'm coming!"

"Well, hurry up, then!" called a voice from below, and Emmy glanced down, startled. Meg and the rest of the girls looked up, their faces oval blurs against the green grass. Mr. Benson started his engine with a roar.

Emmy gave a last, anxious look across the alley. The little girl on the sill was standing perfectly still, her tiny palms pressed against the window glass.

Slowly Emmy backed away. What on earth had

made her shout that she was coming? She couldn't go in the shoe shop again without getting into horrible trouble—and even if she did, there was no way into the attic, not with the key in Mrs. B's pocket.

But there *had* to be a way to rescue the little girls. She would tell the others. Together they'd figure something out. She'd start with Joe.

She rattled down the wooden stairs and burst out onto the porch. But the Bensons' car was already pulling away from the curb.

"Come on, Emmy!" Meg ran up and took her arm.

"Yeah, let's go, I'm starving," added Kate, and the girls surrounded Emmy, chattering all at once.

"But I haven't packed my pajamas and toothbrush," said Emmy, holding back. "And a swimsuit. You go on—I'll be there soon." She glanced at the professor and Brian, who were deep in conversation with Peter Peebles about rodentology and the law. *Someone* should know she had found the tiny girls.

"We'll help you pack!" said Sara, tugging at her other arm. "Come on, I'll give you a ride on my handlebars."

Emmy glanced up at the third-floor window of the shoe shop. She couldn't see anything from this angle.

Had the girl gone away? She turned back in time to see the professor and Brian follow Mr. Peebles into his office, still talking. The door shut.

How was Emmy supposed to go off and have fun at a pool party while the troubled girls were still captive? And yet there didn't seem to be anything else she could do. Something in her quailed at the idea of marching into Mr. Peebles's law office and demanding to speak to the professor and Brian alone, while Mr. Peebles frowned and the girls outside got mad at the delay.

After all, she thought gloomily, settling herself on Sara's handlebars, the little girls had been prisoners for years. One more day probably wouldn't kill them.

She tried to laugh and talk with the girls as they tore along on their bikes, planning the evening and arguing about pizza toppings, but it was hard to keep up the pretense that she was having fun. Still, she put a smile on her face. And by the time they skidded to a stop on her own driveway, the smile was almost real.

"Who wants to—" Emmy began, looking up at her bedroom window. She had been about to say "come up to my room," but she stopped at the sight of a familiar-looking chipmunk with a large sack on his back. As she watched, he leaped from a tree branch to her windowsill and lifted the flap on her screen.

"Who wants to what?" said Kate, letting her bike fall on the lawn.

Emmy turned, anxiously trying to think of a way to keep the girls from looking up. Her eyes fell on the woods behind the lawn, and she had an inspiration. "Who wants to play in my tree fort?" She pointed to the rope ladder dangling from the tallest oak.

"Me!" "Me!" came the cries, and "Last one up's a rotten egg!" called Kate.

Relieved, Emmy trudged inside, gave her mother a hug, and went to her room. It didn't take long to pack an overnight bag.

She stood at her playroom door and watched Chippy fill his sack from a pile of doll clothes. The pile was much smaller than it had been. He must have been going back and forth for hours.

Emmy scuffled her feet, and Chippy glanced up.

"Emmy!" he cried happily. "I've been here ten times without seeing you!"

"You're seeing me now," said Emmy, coldly polite.

Chippy sat up on his haunches, rubbing the back of his neck as if it ached. "I want to thank you," he said earnestly. "Janie—I mean, Miss Barmy—" His ears pinkened, and he cleared his throat. "She said you offered *all* your doll clothes for the beauty pageant. You've been *very* generous," he added, clasping his paws, "and it will mean so much to our contestants. *And* to Rodent City."

Emmy looked at him without expression.

"Don't you think so?" he added, a trifle uncertain.

"Oh, I'm sure of it," said Emmy.

The chipmunk brightened. "And Mother is getting so much sewing! Her paws are almost worn to nubs, she says, but it's worth it. This beauty pageant will bring in business from miles around. And Jane—I mean, Miss Barmy—has even *more* plans for our community. She's got ideas for a beauty salon, and a spa, and a tanning parlor, and she's already asked me to draw up plans for a tail-straightener and a whisker-curler, too."

Emmy felt a little sick. That Chippy, who had designed so many important things for Rodent City, should be reduced to creating a whisker-curler! It was too much. She wondered dully if this had been what Ratty had tried to warn her about when he sent the message through Sissy. Well, Chippy could have the doll clothes, and welcome. She didn't have time for an argument, and she didn't want to burst his bubble. Miss Barmy would do that herself, soon enough.

Emmy wheeled her bike out of the shed and rode off with her new friends through the streets of Grayson Lake, skidding through sand, jumping pot-holes, laughing and talking all the way to Meg's house. But the shine had gone out of the day. And later, after they'd splashed in the pool, and eaten pizza, and baked cookies, and told ghost stories, and giggled back and forth in their pajamas, Emmy found she couldn't sleep.

She lay wide-eyed on an air mattress in the lower level of Meg's house. The moon shone brightly through the sliding glass door that led out to the pool, and laid a pale oblong of light along the car-peted floor.

The pool party hadn't been quite as much fun as she had hoped. Emmy had tried hard to put the missing girls out of her mind. But every so often the image of a tiny girl with her palms outstretched would intrude on Emmy's thoughts, and then she would have to splash harder, or laugh louder, or eat faster, just to make it go away. Now that all was quiet, and everyone was sleeping, the memory returned, stronger than ever.

How could she have left the tiny girls to their fate, just for a sleepover? Emmy cringed at the question. She tried to convince herself there was no way she could have rescued them tonight.

Even if she had managed to tell the professor, he wouldn't have been able to force his way into the Home for Troubled Girls—not without the police and a search warrant. And what would he have said to the police? "We've found the missing girls, only they're four inches tall"?

Emmy moved irritably under the covers. Well, then, what was wrong with letting people know that there was such a thing as a rat who could shrink people? The police would believe it soon enough, once they watched Sissy kiss the tiny girls and make them grow again.

Emmy had a brief, uncomfortable feeling at the thought of Sissy, which she quickly suppressed. The stoning incident was over, and Sissy was safe.

Emmy didn't need to keep beating herself up about it.

Emmy stared at the reflected moonlight on the ceiling. Of course Ratty's powers had to be kept secret. If everyone knew what he and Sissy could do, the rodents would be taken, and caged, and experimented on, and analyzed, and made to run mazes and who knew what else. Ratty would *hate* that. And, it would be pretty hard to keep Rodent City secret, and free, after Raston and Cecilia's powers became known. People would question the professor, and Brian, and investigate and dig and search, and pretty soon all the rodents would suffer the same fate, if they didn't first escape into the wild.

No, it was best to keep quiet about the rodents of power. But that didn't solve the question of how to rescue the tiny, troubled girls.

Emmy rolled over impatiently, dragging the blanket with her, and thumped at her pillow. She had to figure something out. If she thought long enough— if she stared out the window at the moon—maybe something would come to her . . .

She sat up suddenly on the mattress, fixing her eyes on the sliding glass door. There, near the bottom, flattened against the pane, was the familiar silhouette of a rodent—no, two of them. And one looked suspiciously like Raston.

Emmy picked her way among the sleeping forms of her friends. She flipped the lock and slid the door slowly, quietly open.

"What are you doing here?" She slipped outside. "How did you know where to find me?"

Raston shrugged. "Joe told me."

Emmy sat on the flagstones, shivering a little in the cool night air, and wrapped her arms around her pajama-clad knees for warmth. "How did he know I was here?" She glanced at the second rodent, a scruffy specimen with light-colored fur and a habit of holding up one of his hind legs. She didn't remember seeing him before, but she wasn't that interested in meeting new rodents anyway—not after Gus, the dancing gopher.

But the new rat spoke in an oddly familiar voice. "I heard the girls say you were going to sleep over at Meg's, and I knew where she lived."

Emmy stared at the strange rat. "Who are you?"

The scruffy rat grinned. "Criminy, Emmy, I'm not *that* different. Blond hair, broken ankle—" He held up his hind leg, wrapped in a miniature splint.

Emmy's mouth hung open for a full minute. "*Joe?* You let Ratty bite you twice?"

The scruffy rat nodded happily. "I figured a broken ankle wouldn't matter so much to a rat, and I was right! I can hold my hind leg off the ground, and I've still got *three* feet for running."

Emmy shook her head in awe. Joe was braver than she. It took guts to turn yourself into a rat, knowing that the last one who'd done it hadn't managed to change back.

Of course, Joe probably wouldn't have any problems turning into a human again. His blood wasn't like Miss Barmy's, all gunked up with resentment and hatred.

Still, there was no way *Emmy* was ever going to try it. "So why did you come here?"

"Well," said Joe, scratching behind an ear with his paw, "it's been fun being a rat—you can smell everything!—but I've got to change back before Peter gets us up in the morning. We went looking for Sissy, but we couldn't find her anywhere."

Emmy felt a sudden emptiness in her chest, as if something had caved inside her.

"We asked around at Rodent City, but no one has seen her since yesterday morning, since I sent her on an errand to you." Raston's voice wavered with anxiety. "You got my message, didn't you? Where did Sissy go afterward? Do you know?"

"But you *told* me," Emmy faltered, "you said that Sissy gave me your message. You knew she'd found me, so you must have talked to her afterward—"

"Well, of course I assumed she gave you the message! She's so conscientious, I knew she'd never rest until she delivered it! Are you telling me she never did?"

Emmy's fingers trembled slightly, and she clasped her hands. "She started to," she said in an unsteady voice, "but then some kids started throwing rocks."

Raston and Joe looked at her, waiting tensely.

"She ran into a tunnel!" cried Emmy. "I thought she went back to Rodent City!"

"Didn't you check to make sure?" asked Joe.

"I-I went to the crack in the art-gallery steps, but no one came when Thomas called—and then Miss Barmy and Cheswick were measuring a pipe or something, and said something mean to Thomas, and he ran off to the Antique Rat, and I ran after him. And I was going to tell the professor, and ask Buck to check on her, but then Buck was napping under Brian's chin because they were trying to see if he could give a full night's sleep—and after that Thomas kicked a ball through the shoe-shop window, and the professor fell asleep because he got upset when Mrs. B bashed him with her purse, and I had to get Mr. Peebles to help me because Mrs. B was dragging Thomas away . . ."

Emmy decided against telling them about the attic and the tiny girls just now, and soldiered on. "And then Mr. Peebles got us out of the shoe shop, and called your parents, Joe, and then you all came in the car, and then Meg and the other girls came and told me I was late to the party . . ."

Emmy trailed off into silence.

"So all this to say," said the Rat, his voice cold, "that you left Sissy alone in a tunnel after some kids scared her. And you didn't check on her to make sure she was okay. And now she's lost."

"I don't think she's lost," said Emmy desperately. "I can show you the tunnel she went into. At least I think I can; I know almost exactly where it is." She stopped talking, afraid to say any more.

"You'd better tell us where you saw her last," said Joe slowly. "She's been gone a long time."

A foot scraped on the flagstones, and a door slid softly shut.

"What's going on?" asked Meg. "And how come you're talking to rats again, Emmy?"

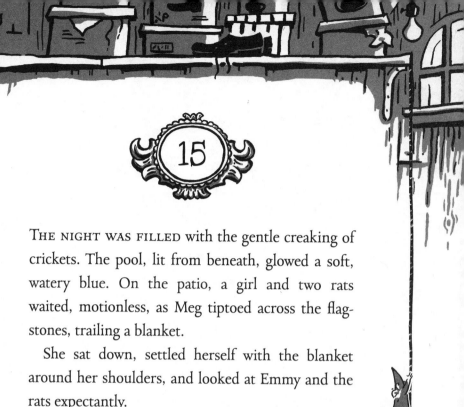

15

THE NIGHT WAS FILLED with the gentle creaking of crickets. The pool, lit from beneath, glowed a soft, watery blue. On the patio, a girl and two rats waited, motionless, as Meg tiptoed across the flagstones, trailing a blanket.

She sat down, settled herself with the blanket around her shoulders, and looked at Emmy and the rats expectantly.

Emmy shut her eyes. This was going to take a *lot* of explaining.

"Get rid of her," snapped Raston. "We have to find my sister."

Emmy looked at Meg helplessly. "Would you just—go back inside and pretend you didn't see anything?"

"Nope," said Meg promptly. "There's something going on, and I want to know what it is. Besides, I've already pretended I didn't see anything. Like that time on the boat when you jumped in after a rat, and

209

in your room when you shouted down a mouse hole, and then yesterday on the field when Kate hit that rat with a rock and you started yelling at us to stop."

"Sissy was *hit?*" cried the Rat.

Joe lifted his pale, furry head and stared at Emmy as if he had never seen her before. "She was hit?" he echoed. "And you didn't tell anyone?"

Emmy looked at him miserably.

"Okay," said Meg after a pause. "And now you can tell me why that rat is speaking English. And why the other one is squeaking."

"Forget it, Meg," said Joe, his voice suddenly flat and emphatic. "There's no time to explain. We've got to find the rat that Kate hit."

"Who *are* you?" Meg exclaimed, staring down at the pale-colored rat. "How do you know my name? And *what* is this all *about?*" She stared Emmy down.

Emmy stood up wearily. "It's too long to explain. Seriously, Meg, just go back inside and cover for me, will you? I'll tell you everything later, I promise."

Meg shook her head.

"Okay, then don't," said Emmy bitterly. "Everything else has gone wrong, why not this? Go ahead, get me in trouble, tell everyone I'm weird, whatever—just move out of my way, because I'm *leaving*."

Meg shrugged. "Then I'm coming with you."

Emmy looked at her, nonplussed.

"I don't want to get you in trouble," Meg said quickly. "I just want to be in on whatever it is you're doing. I mean, talking to rats? Running off in the middle of the night?" She grinned. "That's way cooler than anything I've got planned."

"Come on, come on, *come on!*" cried the Rat, dancing in his impatience.

Emmy looked Meg square in the eyes. "If you're in, then you're in all the way. Will you let the Rat bite your finger?"

"What?"

"You heard me. The Rat bites your finger or you don't come with us. I'm not going to spend the whole time explaining what everybody is saying."

"Can it be the English-speaking one?" Meg frowned.

"Oh, criminy," said Joe. "Stick out your finger and get it over with already."

"*Ouch!*"

"All right, that's done," said the Rat. "Can we get moving now?"

"Hey!" said Meg, pointing. "The squeaking one talks, too!"

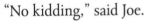

"No kidding," said Joe.

They had gone half a block when Emmy realized she was still in her pajamas.

"Of course we are!" said Meg. "That's what makes it so fun!" She bounced alongside Emmy, holding one end of the blanket that they had slung between them as a carrier for Joe and the Rat.

"What's so great about being outside in your pajamas?" Emmy wanted to know.

"Well, none of my other friends would do it," answered Meg.

Emmy padded over well-kept lawns and smooth driveways, her bare feet pressing on hard asphalt, then damp thick grass, then asphalt again.

"See, you're different," Meg went on. "All I do is ride bikes and hang out with friends and have sleepovers and swim. Your life is much more interesting. You have these weird adventures, and you talk to rats, and it's just so *cool*."

Emmy sighed. "It gets cooler," she said resignedly.

The rodents in the blanket sling made no comment. For once, Raston and Joe weren't complaining, or fighting, or saying anything at all. It put Emmy on edge.

"Do you want to go straight to the field?" she

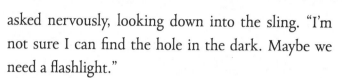

asked nervously, looking down into the sling. "I'm not sure I can find the hole in the dark. Maybe we need a flashlight."

Joe's voice came muffled from the blanket. "I think we should go to Rodent City and get a search party together. There are lots of burrows in that field."

"We should tell the professor, too," Ratty added, his voice high with worry. "He's a doctor, isn't he? Sissy might be hurt."

Emmy immediately suppressed a mental image of Sissy dragging herself into the tunnel. "He's a professor," she said slowly. "I don't know if he's a doctor."

"But he knows all about rodents," said Joe. "He probably knows more about rodents than anyone in the world."

"Are you still talking about the rat that Kate hit?" asked Meg with interest. "Because she'll need a doctor for sure. I mean, she was bleeding and everything."

The Rat gave a sharp, anguished cry. *"Bleeding?"*

There was nothing Emmy could say. There was nothing she could do except just to keep on walking, block after block, hanging on to her end of the blanket. The sling seemed to grow heavier, as if the silence within had weight, like a stone.

At last they came to the park bench on the green. Meg and Emmy set the blanket gently down on the grass. Emmy hardly dared look at the Rat.

"I'm really sorry," she said in a choked voice. "I never meant to leave her."

"Sissy would never have left *you*," said the Rat, slipping into the Rodent City tunnel without a backward glance.

Joe curled his tail, carefully avoiding Emmy's eyes. "You'd better go wake the professor," he said somberly. "We'll meet you at the art-gallery steps in a little while."

Emmy and Meg rang the bell of the Antique Rat until Brian came to the door. He invited them to wait inside while the professor got dressed, but Emmy declined. It was easier to sit outside, in the dark, where she wouldn't have to see the professor's face when Brian passed on the news about Sissy.

The girls sat on the park bench, looking up at the lighted attic window of the shoe shop, and Emmy told Meg everything. Somehow she felt she wanted at least one other person to understand that she really hadn't meant to be so awful.

At last the door of the Antique Rat opened. Emmy

stood up, glancing at Peter Peebles's place. She wondered if his house was as full of mouse holes as her
own. It had obviously been easy for Joe and the Rat
to go in and out. They must have left Thomas still
sleeping . . . For a little while more, then, Thomas
wouldn't know what she had done.

There was a sudden stinging behind Emmy's eyes,
and a tightness in the back of her throat. She held
herself rigidly and blinked. She was *not* going to cry.
She followed Professor Capybara and Meg, with only
a single look back at the lighted attic window in the
Home for Troubled Girls.

She couldn't rescue them. She couldn't even find
out why their light was on in the middle of the night.
Mrs. B or Miss Barmy could be using the little girls
for slave labor, for all she knew, but there was not
one thing Emmy could do to stop it.

Meg took her arm and gave it a comforting
squeeze, but the same stiff feeling that had kept
Emmy from crying was with her still, and she didn't
squeeze back. She felt as if something inside her had
frozen solid.

She sat hunched behind Meg and the professor on
the gallery steps and watched as rodents streamed

from the crack. Each one carried a stick with a bit of greasy rag wrapped around the end.

Buck emerged, a wooden match between his teeth, and scraped it along a chunk of broken sidewalk. It flared suddenly, and he lit the first torch.

One by one the rodent faces were illuminated. The tips of their fur shone golden, and their beady eyes glinted with reflected fire. Emmy recognized Ratty, and Joe, and Mrs. Bunjee, and even Gus the dancing gopher, but Chippy was nowhere to be seen. Cheswick and Miss Barmy were missing, too, a fact for which she was dully grateful.

The torches were all ablaze. The rodents waited, a silent, furry mass. Emmy met their collective gaze and slowly rose. There was a hiss from somewhere in the crowd.

"None of that!" said Buck sharply. "She's here to help. When she brings us to the place where Sissy was last seen, dive into every tunnel and burrow you can find nearby. Use your noses!"

Emmy led the way across the street, through the schoolyard, to the soccer field, and stopped at the great tree where the girls had sat the day before. "I think it was here," she said in a low voice. Meg nodded agreement.

"All right. You humans stay out of the way," said Buck, not unkindly. "With your big feet, and all these rodents running around in the dark . . ."

Professor Capybara bowed gravely, pulled out his pipe, and went to stand in the street.

Emmy followed at a slower pace. She was a little shy of the professor, who hadn't had much to say to her, and she sat on the curb a short distance away. Meg sat beside her, and for a time they watched the small flickering torches moving here and there on the field, low to the ground.

Meg curled up her knees and rested her chin on her forearms. "I'm sorry about throwing rocks with the others. I thought that rat was going to bite you."

"That's okay." Emmy looked intently at the torches. They were clustered in one spot now, unmoving.

"I can see why you didn't protect her at first, though," Meg went on. "It's like, do you help the one getting hurt, or do you side with your friends? It's hard either way."

Emmy cast her a grateful look, and turned back toward the field. The torches were moving again, all together, and getting larger as they advanced. The shifting flames outlined a wedge of bobbing, furry heads, with an unlit patch in the center.

"They've found her," whispered Meg.

"Yes." Emmy forced the word past the cold dread in her throat.

The procession came near. Two burly squirrels carried a limp, gray form on a stretcher. As they passed, Emmy saw the dark blood that crusted Sissy's side and a thin trickle of red coming from the newly disturbed wound.

The professor bent swiftly, putting his ear to Sissy's chest, touching the side of her neck, pulling back the closed eyelids with his thumb.

"She's alive," he said soberly. "Where was she?"

One of the gophers jerked his paw back in the direction of the field. "I found her in an abandoned rabbit warren. It branched off from the main tunnel to Rodent City, but I don't know how she could have missed the signs."

"She can't read." The Rat rubbed his eyes with the back of his paw.

"Why didn't she use her nose, then?" piped up a meadow vole.

"She had a cold," said Mrs. Bunjee. "She couldn't smell *anything*."

"She'll probably have pneumonia by now," said the gopher, shaking his head. "The burrow was damp. That's probably why it was abandoned—poor drainage. Some rabbits just don't know how to build."

Professor Capybara looked at Emmy. "How long was she left in the tunnel?"

Emmy swallowed hard. She looked pitifully at Meg.

"Since noon yesterday," said Meg, her voice barely audible.

There was a hushed gasp from the rodents nearby.

"About fifteen hours," the professor said slowly. "In a damp burrow. Alone and wounded." He gazed down at the unconscious Sissy and covered her gently with his handkerchief. "I don't care if it *is* the middle of the night. I'm going to call the vet."

Emmy stood next to Meg outside the Antique Rat and watched the truck pull away from the curb. Brian, his expression serious, was driving. The professor sat hunched over the small gray lump in his hands, looking tense. No one waved good-bye.

The Rat stared after the receding taillights. "I can't just wait here and do nothing."

Joe threw a furry arm over his shoulder. "We'll wait with you, Ratty."

Buck patted Raston on the back. "Mother will make you some hot cocoa, if you want to come back to the loft."

The Rat shook his head violently. "I don't want to sit around. Isn't there something we can *do*?"

"I know what you mean," said Joe suddenly. "You want to hit somebody, or do something dangerous, or work so hard you can't think anymore."

Emmy looked across the green. The light in the attic of the shoe shop was still on. "I know something we could do," she said slowly. "Rescue those tiny girls."

"Oh, *now* she wants to rescue somebody," said the Rat bitterly.

"What tiny girls?" Joe narrowed his rodent eyes. "And who asked you, anyway?"

Emmy stared at him, stung.

"Listen," Meg said firmly. "Emmy went to the attic at the Home for Troubled Girls, and she saw tiny footprints in the dust. And later, when she was in the attic at Mr. Peebles's house, she saw a girl a few inches tall standing on the windowsill."

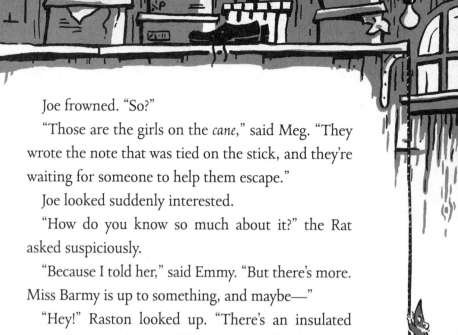

Joe frowned. "So?"

"Those are the girls on the *cane*," said Meg. "They wrote the note that was tied on the stick, and they're waiting for someone to help them escape."

Joe looked suddenly interested.

"How do you know so much about it?" the Rat asked suspiciously.

"Because I told her," said Emmy. "But there's more. Miss Barmy is up to something, and maybe—"

"Hey!" Raston looked up. "There's an insulated wire that goes from Peebles's attic to theirs—we're all rodents, we can run across it—"

"No, we should rig up a sort of pulley, with a basket," interrupted Buck excitedly. "We have to have something to carry the girls back in, right?"

"Yeah!" said Joe, his pale fur sticking out in every direction. "We can go in tonight and get them out by morning!"

"I can help," said Emmy. "I can help you rig the line, and attach the basket, and do anything that needs somebody full-sized."

The rodents were silent.

Emmy pressed on, her voice wavering slightly. "And then maybe one of you can go to Rodent City and try to find out what Miss Barmy and Cheswick are planning. It might be important, you never know . . ."

A sudden spasm of irritation crossed Joe's face. "Stop trying to take over, will you? Why don't you just leave it all to us? Then you can sit around and do nothing. That's what you're best at, anyway."

Emmy flushed.

"We don't need your help," said the Rat bitterly. "If you want to figure out the Barmster's plans, then why don't you just shrink yourself and do it?"

"Fine," Emmy said furiously. "Shrink me."

"Gladly," said the Rat, chomping down on her finger harder than necessary.

"No!" cried Joe, but it was too late. Emmy was already dwindling, down and down. Meg watched in horrified fascination.

"Now you've done it," said Joe coldly. "I hope you don't mind being doll-sized for the rest of your life."

"Oh . . ." said Emmy. She tried to shrug. "So what? Sissy's been found. Even if she's unconscious, all I have to do is put my cheek next to her mouth and it will be just like a kiss."

"Doesn't work," said Joe succinctly. "I already tried it, when we brought her in."

Emmy swallowed hard.

"So if she never regains consciousness, then—" He glared at Emmy, whiskers bristling.

He didn't have to finish the sentence; Emmy knew. He'd be a rat forever. And she'd stay four inches tall.

16

THE LIGHT FLICKED OFF. The heavy attic door shut with a boom. Five tiny girls, alone at last, slumped in weariness and relief in the sudden darkness.

Ana rubbed her eyes, sore from the glare of the naked bulb overhead. Someone—Merry, from the size—pressed close beside her and whimpered.

"Let's not cry," Ana suggested firmly. She coughed, turning her head. "Go on, get in bed. There's a little light from the window; you can find your way."

"Aren't you coming, too?" Merry asked.

"Soon. Go to bed now; you've been up half the night."

Berit touched her arm. "Ana," she said in a low, urgent voice, "why did Miss Barmy and Cheswick work us so hard? I mean, cutting those mirror circles over and over, and you with the archery—why did they keep wanting us to do it faster?"

"Mr. B said the mirrors were for a contest," Lisa said faintly. "Right, Lee?"

"Right," said Lee, sounding exhausted. "A beauty pageant for rats."

"But I still don't get the archery part," Berit insisted. "Then climbing, and hauling that hole saw up and down—what *for*?"

Ana tried to answer and began to cough. "I don't know," she managed at last.

"That's another thing." The worry in Berit's voice sounded like anger. "You've got a bad cough, you're sick, but they never even gave you a rest."

Ana nodded without speaking. She wasn't going to tell Berit, but it wasn't just a cough. As the day had turned to evening, her throat had grown sore, and her head hot. Now, long past bedtime, it was all she could do to keep herself from shaking with chills.

"Come on, Merry." Berit nudged the younger girls toward their beds. "At least they didn't put us in that old shoebox. I guess they know we can get out of it now."

Ana lay on the lowest shelf, listening to the girls' steady breathing. Tired as she was, she couldn't fall asleep. Berit's question kept echoing—"What for?" Mr. B could have cut those mirrors faster by himself. And as for shooting an arrow with fishing line attached over the third shelf, and hauling the circle saw up and down—well, anytime Miss Barmy wanted something on the third shelf, all she had to do was ask her father to reach for it. No, it made no sense at all.

Ana tossed back her covers, suddenly hot again, and looked up toward the window. It shone palely, lit by a moon she could not see.

Had the dark-haired girl come back, she wondered? Hours ago, Mr. B had left them alone while he went down for his supper. Tired though she was, Ana had unhooked the carefully hidden ladders and climbed to the windowsill, longing for a glimpse of freedom. And there had been a girl in the opposite window, calling to her!

Of course, she might have been speaking to the children in the yard below. But for one brief moment, Ana had felt sure that the girl had seen her. Maybe she was waiting at the window this very minute, hoping that Ana would show up again.

Shivering and feverish by turns, Ana crept across the dusty wooden floor and up the shoelace ladder. At last she pulled herself up over the window ledge, breathing hard.

There! A light was on in the attic room!

Ana peered intently through the dirty glass. She could see a lamp, casting a pink glow onto a low table. Next to it was the edge of a bed, and an arm in red-striped pajamas, and the back of a smooth blond head.

She frowned. The girl she'd seen before had dark hair. Who was this?

A spell of coughing shook her. When she glanced up again, there was movement by the half-open window across the way. It was something small. Something with a tail.

Suddenly Ana realized she was gazing at a chipmunk that she had seen once before, through a pinhole in their shoebox. He had been wearing a tux then, and he had been kissing Miss Barmy's paw. What was he called? Chippy, that was it . . . and he had told Miss Barmy that he would do anything she said . . .

Ana looked more closely. *Was* it the same chipmunk? If not, this one was like enough to be his brother . . . No, she was pretty sure it was the same one. And he was doing something with—well, it was hard to see in the half-light, but it might be a pulley.

Now what would one of Miss Barmy's loyal chipmunks be doing with a pulley in the middle of the night?

Two rats suddenly joined him, one gray and one light-colored, hauling a small basket between them. Ana's heart sank. Were *all* the rodents on Miss Barmy's side?

Maybe they were. Miss Barmy was organizing a whole beauty pageant for the rats; they must all think she was wonderful.

Ana closed her eyes, weary to the bone. She didn't know what the rodents across the way were doing, and she didn't care. Her legs trembled beneath her with weakness and fever, and when at last she reached the floor, it was all she could do to drag herself to her pallet on the shelf.

Well, she had learned one thing, at least. She had better not trust *any* rodents.

"Criminy!" said Joe, sliding down from the windowsill on his furry backside and turning an involuntary somersault on the carpet. "I'm glad that's done! I've got a crick in my neck from holding that pulley still while you rigged it."

"Not to mention screwing the hook to the wall on the other house," said the Rat grumpily. "And crawling out on the wire. That was a squirrel's job, if you ask me."

"*I* would have crawled out on the wire, Ratty," said Joe wistfully, "if it wasn't for my ankle."

"Well, you can test the basket," said Buck, wiping the grease off his paws. "And then we can move on to Phase Two."

The Rat sprawled in the glow from a small pink lamp and patted his stomach. "Does Phase Two involve eating? Because I'm *starved*."

Joe pricked up his furry ears. "*Is* there anything to eat around here?"

"Not unless you brought it in your suitcase," said Buck dryly.

Joe thought for a moment. "I'll bet my brother brought something. He never travels without supplies." He trotted over to the bed, where Thomas's pajama-clad arm hung down over the side, and hooked a claw into the red-and-white-striped sleeve.

"Careful," Buck warned.

"Hey!" Joe tugged recklessly at Thomas's pajama sleeve.

Thomas snorted in his sleep and rolled over.

"*Yikes!*" Joe cried, as Thomas's arm flipped him up and across, landing the scruffy blond rat on top of the bedspread. Joe disengaged his claws, and shook his head to clear it. "The kid's stronger than I thought."

"Keep out of range," the Rat advised, "and throw something at him."

"Yell in his ear, but stay alert," Buck suggested.

Thomas flung up an arm, narrowly missing his brother, and rolled on his back, snuffling in his sleep. Joe leaped onto Thomas's chest and dug in his claws. "Wake *up*, you doof!"

Thomas opened his eyes and gave a sudden yelp. "Get *off*!"

"Oh, shut up, Thomas. It's me, Joe. Did you bring any snacks?"

Thomas climbed back into bed, looking rumpled, sleepy, and worried. His suitcase was unzipped, and a bag of chips lay open on the floor. There was a steady sound of crunching from the rodents.

"I don't believe it," Thomas said suddenly, burrowing under the covers. "Emmy's nice. She wouldn't be mean to Sissy, like you said."

"Believe it," said Joe sourly. "She was mean, all right."

"But not on purpose!" Thomas flared. "Emmy *wouldn't*." He stuck his head under the pillow and put his hands to his ears.

"Well, maybe not on purpose," Joe conceded.

"It was just as bad for Sissy, on purpose or not," said the Rat. He dropped a barbecue-flavored chip on the rug. "I guess I'm not that hungry after all."

"What's he doing now?" muttered Joe, watching the Rat as he scrambled to the windowsill and peered out, pressing his nose against the glass.

Buck glanced over. "He's probably checking to see if the professor's truck is back yet from the vet's. Now, listen, about Phase Two . . ."

Joe swallowed a mouthful of chip. "What do you mean? We rigged the whole thing, pulleys and basket and line and all. We should be able to rescue the girls, no problem."

Buck shrugged his striped shoulders. "How do you plan to get in?"

"Well, the window, of course."

"It's closed, though," Buck said, brushing crumbs from his whiskers. "And breaking it would make a lot of noise, and it's dangerous, too."

"We could try to find a way in," said Joe persuasively. "There's probably a hole there somewhere."

"True," agreed Buck, biting into another chip with a crunch. "According to the paper-delivery gopher, there's a way up between the walls to the second floor. But that's watched by the B's, and Barmy and Cheswick, too. And even if we get past them, we still have to bring the little girls down somehow. Humans just aren't built for that kind of work. Their claws aren't long enough, and they have no tail for balance."

Joe looked at his own tail thoughtfully, and nodded.

"They can't scamper," said the Rat with finality, turning from the window. "Not even their wide receivers, no matter *what* the announcers say."

Buck ignored him. "Besides, it will be better to bring them straight back here. They won't be safe in Rodent City—not with Miss Barmy twisting everyone around her paw. Even my own brother loves her," he added, staring morosely at the rug.

Joe lifted a hind leg to his ear, and scratched. "So how do we get in, then?"

Buck straightened. "I think, for Phase Two, we should gnaw a hole in their wall. Beside the window frame, maybe."

"Gnaw a hole? With our *teeth*?" The Rat was aghast. "Do you have any idea what that will do to my dental alignment? And I already have an overbite!"

"Rodent teeth are *made* to gnaw," said Joe, who had already discovered a surprising urge to nibble at the bedposts. "But it's going to take an awfully long time."

"Right," said Buck, dusting off his paws. "We'd better get started, then."

Ana woke up with the sun in her eyes and a confused memory of a dream in which someone had been chewing wood. The dream vanished as soon as she tried to remember it—but the sound of steadily grinding teeth went on and on.

"It's coming from up there." Merry, the only other one awake, pointed solemnly toward the window.

Ana sat up, and instantly wished she hadn't. Her throat was scratchy, her joints ached, and she had a killing headache. She lay back down.

"Are you going to climb up to see?"

"Get Berit to do it," Ana whispered, her throat like sandpaper.

With her eyes closed, she listened as Berit sat up, grumbling, and headed off to the ladder. Ana drifted

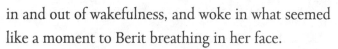

in and out of wakefulness, and woke in what seemed like a moment to Berit breathing in her face.

"It's two rats and a chipmunk!" Berit's words tumbled out rapidly in her excitement. "I think they're trying to get in!"

Ana steadied herself by gripping the sides of her pallet. "All right. We've got to hide." She stared at Merry and Berit confusedly for a moment, trying to clear her head. Something wasn't making sense. Why did they have to hide? Oh, wait—the chipmunk. He had something to do with Miss Barmy, though she couldn't remember just what.

"Do you think they found the note?" asked Berit. "Maybe they're like Cheswick and Miss Barmy. I mean, maybe they can talk, and read, and things."

Ana frowned, confused. "All I know is they're on Miss Barmy's side."

"Then why come through the wall? Why not come in the door with her?" Berit asked reasonably.

"I don't know!" Ana cried. "But I saw the chipmunk kiss Miss Barmy's paw, and he said that he'd do anything she said, anything at all—" She broke off, coughing.

"Okay," said Berit, "but why hide? I could see it

yesterday—anybody that Mrs. B lets in, I'll hide from—but rats are small, and they've got to come through the hole one by one. We could just bash them on the head when they come in."

Merry nodded, her cheeks flushed. *"Bash!"* she echoed, and began to cough. Lisa and Lee sat up in bed.

Heavy feet shuffled outside the big attic door, and a key turned in the lock. Merry muffled her cough. Ana pulled her close. Whatever was planned for them today, she would try to get them to leave Merry out of it. The little girl was getting sick.

Miss Barmy and Cheswick pattered in, followed closely by Mr. and Mrs. B. The vibration of the floor under their weight must have been felt through the walls, for the gnawing sound outside the window suddenly stopped.

"Oh, joy, the gang's all here," muttered Berit.

Ana didn't answer. She was studying Mr. B, who wore a pair of work overalls and carried a metal lunch bucket. He sat down on a stool, unsnapped the buckles, flipped open the lid, and waited expectantly, looking at the piebald rat who was his daughter.

"In you go," said Miss Barmy.

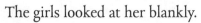

The girls looked at her blankly.

Miss Barmy tapped her claws against the floor. "Wake up, girls. I let you sleep in, but I see it was a mistake. Get—in—the—lunch—pail. You're going to work."

Berit flung herself up and over the side with a disgusted grunt. Lisa and Lee followed.

Ana stepped forward, her arm around Merry. "Please, can Merry have a rest today? She's sick."

Miss Barmy crooked a claw at Ana. "You—the biggest one—come here. Now, listen closely. Here's what I want you to do."

Ana listened carefully, hoping that if she did so Merry would be allowed to stay in bed. She watched as Cheswick loaded the lunch pail with things she recognized from the day before: the metal ring that cut through mirrors, the pencil push-bars, the central pole with a suction cup at the bottom, the small round platform, the bow and arrows, a coil of fishing line. Then he added a cloth sack with a drawstring, and a shoelace ladder that he must have found among their things.

Speaking in Ana's ear, Miss Barmy described, step by step, what she wanted done. Trying hard to concentrate in spite of fever and headache, Ana obediently repeated the instructions, in order. But as she said them aloud, her voice slowed. Suddenly, listening to her own voice, she realized what she was saying.

"What's the matter? Go on!"

Ana stared at the piebald rat, appalled. "No. I won't do it."

Miss Barmy narrowed her eyes.

"You can't make me," said Ana, her voice rising. "I refuse."

Cheswick tapped his clipboard. Mr. B looked alarmed.

Miss Barmy lifted her upper lip and smiled, her prominent front teeth large and gleaming. "Mother," she said, "I'm going to let the littlest girl stay back, after all."

Mrs. B's yellowed, stringy neck twisted. She glanced at the shelf beside her, piled with old kitchen implements, and pulled down a colander.

Ana looked at her, uncomprehending. Then she understood.

Merry seemed to understand, too, for she backed away. But Mrs. B's terrible arm, which had grown in strength and accuracy with every flowerpot thrown, slammed the colander upside down over Merry before she could turn and run.

Ana saw little hands come through the holes of the colander.

"Now," said Miss Barmy, "I'm sure you'd like to see your tiny friend again, wouldn't you? Safe, and unharmed?"

Ana nodded wordlessly.

"Well, then, it's all very simple, isn't it? Just follow the instructions, exactly as I told you. Cheswick will be watching."

Deep within rodent city, Emmy ducked into a shadowed corner.

Two gophers, chatting in high, excited voices, moved along the fourth-level walkway. "Is it true that Cecilia broke a leg?"

"Two legs, I heard, and three ribs . . . and Emmy threw the rock herself."

"No!"

"Well, that's what they *say*. It's probably true. You know how humans are—you can't trust them, it's not as if they were *rodents*."

"Personally, I have never trusted anyone without a tail . . ."

The voices became a murmur in the distance. Emmy tried to shrug off the comments, but she couldn't quite manage it. She'd been hearing the same sort of thing all morning long, and for half the night besides.

Last night, after Emmy had shrunk, Meg had offered to carry her back and hide her until the other girls went home. But Emmy couldn't bear the thought of doing nothing, and so she'd sent Meg home with a promise to meet the next day.

Buck had been kind enough to give her a full night's sleep. He had curled up with his head tucked beneath her chin for fifteen minutes. Then they had gone—he and Joe and Ratty, gone to Peter Peebles's attic to work on their plan to rescue the tiny girls— and they hadn't invited her to help.

She lifted her shoulders, stiffly, and let them fall. She wasn't going to worry about what her friends— her *former* friends—thought of her. Let them go ahead and make their plans, and good luck to them. Emmy had some plans of her own.

First, she wanted to discover what Miss Barmy was up to. That was why, for hours now, she had searched out tunnels, and skulked in corners, and crouched behind twiggy doors to listen, and watch, and learn what she could.

So far, that hadn't been much. If Miss Barmy was doing anything in Rodent City besides running a beauty pageant, Emmy had yet to discover it.

But she *knew* there was more going on. For one thing, it was certain that Miss Barmy's mother had something to do with keeping the tiny girls captive. She had rubbed out the footprints right in front of Emmy. And even though the note wrapped around the stick had been chewed, the word "prisoners" had been quite clear.

Did Mrs. B keep the tiny girls in the attic without Miss Barmy's knowledge? Emmy doubted it very much. Just weeks ago, Miss Barmy had wanted Emmy's parents to send her to the Home for Troubled Girls. It was the same thing she had done to the girls whose faces were carved on her old cane. No, Miss Barmy knew all about the tiny girl who had stood at the window, looking at Emmy; Miss Barmy had put her there.

"They're passing out the mirrors!" squeaked a rodent just behind her, and Emmy flattened herself against the twigs. A horde of gerbils, their fur carefully brushed, went giggling past on their way to the elevator, a birdcage hung from a sturdy cable of vine.

Emmy peered over the railing as the gerbils crammed into the bamboo cage. Some rodent far below turned a winch, and the elevator slowly descended to ground level, where two narrow gleaming rails extended from the mouth of a tunnel.

As she watched, an open boxcar was rolled out of the tunnel and up to the elevator landing. She blinked as the disks inside blazed with reflected light, casting a kaleidoscope of glowing dots over every surface in Rodent City.

So Miss Barmy had kept one promise, anyway. Of course, Chippy had probably done all the work, but Miss Barmy must have ruined a big mirror of her own, to cut the small ones. Could Miss Barmy have a bit of generosity in her somewhere?

"I heard that Emmy left her bleeding and alone, for twenty hours . . . or was it twenty-six?"

Emmy dodged under a bench as a dormouse and a meadow vole trotted past, murmuring in hushed, shocked tones.

"Thirty, I think. And someone told me that *all* of Cecilia's legs were broken, and half her tail was cut off, too . . ."

Emmy glared at their small, plump backs as they moved away. No one knew anything about Sissy's condition, but that didn't stop rodents from gossiping. And each fresh rumor was worse than the one before.

Well, if anyone had the inside story about Sissy, not to mention the latest on Miss Barmy, it would be the Bunjees. Emmy rolled from the dim recess under the bench and slipped from hidden nook to shadowed cranny, making her careful way to the loft she knew so well.

Of course, she had a perfect right to walk right down the middle of any walkway in Rodent City. She had broken no law—no rodent police were going to arrest her. But she couldn't bear the sidelong glances and sneering looks. Emmy tried to tell herself that the opinion of a bunch of rats didn't matter in the least—but it did.

A chipmunk hurried toward the elevator, pulling a red wagon with a squeaky wheel. Emmy quickly stepped behind a trellis and waited for him to pass.

But the wagon rattled to a stop. Emmy peered through the woven slats of the trellis to see Chippy bending over the wagon, tightening a strap on something that looked astonishingly like a soup tureen. He whirled as a voice spoke.

"Chipster, there you are!" Miss Barmy's tone was winsome. "I was just telling—oh, someone, I forget who—what a marvelous big chipmunk brain you have, to think of such clever inventions . . . We got the mirrors cut in record time!"

Chippy mumbled something and turned red beneath his pelt.

"I was looking for you, Chipster, because I have another project that a clever chipmunk might find interesting."

"I-I'm sorry, Jane, but I can't help you just now. I'm going to the Antique Rat, to bring Sissy some soup. We hear she's back from the vet's."

"Oh, well, in that case, she's all better!" said Miss Barmy brightly. "Anyway, she can't possibly have much of an appetite yet."

Chippy murmured something that sounded like "But Mother said . . ."

"Nonsense." Miss Barmy patted Chippy's cheek. "Think of how much use you could be to *me*. Now, have you ever done delicate metalwork?"

"Like with a soldering iron?" Chippy hesitated, glancing at the soup tureen, which exuded a wisp of steam and a salty aroma of broth. "I soldered a wire splice just the other day, when Baby Grebbler chewed through a cord and killed the lights in Section 3-A, but I don't know that you'd call it metalwork, exactly."

Miss Barmy smiled brilliantly, her large front

teeth gleaming. "What about jewelry? Could you set stones in a tiara, for example?"

Chippy considered this. "Well, I did do some filigree repair for one of Mother's brooches. Are you talking about the tiara for the beauty pageant?"

Miss Barmy grasped the wagon handle, her paw over Chippy's, and wheeled it around. "Yes, but I'd like to add some larger stones to it, jewels that have been in my family for generations." She walked off, drawing Chippy with her. "Is the tiara still at your loft? We'll just go and pick it up, and I'll show you what I want done."

Emmy scrambled after them, moving cautiously. If Rodent City hadn't been full of twigs and branching lofts, with twinkling lights and deeper shadows, she would never have been able to remain unnoticed all the way to the Bunjee loft, where a stream of rodents trotted in and out with garments for alteration. Emmy recognized the clothes with a pang. Barbie and Ken weren't going to have a stitch left.

A soft, small paw tugged at her hand, and Emmy turned. "Endear!" she said with relief, as the little mouse hopped by her side.

With its touch, the Endear Mouse's thoughts came easily into Emmy's mind—a bubbling excitement over the beauty contest, uneasiness about Miss Barmy.

"I know," thought Emmy, huddling on a recessed bench. "I'm worried, too. That's the reason I'm following her."

"Is she still bad?" the Endear Mouse asked.

Emmy waited for a lull in the stream of visitors, then wedged herself and the mouse quickly behind the open door. "She *pretends* to be good. But I think she's up to something, and I want to find out what it is." Emmy put her eye to the crack by the door's hinge. "I'd like to know how to help the troubled girls, too."

Mrs. Bunjee had called in her sewing circle to help, and the loft was packed. Emmy could see Chippy's mother seated in an overstuffed chair, her short forearm going swiftly up and down as she pulled a needle and thread through a pile of frothy blue.

Miss Barmy, nearby, tipped the tiara gracefully as she showed Chippy where she wanted the jewels. A few admirers—a gray squirrel, several gerbils—jostled for position around her. There was a lull in the general noise of conversation, and Miss Barmy's voice rose flutingly.

"Of course, I wouldn't *dream* of entering the contest myself. After all, I'm sponsoring the contest. I *couldn't* enter"—she broke off to smile prettily—"could I?"

A chorus of male voices were raised in protest. "All the more reason!" "You should!" "You're prettier than any of them!"

"Your parents can sponsor the contest," said Chippy, "if you want to enter."

"Well," said Miss Barmy, fluttering her lashes, "since you insist, perhaps I will."

Mrs. Bunjee bit off a thread with a snap. "Chipster. Did you get that soup over to Cecilia?"

Chippy jerked his head up guiltily. "Not yet, Mother. Miss Barmy needed me—"

"Come to think of it," interrupted Mrs. Bunjee, shaking out the gown, "I didn't see either of you in the search party last night. Too busy, were you?"

The Endear Mouse pressed close to Emmy. "I can find out if she's still bad," it said, mind to mind, and then the fawn-colored mouse with the big eyes ran from behind the door, went straight to the piebald rat, and leaned against her.

The Endear Mouse's eyes seemed to grow even larger, and a look of horror covered its delicate face. It tried to back away, but Miss Barmy whipped around and engulfed the mouse in a sudden, smothering hug.

"What a love of a mouse!" Miss Barmy cried, squeezing tight. "You're just the thing for the pageant—you'll be *darling* in blue velveteen. Come with me and I'll teach you to bow, and curl your tail, and you can carry the tiara on a golden pillow."

She swept out of the loft, the Endear Mouse tucked firmly under one arm, and stopped only to point at Emmy. "Mrs. Bunjee!" the piebald rat said, loud and accusing. "*Look* who's skulking behind your door! And in her pajamas, too!" And before Emmy could say one word of protest, she was gone, and the Endear Mouse with her.

Emmy emerged, hot all over, to face the disapproving stares. "I was just trying to see what Miss Barmy was up to," she mumbled.

Mrs. Bunjee looked at her. "A laudable goal," she said quietly. "I wonder, Emmy, would *you* like to take the soup to Cecilia? Chippy seems to have something better to do."

Emmy nodded, overwhelmed with gratitude. Mrs. Bunjee hadn't lost all faith in her, then! There was enough left, at least, to trust her with a soup delivery.

"Well . . ." Chippy turned the tiara awkwardly in his paws. "I guess I should get started. Jane said she'd send Cheswick over with the jewels in a little while."

Emmy, hesitating, touched his arm as he passed through the door. "Listen, Chippy. Don't trust her, okay?"

Chippy drew back, his fur slightly raised. "Maybe *you're* the one I shouldn't trust. After the way you treated Sissy . . ." He paused, glancing uncomfortably at the soup tureen. "What do you mean?"

"I'm not sure, exactly," Emmy admitted, "but she's not just putting on a beauty contest, she's doing something else. I *know* it. And besides that, I think she's keeping some little girls captive—"

"You *think*? Where's your proof?"

"Chippy, I *know* her. She was my nanny for a whole year. Remember how awful she was? Remember how she tried to choke Sissy? That's when Raston bit her and she turned into a rat. Don't you remember?"

Chippy stiffened. "That was long ago."

"Yeah, like—what?—four weeks?"

249

"She's a lovely rat now," Chippy went on dreamily, "and she thinks my inventions are wonderful—"

Emmy gripped his furry arm and shook it. "She's just *using* you, Chippy. Can't you see that?"

"Such style, such sharp, gleaming teeth . . ." Chippy peeled Emmy's hand off his arm. "Why can't you forget about the past? Why do you have to be so judgmental?"

"Wait!" Emmy ran after Chippy, panting. "You want proof?"

The chipmunk grunted. "Leave me alone, will you? I'm going to my workshop; I've got a lot to do."

"I *dare* you to listen. I've got all the proof you need."

Chippy faced Emmy, his whiskers bristling. "What do you mean?"

"Find the Endear Mouse," said Emmy, "and touch it. Let it talk to you. And then you'll know for sure who's right about Miss Barmy—unless you're scared to find out."

Emmy pulled the wagon to the elevator and waited her turn in line. She could hardly dodge from shadow to corner with a cargo of soup rolling behind her, sloshing out from beneath the lid.

She stepped into the birdcage, steering the wagon to the side to make room for others. But the rodents behind her stayed in line, whispering behind their paws.

"How could she *do* such a thing?"

"And so young, too!"

Her face burning, Emmy tugged on the cord that signaled the squirrel below to turn the winch. She looked out through the bars of the cage as she made her lonely, creaking descent, feeling as if all eyes were on her.

Fine, then. She wouldn't try to warn anyone. Let them find out for themselves what Miss Barmy was really like.

She rolled slowly past the tunnel entrances on the ground floor. Each one had a chalkboard beside it, and Emmy scanned the warnings as she passed. Cars, soccer balls, children; that one must lead to the playground. But she wanted the passage that led to the backstreets, and at last she found the danger-board on which someone had chalked "(1) Dog, white and yappy, stupid, fast. (2) Hawk, tethered, tattoo parlor: lethal within a two-yard radius. (3) Cat, ginger with white paws: slow, silent, dangerous.

(4) Female human, screechy, shoe-shop window: throws flowerpots, good aim."

Emmy nodded grimly. She turned into the brightly lit tunnel with its brass wall sconces, and rolled down a passageway that grew darker and earthier the farther she went. At last a glow of daylight appeared, and the floor began to rise. Emmy shoved the wagon up the last incline to the surface of the green, and blinked in the sudden light of morning.

It seemed safe enough. Emmy was thankful for the low evergreen that screened her from anyone who might be sitting on the park bench. She grunted slightly as she yanked the squeaking wheel over a pebble and past a scrolled iron leg set in concrete.

Now she just had to figure out how to get to the Antique Rat without being caught by somebody's pet, or hit by a flying flowerpot. Emmy leaned her elbows on the edge of the concrete slab to get her bearings. Which way was the Antique Rat?

There was a sudden whoosh overhead—Emmy felt the push of displaced air—and a loud, leathery *smack*. Emmy shrieked and fell back as pounding feet shook the ground. Get to the tunnel—she had to get to the tunnel—

The yew branches parted overhead. Emmy's breath caught in her throat. Staring right at her, not a foot away, was a pair of gigantic blue eyes.

"Hi, Emmy," said Thomas, reaching for his soccer ball.

18

"SO THE VET couldn't help her?" Thomas looked from Brian to the professor.

Emmy was grateful that Thomas was asking the questions. She had tried to speak once or twice, but somehow the words wouldn't come out.

She stood on the counter at the Antique Rat, close to the lab equipment, and a little distance from Sissy in her blanket-lined box. She had already been close enough to see Sissy's closed eyes, and the paleness of her skin beneath her soft gray fur, and to smell the antiseptic beneath the bandage on her leg. Little by little, Emmy had edged away, and now she stood with her back pressing against the smooth, cool metal of the charascope.

Professor Capybara cleared his throat. "The veterinarian did what she could, but she said that I knew more about rodents, anyway. Apparently it's an unusual specialty."

"When is she going to wake up?" Thomas stared solemnly at the silent gray rat.

The professor and Brian exchanged a quick glance. "We don't know, exactly," said the professor gently. "Soon, we hope."

"Did—" Emmy stopped to swallow, and tried again. "Did she break anything?" She had already taken a good look at Sissy's tail, which seemed intact, in spite of the rumors. But it was hard to tell about bones.

The professor shook his head. "The X-ray didn't show any breaks. But the skin was lacerated, of course—that's where the blood came from. And," he added in a lower tone, "there's a little internal bleeding. We're waiting to see if it stops by itself."

Emmy turned away. Internal bleeding was bad; it could kill. She wondered what a sample of her blood would look like in the charascope, now that she was practically a murderer.

As if through a layer of felt, she dimly heard Thomas explain about Mrs. Bunjee's soup, and the wishing mouse, and his own newfound kicking ability. After a while, the others went outside for a demonstration, and Emmy was alone on the counter except for the still, gray form on the ragged piece of blanket.

It took no time at all for her to prick her arm with a lancet and prepare a glass slide with some drops of her blood. It took a little longer to climb up to the eyepiece of the charascope, but her bare feet gripped the smooth pewter with its brass fittings, and she inched her way up until at last she was looking down into a bright, swirling mass.

The shapes were similar to the ones she had seen before, flipping and joining and swimming in a vividly colored sea. Emmy was just beginning to feel relieved—maybe her character wasn't so bad, after all—when something new came into her field of vision.

It wasn't the green wormy ball of resentments and hate that she had seen in Miss Barmy's blood. But it looked equally difficult to untangle. There before her, wriggling in her very own blood, was a knotted orange rope, thick and barbed.

It looked like a whip, thought Emmy—a whip with thorns.

She looked at it for some time. At last she climbed down and rubbed off the blood with the edge of a paper towel until the slide was quite, quite clean. And then she waited, staring at nothing, until Thomas came in again with his soccer ball under his arm.

Emmy asked him if he would take her to the

art-gallery steps. She had agreed to meet Meg there, she said, around noon, and wasn't it almost lunchtime? Thomas nodded, put her in his pocket, and said his good-byes.

"Did Mr. Peebles wonder where Joe was this morning?" Emmy asked as the door slammed behind them. She felt uncomfortable with silence just then.

Thomas chuckled. "Nope. I turned on the shower and put Joe in the bathroom. Then, when Cousin Peter came up, Joe talked to him through the door. I said I'd bring Joe's breakfast up to him so he wouldn't have to go on the stairs with his ankle, and Peter said okay. And it was all true," he added virtuously. "A Cub Scout never lies."

"Good for you," murmured Emmy, feeling a rumble in her stomach at the mention of breakfast. She hadn't wanted to ask anyone in Rodent City to feed her. Maybe Meg would bring a crumb or two for lunch.

Thomas's steps echoed in the alleyway, and Emmy thought of another question. "Did Joe and Ratty and Buck rig up the pulley and rope?"

Thomas nodded. "It goes between the two attic windows. They're gnawing a hole in the other attic's wall now, but it's taking a long time."

Emmy considered this. "Aren't they worried about—owls and things?"

"One of them stands guard, and they dive for the gutter if they have to. Here's the art gallery. Do you want to wait inside Rodent City?"

Emmy looked out of his pocket at the loose pipes, the dug-up sidewalk, the crumbling crack in the gallery steps, and realized that she did not want to be anywhere near the underground city, or its scornful, whispering rodents.

"Let's go across the street. We can watch for Meg from the playground."

It was high noon. A dull, steady *thwack* came from the schoolhouse wall as Thomas practiced his kicks. Meg, who had brought a bag lunch, sat in the shade under the kiddie slide and laid out pickles, grapes, and a wrapped sandwich. "Sorry if you don't like egg salad, Emmy. I wish my mom had made peanut butter and jelly."

The hot sun beat down on the playground with its scrubby dandelions, but beneath the slide the grass was thick and cool. All around them were the subdued rustlings and chirpings of small creatures, flying and scampering and leaping.

"Egg salad's fine, but I can't eat this," said Emmy, holding up a single grape. "It's like trying to eat a basketball."

Meg cut the grape into quarters with her jackknife and poured some lemonade into a bottle cap. Two flies, each as big as Emmy's hand, went droning by, their shiny eyes staring, and Emmy flapped at them with a bit of waxed paper.

"Hey, this isn't egg salad!" Meg peeled back the top slice of bread. "It's straight jelly—no peanut butter."

"I don't mind." Emmy ducked as the flies circled her head. "I just wish these stupid bugs would leave me alone!"

One of the insects promptly flew off. The other, more persistent, made regular attempts to land on the jelly sandwich. Meg fanned it away as Emmy told her what had happened since the night before, leaving out the charascope. Meg, in turn, told Emmy how she had sneaked into her house, never waking the sleeping girls on the floor.

"Plus, I called your mom to invite you over for one more night, so you don't have to worry about going home!" Meg looked justifiably proud of this detail, but broke off as a small tan mouse bounced out of a patch of long grass, sat up on its haunches, and nodded briskly. "That's two," it said, dusting its forepaws together.

"Wait!" Emmy's heart picked up a beat as she saw the white star-shaped patch on the back of its head. "Aren't you the *wishing* rodent?" She turned to Meg, delighted. "This is the mouse that turned Thomas into a kicking machine, and then Joe broke his ankle when he wished for it, and it got me invited—" Emmy stopped, embarrassed. She didn't really want to tell Meg how much she had longed to be invited to her pool party.

"Anyway," she said hurriedly, addressing the mouse, "what do you mean, that's two? We didn't make any wishes."

"Yes, you did. For a jelly sandwich, and for a fly to go away."

"But we wished for *peanut butter* and jelly," protested Meg. "And there were *two* flies."

"Don't complain," said Emmy hurriedly, as the mouse showed signs of bouncing off in a huff. "We've got one more wish. Let's wish for Sissy to be all right!"

"Or for the troubled girls to be rescued," suggested Meg.

Emmy hesitated. "Joe and Ratty and Buck might have rescued the girls already—and if they haven't yet, they will soon. I think we should help Sissy first."

"Don't bother deciding," snapped the wishing mouse. "Only two wishes today."

"But we got three *yesterday*—"

"Just like a human," said the mouse in disgust. "Are they grateful? No, they are not. Do they say, 'Thank you, dear wishing mouse'—my name is Sunny, by the way, not that you bothered to ask—"

"Thank you—"

"Thank you—"

"—dear, dear wishing mouse!" said Emmy and Meg together, tumbling over their words.

"Don't mention it," said Sunny grumpily, and dived back into the patch of grass.

Meg looked blankly at Emmy. "What's the good of a wishing mouse," she said, "if it doesn't even get the wishes right?"

"Or give us some warning that it was listening," said Emmy.

"Here's a warning," said Thomas, ducking his head under the slide. "Look who's hanging around the art-gallery steps."

Emmy scrambled out and shaded her eyes. Even from this distance, she recognized the dumpling posture and fuzzy white hair of Mr. B. But why was he dressed in a workman's overalls, and what was he doing with a lunch pail?

Meg, carrying a brown lunch bag, strolled casually across Main Street, glanced at the art gallery, and paused by a concrete planter filled with petunias and trailing vines. A white-haired man with a gentle, worried face saw her and suddenly closed his lunch pail.

"Gee, mister! What are you doing with those pipes?"

Inside the paper bag, Emmy stifled a snort of amusement. No one could beat Thomas for artless innocence, but Meg was making an excellent try.

"Oh . . . I'm just . . . checking." Mr. B sat back on his heels and patted one of the copper pipes several times, as if it were a long metallic dog.

"Do you mind if I watch?" Meg set the lunch sack carefully in the planter.

"Yes!" said a small, emphatic voice from somewhere near the ground.

"I do?" The old man seemed befuddled.

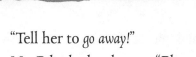

"Tell her to *go away!*"

Mr. B looked unhappy. "Please, go away, little girl. I'm sorry, but . . ."

"I'm really very busy!" finished the commanding voice.

The scrape of Meg's sandals faded as Emmy pressed her eye to a small hole in the paper bag. She couldn't see much—a few petunia leaves, the back of Mr. B's overalls—but she could hear quite well. Was someone coughing?

"Now, then, Mr. B," ordered the voice. "Step one—fit the pipe into the wall."

Emmy poked her finger into the hole and made it bigger. Now she could see a glossy black rat pacing importantly back and forth, consulting a clipboard. A few steps away, where the sidewalk had been broken to bits, pipes were lying on the ground. Mr. B, his overalls sagging in back, pulled a large pipe off the pile with a clank and lifted the temporary flap that covered the hole in the jewelry-store wall.

"That's right—shove it in," said Cheswick, looking up from his notes. "Step two—description."

Mr. B's massive hand reached into his back pocket

and dug out a folded piece of newspaper. As he opened it up, Emmy caught sight of a familiar-looking picture.

Mr. B read in a dutiful voice, "'Originally bought by William Addison as a gift for his bride, these spectacular Kashmir sapphires were worn by his daughter Priscilla when she entered the Miss Grayson Lake beauty contest, shortly before her untimely death—'"

"No, no." Cheswick glanced nervously over his shoulder. "Read farther down."

"'The jewelry will be passed on to his daughter Emmy on her eighteenth birthday, according to James Addison, great-nephew of William and heir to the Addison fortune . . .'"

"Come on, get to the description! We can't stay here all day, it's dangerous!"

"'The cornflower-blue gems, of exceptional quality, are valued at over one hundred thousand dollars, according to Carnegie Peters, local jeweler extraordinaire.'"

There was a creaking sound, as of small metal hinges. "Are you listening to this, girls?" demanded Cheswick.

The black rat had moved so close to the planter that Emmy could no longer see him. Carefully, slowly, she tore the brown paper all the way down until she could step out of the bag. The earth between the petunias was soft and lumpy. A rich smell of potting soil filled her nose.

"'The necklace, a heart-shaped trio of three-carat sapphires surrounded by small diamonds, is suspended from a sterling silver chain—'"

Emmy pushed between the petunia stalks and peered over the edge of the planter. The lunch pail, open now, was just below. Four tiny girls looked up at her, startled.

"Who's that?" blurted one, and was immediately muffled.

"It's me, you nitwit," Cheswick Vole snapped. "Shut up and repeat after me. 'Necklace, silver chain, three blue stones set in diamonds, shaped like a heart.' Got it? That is what Miss Barmy wants you to take."

"Take?" said one of the smaller girls.

"For Miss Barmy?" said her twin.

"He means 'steal,'" said the middle-sized one. "Right, Ana?"

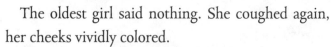

The oldest girl said nothing. She coughed again, her cheeks vividly colored.

"It's not stealing," said Cheswick sharply, "if you're taking something that should have been hers in the first place. Now, step three. Go into the pipe, and drag the equipment behind you."

"Why don't *you* do it?" muttered the middle girl, but the oldest shushed her. Mr. B lifted them out of the lunch box. The doll-sized figures crawled into the copper pipe that led to the hole in the wall, dragging a piece of string behind them.

Cheswick Vole tied the other end of the string to a small, lumpy cloth bag—and soon, jerkily, it was pulled into the pipe with a faint clanking.

Mr. B made an apologetic noise in his throat. "So . . . I'm just wondering. Why *aren't* you and Jane doing this yourself?"

Cheswick drew himself up rigidly. "You can't seriously imagine that I'd allow *Jane* to run such risks?"

"Er—"

"Besides, we can't leave our scent inside. What if the Rodent Police got suspicious?" Cheswick glanced at the store window with its shuttered blinds. "They might not understand that we were only taking what was really Jane's all along."

Emmy, behind a large pink petunia, narrowed her eyes.

Cheswick tucked his clipboard into the lunch pail, and climbed in. "Now for step four. Look busy."

"How?" Mr. B sounded apprehensive. "I don't know anything about plumbing."

Cheswick shrugged. "Fit pipes together, bang around a bit, that kind of thing. I'm going to take a nap. Close the lid, would you? The sun's in my eyes."

His last words echoed hollowly inside the metal box as Emmy stared down at the rounded black lid, fury building inside her. She had never really cared about the sapphires before. But now her family was being *robbed*.

Mr. B put the society clipping in his pocket. Emmy backed up, out of his field of vision, and tripped over the paper bag. There was a loud crinkling.

Mr. B grabbed the bag out of the planter and crumpled it in his meaty hands. "Must've been the wind," he said to himself, tossing it aside.

Across the street, Meg leaped up and came running.

"Excuse me, mister, but I think I forgot my lunch!" She snatched up the crumpled bag, her face pale. "Was—" She swallowed, and tried again. "Wasn't there anything in it?"

Mr. B shook his head. "If there was, it's squashed now."

Meg stared in horror at the bag in her hands— and then came to her senses. It was far too light to contain even a very small body. She looked about her wildly, and began to dig among the petunias. "Maybe my lunch fell—ulp!"

Emmy, hanging from a vine off the side of the planter, was tickling her ankle with the trailing end.

Meg's face sagged in relief. She shielded Emmy from view and picked her up gently. "Thanks anyway," she said, and headed for the kiddie slide, where Thomas waited with his ever-present soccer ball.

Emmy had time to think on the way to the playground. And by the time Meg set her down in the long cool grass, she had a plan.

First, of course, she told Meg and Thomas that the girls whose names were on Miss Barmy's cane had been found.

"All of them?" Thomas's round face was polished with joy.

"Well, actually—"

"Are they okay?" Meg interrupted, just as excited as Thomas.

"One of them has a cough. But listen, we've got to hurry—they're in the jewelry store right now. Here's what I think we should do."

19

Mr. b tried to look busy. He picked up one pipe
and tapped it against another. He fit two together,
and took them apart again. He rolled a pipe over to
see if any slugs were attached to the bottom, and
picked them off. Then he scratched his head.

Footsteps sounded behind him. He turned with an
air of relief.

"You look *very* busy," said Meg.

"What are you doing?" asked Thomas. "Can I see?"
He squatted next to Mr. B, blocking the man's view
of the transit pipe that led to the jewelry-store wall.

Meg bent swiftly behind him, lifting something
from her pocket onto the ground. Then in one
smooth motion she patted Thomas's head. "He likes
to see how things work," she said to Mr. B with an
apologetic smile.

Behind Meg's feet a small figure in pajamas dived
into the mouth of the pipe. Meg spoke to mask the
sound of tiny echoing footsteps. "Look, Thomas. See

how they fit together?" She grabbed two pipes with a clatter, hauled them in place with a clank, and bumped the pieces together a few more times for good measure. "Let's put them end to end and see how far they go!"

Mr. B looked unsure. "Well, I don't know," he began, glancing back at the transit pipe, now abutting another copper tube at right angles.

Thomas, ignoring this, lined up more pipes with great enthusiasm, while Meg knelt by the planter, pretending to sniff the flowers. She reached stealthily behind her and latched the buckles on the lunch pail, taking great care not to jostle the sleeping rat inside. She eased her fingers away just as Mr. B turned.

"Now, children, that's enough." Mr. B made a valiant attempt to sound firm.

Meg rose promptly. "Okay, Mister. Come on, Thomas—let's play soccer."

Emmy lay just inside the open end of the pipe and gazed into the jewelry store. The blinds were shut, and the interior was dim, but cracks of sunshine leaked around the edges, running along the floor

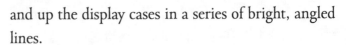

and up the display cases in a series of bright, angled lines.

A small bow and arrow lay discarded on the floor. Emmy could see the fishing line still attached to the arrow, and then the knotted shoelaces attached to that. . . . Someone must have shot the arrow all the way over the display case, and then they had all pulled the ladder up from the other side. It was ingenious, she had to admit.

She could see the girls now, busily hauling a lumpy bag up the side of a glass display case. The girl named Ana seemed to be giving the orders, in between fits of coughing, but as the others pulled out metal and wood and worked to fit the pieces together, Emmy couldn't help noticing that they seemed terribly practiced and efficient, as if they had done the same thing many times before.

An odd grating noise came to Emmy's ears. Two girls went round and round in a circle, pushing a crossbar, while two stood on top of a little platform, adding weight.

Were they truly troubled girls, after all? Emmy hadn't expected a gang of *thieves*. How could they do such a thing? And so young, too . . .

Emmy felt suddenly ashamed. Those very words had been whispered about her, just hours ago. She had judged the girls without hearing their side of the story—the same thing she had hated when it was done to her. And—it occurred to her now—if they were happy to be stealing for Miss Barmy, why had they sent a note begging to be rescued?

No. She would give them a chance. She would rescue the girls, troubled or not. But in the meantime, they had already cut a hole in the glass countertop with the circular metal piece. A hole saw, that's what Chippy had called it—

There was a sudden coldness in Emmy's chest, as if her heart had been plunged into ice water. The night of the party, she and Joe had overheard Chippy talking with Miss Barmy about this very thing. Had Chippy known how his invention would be used?

The tiny girls lowered a bent paper clip into the display case, and pulled up something that glittered blue and silver and ice. Emmy watched them narrowly.

Of course Chippy had taken her doll clothes, but he'd thought Emmy had given permission. This was different. This was actually planning a burglary . . .

This was using little girls to do something really bad, something he didn't dare to do himself.

The girls lowered the necklace over the side of the display case. The gems caught the light that filtered in through the blinds, flashing a brilliant, vivid blue. It was a living color, velvety and deep, and Emmy caught her breath. All at once she longed to be eighteen so she could wear them.

It was time to stop this burglary. Emmy swung her legs out of the pipe and jumped to the carpet.

The little girls dropped the necklace in their surprise.

Ana stepped forward, coughing. "Who are you? What are you doing here?"

"My name's Emmy Addison, and I've come to rescue you. Climb in the pipe."

The two smaller girls, apparently used to taking orders, obeyed at once. The next girl glanced back at Ana, who made a sound halfway between a sob and a laugh.

"That's just great," said Ana bitterly, draping the necklace over her shoulders. "What are *you* going to do? Fight Cheswick and Mr. B all by yourself?"

Emmy stared at her.

"Because if that's your plan, you can count us out. Cheswick has very big claws, and Mr. B is basically a giant, in case you hadn't noticed."

"Don't be stupid," Emmy said. "I've come to rescue you, and I've got a plan, and friends helping. All you have to do is drop the necklace and come with me."

"I'm *not* leaving without the necklace." Ana glared, her eyes bright with fever.

"Oh, yes, you are," said Emmy grimly, grabbing for the silver chain. She got hold of the clasp, heavy and smooth, and tugged hard.

Ana pulled back even harder, the necklace wrapped around her body. She had more size than Emmy, and more leverage, but she was shivering, and coughing, and altogether looked so ill that Emmy couldn't find the heart to pull anymore.

"What is *wrong* with you?" Emmy demanded, slacking off. "I thought you wanted to be rescued. Do you *like* stealing for Miss Barmy?"

"I *hate* it!" Ana cried passionately. "But she's got Merry, and if I don't bring back the necklace—"

Smash! The window exploded in shattering glass. Something twanged through the metal blinds,

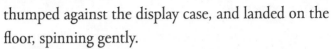

thumped against the display case, and landed on the floor, spinning gently.

Shaken, Emmy glanced at the soccer ball. *That* hadn't been part of the plan.

An alarm started to beep, loud and insistent. Outside, there came the faint sound of a distant siren. Ana, completely overcome, let the necklace slip and started to sob.

Emmy put an arm around Ana's shoulder and urged her up into the pipe. "We'll rescue Merry, too," she whispered. "But one thing at a time."

All at once there was light—dazzling after the dim jewelry store and the long dark pipe. The tiny girls spilled out of the transit pipe and huddled on the ground, frightened and confused. The siren was suddenly louder, and somewhere nearby, Cheswick's voice echoed furiously, as if he were swearing inside a tin can.

Emmy tumbled out last of all. She squinted against the brightness, and watched the lunch pail jump as something—Cheswick, by the sound of it—bounced and banged at the inside walls. Mr. B's feet, massive in leather work boots, turned around and around as if he, too, might be confused.

"Listen." Emmy's voice was low but commanding as she gathered in the troubled girls. "Follow me through the pipes on the ground, as fast as you can." She looked sharply at Ana. "You—come last. Keep them moving." She glanced at the lunch pail; Mr. B's hands were fumbling at the buckles. "Let's go!"

Dark. Cool metal beneath her hands and knees, hard copper rounding overhead, and the ragged sound of breathing. Then light again—brief, bright, a space between the pipes—and back into dark and endless crawling, with the soft, urgent pat-a-pad of four sets of hands and feet behind her.

Light once more: a flashing of red and blue, a glimpse of shiny police shoes, and then another long, dark passage inside curving walls, a metallic smell that Emmy could almost taste. Just as she was wondering if it would ever end, she saw a round of light ahead, unimpeded by another pipe, and a row of toes in a sandal.

"Quick!" breathed Meg at the pipe's end.

Emmy scooted out onto a huge red bandanna, and pulled the rest of the girls out like candies from a roll. She grasped Ana's hands last of all. The palms were hot with fever.

Red cloth billowed overhead, gathered in a peak, and five small bodies jumbled together. Emmy got a knee in her chest and an elbow in her mouth, and then there was a sudden swift rising as Meg stood up. Emmy felt it in her stomach, violently, and one of the little girls started to cry.

"Hush, hush," Emmy soothed, "it's all right, it's my friend Meg, she's taking us away, it will be over soon." They swayed together like babies in a cradle.

"Stop! Yes, you!"

The swaying halted with a sickening turn as the deep official voice spoke. Emmy waited, trembling herself but whispering "Hush, hush," over and over, like a prayer.

"Let's see what you've got in your kerchief," the stern voice demanded. "Can't hide anything from the Law, you know. Got to make sure no one's taking anything away from the scene of the crime."

Frozen, unbelieving, Emmy watched as the corners of their swaying hammock opened to reveal blue sky, leaves a mile off, and suddenly a massive nose, a brown mustache, a blue hat with a badge.

"They're just my dolls," said Meg in a high, breathless voice.

The giant face relaxed into a smile. "They sure do make them realistic nowadays. Do they say 'mama' if you squeeze them?" He put out a loglike finger.

"No." Meg hurriedly closed the kerchief.

"Hey, Carl! Stop interrogating little girls and get over here—we've got a break-in to investigate!"

"Nobody broke the window on purpose, officer." It was the anxious voice of Mr. B. "This boy was playing, and he kicked a soccer ball through the window. That's all."

"What? This little feller? I don't believe you. How old are you, sonny?"

"Six," said Thomas's pure, innocent voice. "But I'm *almost* seven, sir."

Emmy peered out between folds of cloth. Thomas, looking particularly sweet and pudgy, was giving his Cub Scout salute.

"A *six*-year-old," said the policeman, with emphasis. "Sir, you have *got* to be kidding. I don't know a six-year-old who could even get a soccer ball across the street, much less with enough force to break a window."

"But you should have seen his kick! It was like a cannon!"

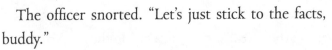

The officer snorted. "Let's just stick to the facts, buddy."

"Hey, Andy! Look at the counter! It *was* a break-in, after all!" Officer Carl's voice floated out from inside the jewelry store.

"Whaaat?" The policeman named Andy moved closer to the shattered window, keeping a firm grip on Mr. B's arm. They both peered within.

Behind their backs, a black rat's face poked out of the transit pipe and looked both ways. Then, with a rattle and a scamper, Cheswick Vole streaked across the broken sidewalk and disappeared into the crack beneath the art-gallery steps, trailing silver and diamond and a flash of sapphire blue.

Emmy stood on the laboratory counter at the Antique Rat and gazed at Sissy where she lay, still unconscious. "If only I'd wished for her to get better," she said heavily. "The flies and the sandwich didn't really matter."

Brian filled an eyedropper with milk from a cup. "There, now, little girls. Didn't they give you any breakfast? Open wide . . ."

Lisa, Lee, and Berit stood with their mouths open,

like baby birds, gulping milk from the eyedropper. Then Brian fed them bacon crumbles and one Cheerio each, and helped them into a drawer padded with dish towels. Exhausted from their labors, they fell asleep almost instantly.

A few feet away, Professor Capybara took Ana's temperature, his face grave, and tucked her into a notepaper box lined with cotton balls.

"I, too, wish Cecilia would recover," he said quietly. "This little girl is ill. It would be easier to treat her if she were larger."

Emmy looked at him bleakly. Professor Capybara would never say it, but if Ana died because Sissy couldn't make her grow, Emmy knew whose fault that would be. The frozen feeling, which she had almost forgotten in all her activity, was still there. It settled in the center of her chest, a solid hard weight, colder than sleet.

She gazed dully at the charascope. She didn't need to look at a sample of her blood to know that the whiplike thing with thorns was getting larger.

Meg leaned her elbows on the counter. "Maybe Sissy's still unconscious, but I think she's looking better. She's not so pale under her fur."

"I believe you're right," said the professor, peering at her closely.

"Merry . . ." Ana lifted her head from the cotton pillow.

Emmy made an effort. "Don't worry," she said, speaking with simulated cheer. "We'll find her somehow. Is she in the attic of the shoe shop?"

Ana coughed deeply. "Yes, but Mrs. B caught her."

The professor looked suddenly alarmed. "Mrs. B? The old lady with the purse?"

"Calm down, Professor," said Emmy anxiously. "You can't fall asleep—not while Sissy and Ana need you."

"Maybe Ratty and Joe and Buck have already rescued her," Meg put in. "Thomas said they were gnawing a hole in the window."

Ana's eyes shot open. "Gnawing?"

"Well, they're rodents, that's what they do," said Emmy.

"They're *your* friends? Not Miss Barmy's?" Ana rasped.

Emmy thought of the last time she had seen the three rodents, and hesitated. *Were* they still her friends? "Well, they're not Miss Barmy's friends, that's for sure."

Ana shook her head, agitated. "The chipmunk—I saw him taking orders from Miss Barmy. I told Merry—not to trust them—" A violent series of coughs made further speech impossible.

The professor drew a handkerchief gently up to Ana's chin. "Here, Brian, give me that eyedropper. I'm going to calculate a dose to bring down her fever. Grind this pill into fine dust, will you?"

"Put me in your pocket, Meg," said Emmy. "Let's go find out for sure."

Carl the policeman was there before them. Standing on Mr. Peebles's porch with a hand clamped on Thomas's shoulder, the officer was telling the lawyer what had happened. Thomas, who seemed to have the situation well in hand, was looking up at the officer with his best blue-eyed gaze.

Meg asked politely if she could visit Joe in the attic. Mr. Peebles nodded, distracted, and in moments Meg was in the house and up the stairs.

But the attic was empty of rodents.

"Look across," said Emmy urgently. "Did they get in?"

Meg peered through the half-open window to the house across the way. Emmy climbed from her pocket to stare at the pulley and basket, hung on a wire that stretched between the two houses.

"See that dark spot beside the frame?" Meg pointed. "That must be the hole. And they must have gone through it; otherwise, why aren't they here?"

"So all we have to do is wait for them to come back," said Emmy. She sat down on the windowsill, her legs dangling.

Time passed. After a while, the girls saw Mr. Peebles leave with the policeman and Thomas, presumably to visit the scene of the crime. The lawyer waved up at Meg, calling something or other, and she waved back.

They waited some more. Emmy swung her legs and wondered if they were having trouble finding Merry. No, of course not! Three rodents would certainly be able to sniff out one human, no matter how small.

But what if Merry had refused to go with them? What if Merry was afraid of rodents?

Emmy looked at the basket again. It looked sturdy . . . but it was a long way down.

"Don't even think about it," said Meg, following

her gaze. "Joe and Ratty and Buck can take care of themselves. And I wouldn't let you ride in that basket for a million dollars."

Strangely enough, now that Meg had put it into words, Emmy wanted to argue. "If the basket was strong enough to carry rats, it'll be safe enough for me."

"But you don't know what's happening in the attic," Meg pointed out. "It might be dangerous."

"If it's dangerous for me, then it's dangerous for Merry, too. And she's only five."

"Emmy! Don't!"

"I'll just peek through the hole," Emmy answered as she hung from the windowsill. "Just to see what's going on. That'll be safe enough."

She dropped onto the short overhanging roof, ran across the asphalt shingles, and reached for the wire looped between two pulleys. "Haul it in, will you, Meg?"

Meg reached out of the window and tugged on the lower wire. The basket came smoothly up to the wall of the house. Emmy climbed in.

She was *very* high up. The light breeze, so refreshing near the ground, was stronger at this level, and the basket swayed. The wicker seemed sturdy enough, but there were disconcerting gaps in the weave. Emmy gripped the basket and kept her eyes straight ahead, determined not to look down.

"Watch out for the power line!" Meg's voice was full of worry.

Emmy grinned a little. It was a telephone line, insulated of course, and it was a good two feet away. Meg sounded just like a grown-up.

"Keep your hands inside the basket!" Meg added as she pulled on the upper wire, and the basket began its slow, inching way over the yawning gap.

Emmy looked down only once, and that glimpse was enough to make her head swirl. She closed her eyes until she felt the basket bump lightly against the far pulley. She had arrived at the Home for Troubled Girls.

The hole in the window frame had clearly been gnawed; the wood around the opening looked as if it had been attacked by a hundred tiny chisels. Emmy put her head cautiously through, her hands rubbing the rough tooth marks, and saw rows of tall, cluttered shelves stretching almost to the ceiling.

The attic was quiet. Was Merry hiding somewhere? Emmy looked back at Meg, waved briefly, and wriggled through the hole.

She paused on the windowsill, catching her breath. This was where Ana had stood looking out. This was the window from which she'd dropped the note. There was history in this place, a feeling of long, prisoned hours, and Emmy shifted uneasily.

The sill was as broad as a sidewalk. Emmy paced it slowly, scanning the room. Ana must have had a way to get up and down . . . Yes, there was a shoelace ladder, hooked under the shelf by the wall, just like the one they'd used in the jewelry store.

Well, this was easy enough. Emmy descended carefully, her hands gripping the wide, soft shoelaces, her feet finding the swaying rungs. Though how she would ever find Merry in this huge place, she didn't know.

Emmy stopped with one foot in the air. At first she heard nothing but the tick of settling wood, the soft creaking that all houses made if you were still enough to listen. Then the sound came again, so quiet she almost didn't hear it at all. It was a sob.

Emmy crept along the floor, listening, watching, her eyes searching all directions. She stopped frequently, her head cocked.

Shoes were everywhere, in boxes and out, along with mounds of assorted junk. Emmy skirted a pair

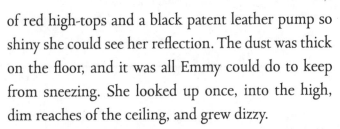

of red high-tops and a black patent leather pump so shiny she could see her reflection. The dust was thick on the floor, and it was all Emmy could do to keep from sneezing. She looked up once, into the high, dim reaches of the ceiling, and grew dizzy.

Sticking out from behind the next shelf was the toe of an old-fashioned lizard-skin pump, two shiny green purse straps, and half of a big upside-down bowl with holes. A colander, that was it—her mother used one to drain spaghetti. Emmy walked stealthily—the sobbing was very close now—and stopped.

Huddled on the open floor, just past the shiny purse on its side, was a tiny girl dressed in white. The sun slanted through the window and lit up her wispy brown hair, turning it to gold. As Emmy watched, the little girl sniffed, drew the back of her hand across her nose, and looked up.

"Oh!"

Emmy was at her side in an instant. "Hush," she breathed. "Come with me."

"Where's Ana?" The little girl's mouth trembled.

"I'm taking you to her. Come on."

Tears welled up in Merry's eyes. "I can't. My feet won't move."

Emmy frowned, stood her up, and tugged. Merry almost fell over, but her feet remained stuck to the floor.

"What, did you glue them?"

Merry shook her head. "Not me," she whispered. "Her." She pointed upward.

With dread, Emmy followed Merry's gaze. Above the lizard-skin shoes rose two shins like aged trees. Knees, big as boulders. A landscape of red and orange cloth, a withered hand hanging; and far away was a face, eyelids like tissue paper, mouth slack.

Mrs. B was asleep in her chair. Emmy's heart beat twice, hard, with a boom like thunder.

"We'll untie your shoes," Emmy mouthed as she fumbled at the laces.

"I tried that already." Merry sniffled again.

The laces were tightly knotted. Merry must have yanked and yanked at them. Emmy stifled an exclamation of impatience and looked around her for something she could use. If only she had Meg's jackknife!

The shiny green purse was on its side, its clasp open. Just inside, Emmy could see a jumble of makeup, bottles of nail polish, a comb, a tube of Super Glue . . .

There. Emmy grabbed a nail file, metal and jagged, and sawed at the laces. Above them, Mrs. B mumbled in her sleep. Her clawed hand twitched, and Emmy worked faster.

At last she was through. Carefully, gently, she pulled Merry's feet out and left the tiny shoes stuck where they were.

"Bye, bad rats!" said Merry gleefully, pressing her face to one of the colander's many holes.

There was a sudden scuffle from within, as if something inside had woken up. Emmy stared at the colander, aghast.

"Emmy!" cried a voice.

"It's us!" shrieked another.

"Help!" shouted a third, loudest of all.

"*Don't wake her!*" whispered Emmy furiously, but it was too late. Mrs. B's eyes popped open. She sat up in her chair with a bang.

"Oh. Sorry," came the contrite whisper, but Emmy was already galloping toward the shoestring ladder, dragging Merry by one arm. "Up you go! Hurry!" she said under her breath, and Merry, obedient, climbed as fast as she was able.

The lizard-skin shoes slid back. The floor creaked. There was a whisper of cloth.

"Faster!" urged Emmy. "Grab the nail at the top—go out through the hole. I've got you, don't be afraid—"

"Oh, little *girl* . . . where are you? Where is Mrs. B's little dolly?"

Emmy and Merry scrambled and tumbled across the bit of roof, their hands and knees burning from the gritty asphalt shingles. They could feel the roof shake lightly, in time with the heavy footsteps on the attic floor.

Emmy lifted Merry into the basket and leaped in after her. She grabbed the upper wire and pulled it hard, calling out for Meg. Where *was* she?

The window behind them banged open. Two scrawny arms reached out, clutched the wire, and pulled it hand over hand. Inch by inch, the basket came shuddering back.

Emmy's heart pressed into her throat. She glanced across to the phone line—could she leap to it? Maybe by herself, but never with Merry.

The little girl buried her head in Emmy's side as Mrs. B's strong, sinewy fingers came closer. The polished red talons curved around them, smelling leathery and stale. The girls were lifted from the basket.

Emmy gripped Merry tight as they fell sickeningly

into a pocket, and twisted up to watch as Mrs. B yanked the zipline down—basket, wire, pulleys, and all. It fell, the wire singing, and landed with a discordant twang on the grass.

"Can't get back now," Mrs. B gloated, and banged the window shut.

Mrs. b was terribly methodical. She ripped the shoelace ladder from the windowsill. She pulled down shoeboxes and made a corral, enclosing her chair and the colander. And last of all she set the girls down inside the shoebox fence.

"*Naughty* dollies," she said, "to make me run. I think I stubbed my toe." She pulled off her shoes and stockings and peered at one foot with rheumy eyes.

The odor of unwashed feet was powerful. Emmy tried to keep from gagging.

"I know! You can give me a pedicure!" Mrs. B stretched her thin lips in a spiteful smile. "Take that file and start on my left foot." She leaned back in the chair, humming to herself.

Emmy, whose hands were pressed over her nose, looked at Merry in alarm. "She *can't* be serious."

Merry nodded sadly. "We do whatever she says." She knelt to pick up the nail file, and staggered with it over to Mrs. B's leathery, reeking feet. "Which is the left one?" Merry whispered. "I forget."

Mrs. B waggled her left big toe lazily. Merry did not look at Emmy as she leaned the file against the toenail and began to move it doggedly back and forth.

Emmy glanced at the bits of fur she could see through the colander's holes and turned away. *They* weren't going to be any help. Merry would have been safe by now, if those friends of hers—*ex*-friends, she reminded herself—hadn't yelled loud enough to wake the dead.

Emmy examined the shoebox fence that enclosed them. The boxes were higher than her head. But suppose she could get over them, then what? How was she going to get up to the windowsill without a ladder? Climb from shelf to shelf, and then leap?

Even if she managed all that, there was still the little matter of getting across to Mr. Peebles's attic, and she couldn't do that with Merry on her back. In fact, none of it could be accomplished if she brought the little girl along.

"You know," said Mrs. B from a great height, "I could squish you if you'd rather not work. The choice is *completely* up to you."

Gritting her teeth, Emmy took the heavy end of the file and helped scrape at the thick yellow toenail.

A flake of old crimson polish chipped off and flew up into her face.

"I have *never* done anything this gross," Emmy muttered, sawing away. "Never, never, never!"

"*Emmy* . . ." The whisper sounded ghostly, hollow, coming through the holes in the stainless steel colander.

Emmy looked over her shoulder. Six small paws were extended to her through the holes.

The sight softened her heart, but only slightly. So they'd changed their minds about needing her help, had they? It was just too bad they'd waited until she was trapped, too.

"We're really sorry." It sounded like Buck.

Emmy flushed. She had been sorry, too, about what had happened to Sissy, but no one had forgiven *her*. She turned back to her loathsome task, bearing down hard on the file.

"We didn't think," pleaded Joe.

"We didn't mean for you to get caught," the Rat added, sniffling a little.

"Yeah, well, I didn't mean to abandon Sissy either," said Emmy, unable to keep the bitterness from her voice. "So now you know how I feel."

The rasp of the file was loud in the quiet attic room.

"Hey! That tickles!" Mrs. B jerked her foot, and Merry fell down with a whimper.

Emmy, already upset, now lost her temper entirely. "Why don't you pick on someone your own size?" She dusted Merry off and glared upward. "And why don't you lose the red polish while you're at it? It's—" She cast around in her mind for something cutting. "It's *so* last year!"

There was a ghastly silence.

Emmy took a step backward. How could she have been so stupid? "I mean, why don't you try pink?" she added hastily, attempting to smile. "Or fuschia? Or maybe brine shrimp? I hear that's fashionable this year."

Mrs. B hung over them. A dusting of face powder drifted down like dirty snow. "Rude, ill-mannered little dollies," she murmured, "must be taught a lesson." She reached a scrawny hand into the shiny green purse and fumbled inside it, pulling out a small container of cotton balls.

Dread fought with hysteria in Emmy's stomach. What was Mrs. B going to do with those? Pat them to death?

Mrs. B rummaged in her purse and drew out a clear bottle, gazing at it dreamily. "I'll just soak a cotton ball, and little dollies can rub and rub my toenails until the old polish comes off . . ."

Merry stopped in mid-whimper, her eyes round. "Mr. B says that's dangerous for little girls."

The yellowed, bony fingers tilted the clear bottle up, then down. The liquid swirled, catching the light, and Mrs. B smiled. "But Mr. B isn't here, now, is he?" she said, and set the bottle gently on the floor.

Emmy stared at the bottle of nail-polish remover. Its label was at eye level. "Acetone," it said in bold letters. "Avoid breathing fumes. Toxic to birds. Keep out of reach of children."

Emmy blinked. Toxic meant . . . poisonous.

If acetone fumes were poisonous to birds, what might they do to someone bird size?

Fear stabbed through her like silver ice, turning her skin cold. She leaped for the farthest shoebox and grabbed the edge of the lid with fumbling, numb hands. She levered up a foot, a knee, an elbow. She heaved, she rolled, she was on top of the box, she was almost out of reach. She would run—she would hide—

She would abandon Merry.

On the very edge of the box, Emmy turned.

From three feet away, Mrs. B looked at her, smiling dreadfully. Her hand was cupped around the little girl.

Emmy felt the strength run out of her bones. There was nothing she could do. If only the rodents under the colander were free—*they* would have no trouble scampering over the boxes, swarming up the shelves, even with Merry on one of their backs. If only Emmy were a rat, *she* could do it . . .

If she were a rat. The words seemed to sizzle on her brain.

Mrs. B was unscrewing the cap. "Dolly," she said carelessly, "do you remember which is the left foot?"

Merry nodded. She put her thumb in her mouth.

Emmy felt a great pain, as if something inside her was squeezing, squeezing . . . She saw vividly the thick, orange twisted rope, the spiking thorns of the thing in her blood. It was just as knotted and horrible as the green wormy mass that had kept Miss Barmy a rat—it would keep Emmy a rodent, too, if she was foolish enough to become one.

She couldn't risk it. She *couldn't* be a rat for the rest of her life.

Mrs. B was dripping clear liquid onto a cotton ball. A sharp, dizzying scent wafted past Emmy's nose, lifting the tiny hairs inside. Merry, closer to the bottle, coughed.

And suddenly Emmy saw, with piercing clarity, that if she didn't turn into a rat—if she didn't rescue Merry right now—then, for the rest of her life, it wouldn't matter that she still looked human. She would *feel* like a rat until the day she died.

A small sound—it might have been a sigh—worked its way up from Emmy's chest and out her throat. She slid down off the box. She pushed her hand through one of the colander's holes.

"Bite it, Ratty," she said, and shut her eyes. "Hurry!"

She was thickening. No, parts of her were thinning. Everything was different—her arms grew short and furry—and instinctively Emmy sniffed the air. The harsh, stinging acetone was overpowering, but there were a hundred other smells, too. Each of the three rodents beneath the colander had his own unique scent; the musty attic had odors of mold and leather; and somewhere a banana was rotting slowly.

She could smell the strong human odor of Mrs. B, and Merry's scent, too, more faint . . .

Merry. Emmy opened her eyes—even the colors looked different!—and located the child. She was swaying dizzily, her white dress sagging. The soaked cotton ball fell from her hands.

Emmy's hindquarters bunched, and she leaped powerfully. Her sharp claws dug into the soft wood of the floor. With a snarl she darted past Mrs. B's nasty yellowed feet and snatched up Merry, clenching the little girl's shoelace belt in strong rodent teeth.

It was rat's play to scrabble up on top of the boxes; it was the work of a moment to leap down and scurry along the floor. Emmy scaled the shelves by the window with the agility of a rock climber, and before Mrs. B had recovered enough to stand and pursue, Emmy had pushed Merry through the hole in the wall, and wriggled after her.

Emmy's whiskers brushed the asphalt shingles, giving her precise information about the surface, the slant, the amount of traction. Her sensitive ears picked up the humming of the phone line, and in an instant she had leaped onto it, balancing like an acrobat.

It was amazing, Emmy thought, what a difference a tail made. She would have gotten a much better grade in gymnastics with one. All she had to do was stick it out to one side or the other—just a flick—and she was completely stable. She didn't even have to think about balancing.

But she did have to decide what to do next. Emmy crept along the swaying wire as easily as if it were a sidewalk three feet wide, carrying her precious burden, thinking hard. And suddenly there was Meg at the window, biting her nails.

Emmy lowered the limp white form to the windowsill. "Meg," she said, as the girl opened her mouth, "see those fishing rods in the corner? And the tackle box? Find me a spool of fishing line and a big paper clip. Hurry!"

"Who are you?" Meg demanded. "You're not— *Emmy*?"

"Yes! Hurry!"

Meg obeyed without question, tying the line to the paper clip as Emmy directed. "Remember—wait for two sharp tugs. Got it?"

Meg nodded.

"And then take Merry straight to the professor.

Tell him she got a whiff of some nail-polish remover. And *please* send someone to let me know if she's all right."

Emmy grasped the paper clip between her teeth and headed for the phone line again. She could not see much into the distance, which was actually a relief. She was just as happy *not* seeing how far down it was to the ground.

But her sense of smell was keen. As Emmy crept up to the hole in the window frame, one sniff was enough to tell her that no one was hiding on the other side.

Emmy squirmed through the hole and into the Home for Troubled Girls once more. Quietly, carefully, she pulled the fishing line behind her, and dangled gently to the floor. She moved into the shadows.

The chemical smell of acetone was pungent in the attic room. As she moved closer, she could see that Mrs. B was doubled over in her chair.

Had she been overcome by the fumes, too? wondered Emmy. But as she peeked through a gap in the shelves, she had to bite down hard on her paw to keep from squeaking with laughter. Mrs. B had apparently taken Emmy's advice, and was carefully painting her toenails pink.

Emmy crept softly to the back side of the colander, put her muzzle up to a hole, and whispered a few brief words.

"Got it," whispered Joe. "Get ready, you guys."

Noiseless and swift, Emmy climbed to the second shelf and lay flat on her furry stomach. She edged around a brown leather brogue and lowered the fishing line, with its dangling paper clip, all the way down to the colander.

The paper clip made a tiny *ting* as it touched the stainless steel. Instantly a paw reached through and drew it inside.

Mrs. B lifted her head. She glanced at the colander, but after a moment went back to her toenails. The translucent fishing line was all but invisible in the dim attic light.

Emmy watched narrowly as one end of the paper clip was stealthily threaded out through another hole, and then back. She nodded—braced herself—and tugged on the line, two sharp tugs.

On the other end, Meg felt them. At once she yanked back hard, pulling the fishing line until it stuck. And in the attic room, the colander flew up, the rodents dashed out, and Mrs. B began to screech.

They glued her feet to the floor.

Mrs. B was small by that time, naturally. While Joe and Buck and Emmy distracted her from one side, snapping and squealing with high-pitched, nerve-racking cries, Raston dashed in from the other side, settled his claws firmly into her right ankle, and got in two good bites.

After the first bite, of course, she was able to understand what Raston and Buck were saying; it wasn't very flattering. And as she was bitten a second time, she shrank with an ear-piercing shriek that was music to Emmy's soul.

But it wasn't until Mrs. B was safely glued down, and under the heavy steel colander, too (they gnawed the fishing line until the cage fell over her with a satisfying clang), that Emmy felt the situation was fully under control.

The four rodents sprawled some distance away, catching their breath. Now that the battle was over, Emmy felt a little awkward. She rested her furry chin on her forepaws and risked a quick glance at the others.

They were all grinning at her.

Relieved, Emmy grinned back. Somehow after

combining forces to capture the terrible Mrs. B, they had become good friends again without needing to say anything at all.

But of course there was still the problem of the necklace.

"And Sissy, too," said the Rat after the jewelry-store burglary had been explained.

"She's a little better," Emmy said earnestly. "She hasn't woken up yet, but she's not so pale."

"I want to see for myself." Raston sprang up.

"Maybe we shouldn't go," Joe objected. "Maybe she needs her rest."

Buck nodded his striped head. "And remember, we've got to find Emmy's necklace and get it back."

"Chippy's going to put the jewels in the tiara for the beauty contest." Emmy tapped the floor with her claws.

The fur on Buck's back stood up. "Are you telling me," he demanded, "that my brother *knows* those jewels are stolen? That he's helping *criminals*?"

"I'm not sure," said Emmy. "But Miss Barmy did tell him the jewels had been in her family for generations. And he believes everything she says. Maybe he's just a—what do you call it?"

"A dupe," said Buck grimly.

"A pigeon," added Joe.

"A patsy," said the Rat.

"Downright stupid," finished Buck. "And so is everyone in Rodent City. They've let themselves be blinded by a pretty rat—"

"She's kind of blotchy," said the Rat. "I like a nice smooth gray myself."

"—and a beauty pageant, and all those seeds and nuts she's been handing out."

Emmy nodded. "You know those seeds that the rodents think are so rare? That you use for money? The kitchen downstairs has whole jars full. They only cost a few dollars in human money at any grocery store."

"Let's go to Rodent City and tell them!" cried Joe. "We'll tell about the jewels, and the troubled girls, and the seeds, and everything. The Barmster won't get to run her old beauty contest after all!"

"I wonder if they'd listen," said Buck slowly. "Everyone is so thrilled about the pageant. Even Mother has been sewing dresses. They won't want to believe us."

"I have an idea!" the Rat said brightly. "Let's wait until *after* the pageant to tell them! Everyone is *so* looking forward to it . . . and there's going to be a *theme song* . . ."

Emmy hid a grin. "What? Were you asked to write one?"

"Well, yes." The Rat lowered his eyes modestly. "And sing it, of course."

"Of course," said Joe.

"Don't tell me you want to be a part of that three-ring circus," Buck said with disgust. "It's bad enough that Chippy's involved. And that everyone else in Rodent City thinks Miss Barmy is Queen Princess Biggypants."

Joe snorted out loud.

The Rat's head shot up defensively. "It's a good song. I spent *hours* getting it to rhyme."

"Let's hear it, Ratty!" Emmy rolled on her stomach and propped her furry cheeks on her paws.

The Rat stood up shyly, and dug a toe into the floor. "This is to the tune of 'There She Is, Miss America,' you know." He clasped his paws behind his back, swelled his chest, and sang:

There she is, Princess Pretty—
There she is, your ideal . . .
The dream of each lovely rat
Here in Rodent City—

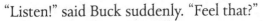

"Listen!" said Buck suddenly. "Feel that?"

They all fell silent as a slight vibration shook the attic floor. Heavy footsteps sounded on the stairs, and the rodents dashed beneath a shelf and waited, panting, in the shadow it cast. The door creaked open.

"Addie, dear? Where are you?" Mr. B's heavy feet shuffled past the rodents' hiding place.

A tiny, shrill cry could be faintly heard under the colander.

"I'm sorry, little girl, but you just have to stay there." Mr. B put his hands over his ears. "I hate it when the little ones cry," he mumbled to himself. "Jane and Addie will be so mad that the other girls got away . . . and the police keep asking questions . . ." His footsteps receded to the far end of the room. "Addie? Addie, where have you gone?"

The four rodents looked at one another and nodded. In an instant, they scampered out the open door and down the stairs. They bunched in a furry heap on the second-floor landing and listened at the apartment door that Mr. B hadn't quite shut, their sensitive ears cocked. They heard voices.

21

"BUT WHERE IS HE, Cheswick? He *promised*."

"Now, Jane," soothed Cheswick Vole, "I'm sure he'll turn up in time for the pageant. And if he doesn't, you can ask someone else to sing."

Miss Barmy's claws tapped on the floor of the dollhouse. "You don't understand, Chessie. I can't have just anyone. I need a rodent with a *voice*."

Raston grinned cheekily. Buck and Joe pretended to gag, but Emmy listened intently as the conversation continued.

"Do you have the ballots ready?" Miss Barmy sounded uneasy.

"All marked and ready, my little kumquat," said Cheswick.

"And the mouse? The one that doesn't talk?"

"Locked up with the ballot box and a satin pillow. Don't worry, princess—the pageant will go exactly as you planned. I will take care of *everything*."

Emmy scuttled around the baseboards to an

overstuffed chair with a skirt that went to the floor. The three rodents followed her silently, slipping under the curtain of fabric. They gathered in the dim space beneath the sagging upholstery, and put their heads close together.

"You heard them," said Emmy quietly. "They've marked the ballots for the beauty contest—*before* the voting. That means they plan to cheat."

Raston's ears drooped. "I suppose you're going to say I shouldn't sing for them."

Emmy shook her head. "No, I was actually thinking that you *should*."

Buck pulled back. "*What?*"

"Just listen to her." Joe looked around the circle. "What's your idea, Emmy?"

Emmy lowered her voice. "Miss Barmy knows that everyone in Rodent City blames me for what happened to Sissy, including you guys."

Joe rubbed a paw over his whiskers, looking uncomfortable. "We don't blame you now," he said, and Buck and Raston nodded quickly.

"But there's a lot she doesn't know," Emmy went on. "She doesn't know that I was the one who stopped the burglary and helped the little girls escape. I mean, Cheswick was locked in a lunch pail the whole time."

"She doesn't know that Mrs. B is under the colander, or that Merry is gone," said Buck, realization dawning. "Not yet, anyway."

"She doesn't know that we're not still mad at you," added Joe.

"Well, I'm still kind of mad," said the Rat.

Emmy ignored him. "And best of all, she doesn't know who I am."

They looked at her blankly.

"She won't recognize me," Emmy said patiently. "I'm a rat now, see?"

They saw.

"You can be a spy!" said Raston.

"And you three can be double agents. Miss Barmy already thinks you hate me; she'll think it's natural if you switch to her side, like everyone else in Rodent City."

"We never *hated* you," Joe said earnestly.

Buck sat back on his haunches and nodded approval. "I like it. Miss Barmy won't be on her guard, but all the time we'll be undermining her."

"The Underminers!" said Joe. "Cool name!"

"Can we have a secret handshake?" asked the Rat.

Emmy and Joe moved quickly from the chair to the hole in the baseboard. Buck watched until they disappeared behind the wall. He gave Raston the signal.

The Rat bounded up the table leg to the dollhouse. "I'm here!" he announced.

"Rasty!" Miss Barmy gave a charming little squeak. "Just the rodent I wanted!"

"I have my song all ready," said the Rat. "Do you want to hear it?"

"I'm afraid you misunderstood," said Cheswick stiffly. "We have the song here. It's already written." He passed a folded sheet of paper to the Rat.

Raston's whiskers fell. "Oh, really," he said without enthusiasm.

"Let's hear it, Raston! Let's hear your marvelous voice!" Miss Barmy crooned.

"Well . . ." The Rat weakened. "I'll try." He hummed a note, looked down at the paper, and began:

> There she is, Princess Pretty—
> There she is, your ideal

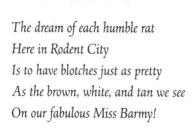

> The dream of each humble rat
> Here in Rodent City
> Is to have blotches just as pretty
> As the brown, white, and tan we see
> On our fabulous Miss Barmy!

The Rat hesitated, glanced up, and went on:

> There she is, Princess Pretty—
> There she is, your ideal
> For though you may dream,
> You know you can never be her
> She does you a favor
> Even to let you see her . . .
> And there she is!
> Rarer than rare, she is!
> Worthy of stare, she is!
> Princess Pretty!

There was a muffled sound of clapping. "Lovely! Lovely!" cried Miss Barmy. "Don't you think so, Cheswick?"

"Well, I wrote it, after all," said Cheswick.

The Rat stared down at the paper in his paw. "But this seems to assume that Miss Barmy will be the winner."

"But of course!" cried Cheswick gallantly. "Don't *you* think she'll win?"

"Uh—sure, maybe." The Rat scratched his head. "But shouldn't we have a song that could work for someone else, just in case?"

"Certainly," said Cheswick. "By all means. Just make sure to practice *this* one."

There was an awkward silence.

"You'd better go put on your tuxedo," said Miss Barmy, with a winning smile.

Buck waited until everyone had left. Then he bounded to the kitchen, leaped onto the counter, and scrambled into the cupboard. What he found left him gasping. Not just jars of seeds and nuts, but a whole *box* of peanut-butter cups!

He made numerous trips between the kitchen cupboard and an underground storage room in the tunnel to Rodent City. Then, on his last visit, he stopped abruptly at the kitchen door, his head cocked. There was an odd ringing sound overhead— *wang*-wang-*wang*-wang—as if something round and metal had been cast aside and was spinning fast, and faster. Suddenly it rattled to a final stillness.

Buck tucked his carrying pouch under the uphol-stered chair. He scampered out to the landing and up thirteen steps. He peeked around the edge of the attic door.

Mr. B was on the chair, looking down in fascina-tion at his miniature wife. "I'm afraid you're stuck, Addie dear. At least until the glue wears off your feet."

A tiny, shrill whine, like that of a furious mos-quito, rose from the small figure and went on for some time.

"Eh?" Mr. B cupped a hand to his ear. "I can't hear so well as I used to, Addie. But never mind," he continued, "I'll take good care of you. I'm used to tak-ing care of little dollies." He got up, beaming, his white hair surrounding his soft, gentle face like a puff of cloud. "I'll just see what I can find . . . Why, look here! A nice little bed for you!" He pottered happily among the shelves, chuckling to himself, as the thin, reedy whisper of his wife's voice persisted. It had a distant, almost pleasant sound, like wind in the rushes.

"You know, I kind of *like* her small," he said to no one in particular.

Mrs. Bunjee was delighted to see Joe. "My, you make a handsome rodent! And you can help me, too. Would you please deliver this to the Antique Rat? It's for Cecilia, in case she feels better."

"Sure," said Joe. "What is it?"

Mrs. Bunjee peeled back a corner of the soft, squashy package to reveal a soft bathrobe of a beautiful royal blue. "I ran across this in the pile of clothes that Chippy brought—you know, the ones that Emmy donated—and I made a few alterations. Perhaps she'll be glad to have it."

"Has she woken up yet?" Joe asked.

Mrs. Bunjee shook her head. "The last messenger said she was still asleep. But that's good, you know. There's nothing so healing as sleep."

She leaned forward to look past Joe. "And who is your pretty little friend?"

Emmy shrank back.

"Oh," said Joe, "this is—uh—what did you say your name was? I don't know her very well," he added in an aside.

"Mm—Olivia," said Emmy in a panic, saying the first name that occurred to her.

316

"Molivia? What an interesting name, dear. And where are you from? I haven't seen you around."

"She's new," said Joe, on his way out the door. "And *very* shy. I wouldn't ask her a lot of questions."

"I won't, then." Mrs. Bunjee appraised Emmy from ears to tail. "But I can see that we'll have to hurry to prepare you for the beauty contest."

"M-me?" stammered Emmy.

"My dear," said Mrs. Bunjee, "you may be shy, but you're also one of the loveliest rats I've ever seen. And we *need* you in the pageant." She bustled about in the piles of finery that were left from the day's frantic sewing. "Here's just the thing. It was too small for the rat that ordered it, but it will be exactly right for you."

She lifted a soft, silky dress of the palest pink, with long flowing sleeves and trailing satin ribbons, and held it up to Emmy. "Look in the mirror, Molivia."

Emmy looked. She saw a small, worried-looking rat of dove gray, with tidy white paws and a furry white bib under her throat that encircled her shoulders. On her forehead was a soft white star, and in front of her was a dress she had always loved on Barbie.

"Why do you need me in the beauty contest?" she

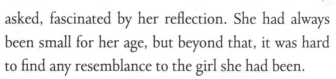

asked, fascinated by her reflection. She had always been small for her age, but beyond that, it was hard to find any resemblance to the girl she had been.

"There's something fishy about this pageant." Mrs. Bunjee lowered her voice. "I don't know what it is, but I'd like someone to win besides Jane Barmy! And you might be just the rat to do it."

Emmy stood in the wings of the stage and waited for her turn to go on. Unlike the other rodents around her, she wasn't at all nervous. She didn't care in the least whether she won or not—she had another goal.

It had surprised her, though, when she was chosen as one of the top twenty contestants.

She hadn't thought her answer to the question "What is your greatest wish?" was that good. Everyone else had said "world peace." Emmy had thought of that, too, but remembered that the wishing mouse had said, "World peace is for everyone. Pick something for *you*," and so she said, "I wish Sissy would get well soon." The judges wiped their eyes with their handkerchiefs and gave her the best score.

It had surprised her even more when she made the top ten.

She hadn't expected to succeed in the talent contest. The only thing she could think of to do was tap-dancing. She was just a beginner, but it was a skill that no one else in Rodent City seemed to have, and it wowed them. She even got a higher score than Miss Barmy, whose ability to bat her eyelashes 240 times in a minute was nothing short of remarkable.

And now that she was among the top five contestants (after the evening-gown competition), she was beyond surprise. The best thing was that she had a perfect opportunity to observe Miss Barmy. Unlike Emmy, Jane Barmy seemed to be getting more and more anxious as time went on.

"What's Buckram Bunjee doing now?" the piebald rat muttered, biting her claws. "*I* didn't tell him to pass out refreshments."

Emmy glanced at Buck, who was quietly moving among the audience, passing a gunnysack pouch from row to row. Where he had been, rodent cheeks bunched and rodent jaws moved in a steady, rhythmic chewing.

"Maybe he's just getting into the spirit of the pageant," Emmy ventured, secure in her identity as Molivia. "Giving back to the community, you know."

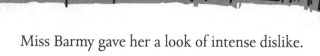

Miss Barmy gave her a look of intense dislike.

"Who do you think will win Miss Congeniality?" asked Emmy brightly.

Buck moved to the stage, wiped some excess chocolate from his mouth, and picked up a sheaf of papers.

"And now," said Cheswick Vole into the microphone, "a little musical interlude as our judges mark their ballots. Ladies and gentlerats, Gerry and his Swinging Gerbils!"

The band swung into a brassy number. Miss Barmy clutched at Cheswick as he walked offstage. "Chessie! Buck Bunjee has the ballots!"

Emmy drifted back behind the curtain, where she could hear without being seen. She pretended to adjust her sash.

Cheswick straightened his red bow tie, which had been bumped askew by Miss Barmy's eager paws. "Of course, my little sugar lump. I asked him to pass them out." He lowered his voice. "It looks better if I'm not the only one handling them."

"But Buck's never liked me! He'll be suspicious!"

"I think you'll find—" Cheswick had begun when Buck's voice interrupted.

"You're looking mighty fine tonight, Miss Barmy!"

Emmy hid her face in her sleeve until she could stop laughing.

"Why—thank you, Buckram," said Miss Barmy, clearly taken aback. "This is . . . unexpected."

"Ma'am, I've been wrong about you, and I've come to apologize. All this that you're doing for Rodent City—well, it just goes to show what a nice rat you really are. And pretty, too! *Dang* pretty!"

Miss Barmy gave a bleating sort of giggle.

"I'd kiss your paw, but I might get chocolate on your dress. Peanut-butter cups don't go with pretty dresses, you know—whoops, there's my signal, I'd better go—"

Buck picked up a padlocked ballot box and carried it to the judges' table. One by one, they pushed their folded pieces of paper into the slot. Buck mounted the platform and set the box on the boards with a thump.

"Now, where did *he* get peanut-butter cups?" Miss Barmy said to herself, tapping her claws together.

Chippy appeared on the far side of the platform. Emmy saw with a pang that he was staring at Miss Barmy in mute adoration.

Buck glanced once at his brother, scowled, and walked off. Chippy trotted on, wheeling several brightly wrapped boxes in a red wagon.

"The prizes!" he announced with a sweeping gesture. "Third place, two tablespoons of slivered almonds!"

No one applauded. They were all too busy chewing.

"Second place," said Chippy, somewhat surprised, "eleven macadamia nuts. First place, three bottle caps of poppyseeds, and"—he consulted a paper in his hand—"seventeen pecans for the lovely rat who is voted Miss Congeniality by her peers!"

There was a scattered round of polite applause. Miss Barmy, standing next to Emmy, seemed to swell visibly. "The ingrates!" she hissed. "Those are valuable nuts and seeds, terribly rare and expensive!"

Emmy put up a paw to cover a smile as she walked onstage with the five final contestants. Rodents who had just been stuffing themselves with the very same seeds and nuts—not to mention peanut-butter cups, too, courtesy of Buck—weren't likely to be impressed by such cheap prizes. No doubt Buck had made sure to mention just how plentiful they were at the local grocery store.

There was a rustle behind the curtain. Cheswick

Vole came through, nudging before him a tiny, timid-looking mouse in knickers. The Endear Mouse, looking stiff and uncomfortable in blue velveteen, carried a gold satin pillow.

There was an expectant hush. The band played a flourish. Chippy opened the last box, lifting out something that caught the light in a brilliant blaze and shimmer of blue.

There was a collective intake of breath. The crowd, like one huge, eager animal, craned their necks all together. Chippy set the tiara delicately on the golden pillow where it glimmered like bits of the evening sky, sprinkled with stars. He gazed at it proudly.

Emmy, too, was proud. These were the Addison sapphires, bought by Great-Great-Uncle William for his bride. They were a piece of her own family's history, and they were beautiful. None of the assembled rodents needed to be told that here was something truly rare and precious.

"The jewels in this crown were generously, selflessly donated from the family vault of Miss Jane Barmy," said Chippy, his voice cracking with emotion. "Jane dear, we don't deserve you."

Miss Barmy inclined her head with a satisfied smile,

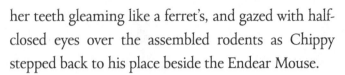

her teeth gleaming like a ferret's, and gazed with half-closed eyes over the assembled rodents as Chippy stepped back to his place beside the Endear Mouse.

A murmuring rustle rose from the back rows and swept forward, but Cheswick held up a paw for silence and unlocked the ballot box. He reached in. He tabulated the ballots, adding the scores as Buck looked over his shoulder, and nodded to the band. The musicians played a continuous chord, with muted drums.

"Second runner-up, Miss Letitia Lemming!"

An earnest-looking brown rodent, furry-tailed and small of ear, stepped from the line amid hearty applause, picked up her prize and a kiss from Cheswick, stepped around the Endear Mouse, and stood to one side.

The band played an ascending progression of chords. The tension mounted. Off in the wings, Raston took a last look at the words of his song, and took a step forward.

"First runner-up, Miss Denilda Dormouse!"

Denilda's large eyes got even larger, and her delicately fluted ears quivered as she acknowledged the honor and clutched a bouquet of flowers to her chest. She wasn't quite as adroit as Letitia, though, for her box of macadamia nuts swung wide and bumped the Endear Mouse off its feet. Chippy helped the little mouse up and dusted it off.

The rising chord changes quivered and died. The drummer began a slow but steadily accelerating drumroll.

"And the winner is—"

The squirrel to Emmy's right was breathing in short, gasping pants. On the other side, Miss Barmy was clenching and unclenching her paws.

"Miss *Jaaaane* Barmy!"

The drumroll stopped with a flourish. The trumpets blared. The audience of rodents began to clap as Miss Barmy shrieked girlishly, fluttering her paws.

Emmy glanced worriedly at Buck. Should she say something? Would anyone believe her if she grabbed the mike and told them what Miss Barmy was really like?

Cheswick advanced with the crown, a mesmerizing glitter of silver and blue in his glossy black paws. He lifted it up. Miss Barmy's eyes flashed triumphantly around the room. She smiled like a conquistador.

"*Stop!*" cried Chippy. "Those jewels are *stolen!*"

CHESWICK'S ARMS FROZE in midair.

Chippy looked at Miss Barmy with bleak condemnation. His paw rested on the Endear Mouse's shoulder.

Miss Barmy's lips stretched thinly over her polished teeth. "What an absurd thing to say, Chipster!" Her tinkling laugh sounded like ice crystals falling. "They are Addison family heirlooms. My mother was born an Addison. Therefore, they are *mine*."

"So why did you make us steal them?" challenged a young voice from the back.

Emmy strained her eyes past the spotlights to the dim figures beyond. Footsteps pattered down the central aisle, and suddenly there they were—five little girls, their faces pale and determined, staring up accusingly at Miss Barmy and Cheswick Vole.

Five. They were all there, Merry and Ana included. True, Merry looked paler than the rest, and Ana was coughing a little. But they were looking much better, they were going to be all right, and Emmy's heart gave a skip of joy.

Miss Barmy's eyes darted from face to face. She spoke into the microphone. "Do you feel you have to *lie* to get attention, girls? Haven't I done enough for you, giving you all a home?"

"No," said Merry, taking her thumb out of her mouth.

"You see why I call them troubled?" Miss Barmy shrugged prettily and looked out over the crowd. "I have given them food, a home, the clothes on their backs—"

"Handkerchiefs!" interjected Ana.

"Of the finest Egyptian cotton. And now they *lie* about me." She gave an affecting sob, dabbed at her eyes with the tip of her tail, and bent forward with a smile like a razor's edge. "You're just little *girls*," she hissed. "Who's going to believe you?"

"I, for one." Professor Capybara stepped forward into the light, tucked his thumbs into his waistcoat, and beamed at the audience.

Emmy glanced at him, startled, and then at the Rat, who was behind her, waiting to sing. How had the professor shrunk without the Rat to bite him?

"Dear friends," Professor Capybara said, and his amplified voice echoed in the empty spaces of Rodent City, "I am sorry to tell you that Miss Barmy is not the rodent you think she is. The jewels in this crown *were* stolen, and she forced four of these girls to steal them, while she kept the fifth hostage."

Miss Barmy sucked in her breath through her teeth. All at once she looked very ratty. "*I* didn't do it! It was Cheswick!" She whirled to point at the stricken black rat. "*He* took them to the jewelry store. I was here the whole time—tell them, Chipster!"

Chippy looked at her stonily.

"Besides, I'm still the winner! I'm Princess Pretty, so *crown* me!" She clutched the sparkling tiara. "Hold up an applause sign!" she hissed to Cheswick. "Tell the band to play the theme song!" She set the flashing blue-and-silver circlet on her head with her own hands, and pasted on a false, brilliant smile.

The Swinging Gerbils stirred uneasily. Gerry raised his trumpet, puffed out his furry cheeks, and blew a great *blaaaatt*. It sounded remarkably rude.

The audience erupted in laughter. Miss Barmy's smile took on the frozen, rigid look of a cramp.

Behind her, Buck lifted the crown from her head with one swift movement. He leaned in to the microphone. "Actually," he said with calm authority, "Miss Barmy did *not* win. These are not the ballots that the judges marked."

The audience gasped. The rejected contestants, sitting off to the side in a mass of brightly colored dresses, rustled indignantly.

Cheswick looked sick, but he managed to sound outraged. "Explain yourself, sir!" He turned to the crowd. "You all watched the ballots being put in the slot. The padlocked box never left the stage. I unlocked it in front of everyone, and Buckram himself watched me add the scores. How *dare* you!"

Buck shrugged. "Look here." He held up his chocolate-smudged palms to the spotlight. "I cut up peanut-butter cups and passed them out. And I didn't wash my paws before I gave the ballots to the judges. Hold those ballots up, Chippy."

The paper ballots reflected the light as Chippy held them up, one by one.

"See?" said Buck. "Every one is clean. Now, the ballots I handed to the judges each had a chocolate paw print in one corner. I made sure of it."

Cheswick snarled. "And just where are these mythical ballots?" He opened the ballot box and showed an empty interior to the crowd.

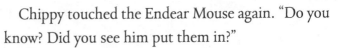

Chippy touched the Endear Mouse again. "Do you know? Did you see him put them in?"

The little mouse looked at Chippy with great concentration. Chippy nodded, reached into the box, and pressed a hidden panel. A false bottom sprang open. A sheaf of paper spilled out.

Chippy held them up. Plainly marked in one corner of each ballot was a chocolate paw print, smudged but obvious even to the back row of chairs.

Miss Barmy, for once, had no retort. Her paws hung. Her mouth twisted sharply.

But the other contestants had a great deal to say.

"You mean this pageant was *rigged*?" A mole rat, dressed in frothy orange, stood up and squinted her tiny eyes accusingly.

"I spent a whole week's seeds to get my fur done," squeaked a tuco-tuco, tawny and beautifully fluffed. "It's not fair."

"You had no right!" A flying squirrel flapped her pale-green sleeves as if about to take off.

A gundi, looking like a fierce powder puff, whistled the rodent signal for attack. "Get 'em, girls!"

The rejected contestants rushed the stage in a pack, their silks and satins whipping behind them. They descended upon Miss Barmy and Cheswick in a frenzy of glitter and sequins and feather boas, squealing and clawing in fury.

Miss Barmy yelped, picked up her skirts, and ran. Cheswick, after a moment's hesitation that cost him dear, scampered after, hanging on to what remained of his shirt. The crowd of enraged would-be beauty queens chased them up the steps to the second level, then the third. Round and round they ran, Miss Barmy and Cheswick in the lead, the rats in Barbie dresses stampeding behind. A last mad dash up to the fourth-level walkway, a frenzied burst of speed, and Miss Barmy and her faithful sidekick tore past the Bunjee loft to the exit tunnel, their shrieks and imprecations fading with distance.

The professor straightened the flower in his buttonhole and dusted glitter off his lapel. "That's the last we'll see of *them*," he said with deep satisfaction.

Emmy, a little shaken, hoped so with all her heart.

The crowd of rodents on the main floor, craning their necks upward, burst into cheers. The disheveled contestants helped one another straighten sashes and pat ruffled fur into place. Then they filed down the winding staircase, level by level, waving to the audience as if each one wore a tiara.

"Let's see who *really* won!" Buck and Chippy bent

331

over the chocolate-smeared ballots and began to count. The band, recovering from their astonishment, picked up their instruments again.

There was a second drumroll. Buck straightened. "Ladies and gentlerats," he announced, "we have a winner. I give you Princess Pretty of Rodent City—Molivia!"

Emmy blinked. This was all happening too fast. Someone led her forward, and someone else put the crown on her head. It felt strangely heavy.

The band swung into a lush, sweeping intro, and Raston stepped up to the microphone, his ears pink from excitement. "Heeere she is, Princess Pretty," he began. "Here she is, your ideeeel . . ."

Emmy flushed. She wasn't anyone's ideal. She wasn't even a citizen of Rodent City. And if these rodents knew who she truly was, they'd never let her wear the crown.

Of course, she could just pretend to be Molivia. If she had to stay a rat, it might be better to start with a new identity.

Except that she didn't want to. She didn't want to be a fake like Miss Barmy, pretending that she was someone she wasn't. She wanted to be real.

And if they hated her for who she really was?

Emmy tried not to let that matter. She stepped forward and took the microphone from Ratty's paw. The band fumbled and faltered into silence.

"I'm sorry," wavered Emmy. "I can't be your Princess Pretty." She waited a moment, trying to calm the hammering in her rib cage. "I'm not even a rodent. My real name is Emmy Addison, and before I turned into a rat, I was the one who didn't stop my friends from throwing rocks at Sissy."

She looked out at the audience. She saw shock and horror and revulsion on their faces. She was not surprised.

The microphone was wobbling in her paw. She fit it back in its socket and held on to the stand to keep herself steady. "I did try to stop them, but only after it was too late. I didn't mean to abandon her," Emmy went on in a rush. "I thought she'd go straight to Rodent City. I didn't realize she would get lost. And then I kept thinking that I should tell someone about her, or go back to check on her, but things kept happening and I just . . . never did."

Her voice cracked on the final word. She waited a moment, until she could speak again. "I'm really sorry," she whispered.

Her words fell like a hesitant rain into a listening,

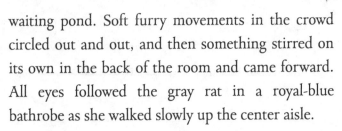

waiting pond. Soft furry movements in the crowd circled out and out, and then something stirred on its own in the back of the room and came forward. All eyes followed the gray rat in a royal-blue bathrobe as she walked slowly up the center aisle.

It was Sissy.

Emmy found it hard to breathe. A surge of emotion welled up inside her, almost too big to contain. She wanted to leap and shout for joy and relief. She wanted to run and throw herself in Sissy's arms and cry. She wanted to drop to her knees and say a prayer.

She did none of these things. She leaped, and cried, and said thanks in her heart, overwhelmed with gratitude. Now the little troubled girls could grow and be reunited with those who loved them. Now Joe could stop being a rat and turn into his old self once more.

She knew that she would likely remain a rat. The horror and disapproval on the faces in the crowd had convinced her. But she could still be happy for others, and most of all for Sissy, who was mounting the steps to the platform, who was looking at her kindly, who was drawing her into a furry embrace.

"Don't," said Emmy, pulling back. She stared out at the audience, now a blur to her. "They know I don't deserve it."

Sissy shook her head. "Does it matter what the crowd thinks? They don't know what's inside of you."

Emmy shrugged painfully, looking away.

"Listen, Emmy," Sissy said earnestly. "The crowd thought Miss Barmy was wonderful, but they were wrong. And they thought you were terrible, but the whole time you were taking brave risks and rescuing little girls. It was just a mistake, that you didn't stop those humans from throwing rocks at me. You just froze—it could have happened to anyone—"

Emmy shook her head. "It was more than that," she said miserably. "It was a *betrayal*. I didn't protect you because I was afraid the other girls would laugh at me."

"Oh," said Sissy. She looked at her paws.

"I wasn't a very good friend to you," said Emmy humbly.

Sissy smiled. "But you're my friend *now*." She threw her short arms around Emmy, and squeezed. "I forgive you," she whispered in Emmy's ear, and then somehow her nose bumped into Emmy's cheek, and her whiskers tickled Emmy under the chin, and Emmy started to laugh. The last grim vestiges of the frozen, tight-fisted, stone-hard thing inside her softened, and melted, and ran dribbling away. She blinked away the blurriness, and lifted a hand to wipe her eyes.

A hand.

And her cheek was smooth. Emmy stretched out her arm—her human arm—and wiggled her five fingers.

Sissy was beaming. "Kisses go with hugs," she said, and then there was a roar of cheering, and a batting sound of paws clapping, and suddenly the crowd surged forward and the ballot box spilled and everyone was hugging, Buck and Chippy and the professor and the little girls and Sissy and Mrs. Bunjee, and then all at once Joe was there, too, telling Emmy that he was the one who had brought the girls and Sissy to the pageant.

"As soon as I saw that Sissy was awake, and Ana and Merry were doing better, I got the professor to let them come," Joe explained, his pale fur rumpled every which way.

"I wouldn't allow it at first," said the professor.

"But I said, what if he went with them? He was their doctor, after all—"

"And then I remembered that I had a little of Raston's saliva left in a vial," finished the professor. "So I poked myself with a needle and shrank, and Brian brought us to the front door. That boy is a treasure, I must say."

Flushed and happy, Emmy remembered to ask Joe about the others. "Where are Meg and Thomas? Did they stay with Brian?"

"Meg had to go home, and Thomas is covering for me with Peter Peebles. But he can't do it for long—my parents are coming back tomorrow."

"We still have to choose a Princess Pretty," Emmy said. She caught sight of Mrs. Bunjee in the crowd, and waved, her silk sleeves falling back to her shoulders. The dress was a terrible fit, now that she was no longer a rat.

Buck and Joe and Ratty—the Underminers—crowded around. "But *you're* Princess Pretty," said Buck.

"I can't be Princess Pretty. I'm not a rodent." Emmy took off the tiara and tilted it back and forth, watching the sparkles reflecting on the surrounding

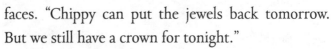

faces. "Chippy can put the jewels back tomorrow. But we still have a crown for tonight."

"Well, then, who can we pick? The ballots are all torn and mixed up on the floor."

Emmy looked around for inspiration. Her eyes fell on Sissy, standing straight and tall in her royal-blue robe.

"Sissy," she said. "Sissy is the one who deserves it."

The Underminers looked at one another with raised eyebrows, considering this.

"But she's not just a pretty princess," said Buck thoughtfully. "She stands for something different."

Joe nodded. "She was wounded and cold and wet for fifteen hours, and she still came out fighting to live. She's got guts. She's got grit."

"She's . . . Princess *Gritty* of Rodent City!" said the Rat.

"That's it!" cried everyone at once.

"Except I haven't written a song," Raston said worriedly.

Emmy threw an arm around his shoulders. "Just sing from your heart, Ratty, and make it up as you go."

The audience were back in their seats. Mrs. Bunjee was seated in the front row with Sissy, Endear, and the five troubled girls, who were not at all troubled anymore. And now, when Emmy looked at the rodent faces in the crowd, their expressions seemed kinder, too.

"It's because you were so brave," said the professor, standing beside Emmy on the stage. "Your friends have been telling everyone what you've done."

"It wasn't so much," Emmy mumbled, embarrassed.

"Nonsense." Professor Capybara fixed her with a penetrating eye. "You rescued four little girls, and stopped a robbery. You saved Merry from almost certain death, and you returned to face the terrifying Mrs. B in order to free Joe and Buck and Raston. After all that, no one can say that you don't care about your friends."

Professor Capybara nodded approval as Buck and Chippy, arm in arm, announced the new princess. He winked at Raston, who stood nervously in the wings, scribbling last-minute changes to his song. And he smiled as the Swinging Gerbils swelled into the theme song of the evening.

"Go ahead," he said to Emmy.

She walked slowly toward Sissy, carrying the precious tiara on its golden pillow. The professor was right behind, and when they reached the gray rat with the gentle expression, he raised the glittering crown and set it carefully on Sissy's head.

The vivid sapphire blue and the wink of diamonds were all reflected in Sissy's bright eyes. With her silky gray fur and regal blue robe, she didn't look like a rat who had no education and couldn't read. She looked like a queen.

Emmy stepped back, filled with the kind of happiness that comes when you have come through great dangers with good friends, and been forgiven, too. And the Rat stepped up, handsome in his tuxedo, and sang:

> There she is, Princess Gritty—
> There she is, your ideal
> Her dream isn't for the whole
> World to call her pretty
> Or to act like a victim, soaking up lots of pity
> No, she'd much rather be
> Known for her tenacity.
>
> There she is, Princess Gritty—
> There she is, your ideal
> For though she was lost and hurt,
> She kept right on trying

Refused to give up, and stoutly avoided dying . . .
And saved, she is!
Everyone's fave, she is!
Worthy of rave, she is!
Princess Gritty!

The applause rang, echoing among the rafters. Gerry, with a nod and a grin to the Rat, launched the Swinging Gerbils into "You Ain't Nothin' but a Rodent"; and within three bars a striped gopher appeared at Emmy's side.

"May I have this dance?" asked Gus.

THE MORNING SUN LINGERED just below the horizon, then popped up, big and pink, and patted the rooftops of Grayson Lake with melon-colored light. It fanned across the triangular green and shone a ray into the window of the Antique Rat, touching seven small boxes laid end to end on a counter.

In the middle box, a tiny Emmy yawned and sat up, rubbing her eyes.

Last night had been fun. After Joe had grown and gone to Mr. Peebles's attic, after Chippy had returned the jewels through the transit pipe (luckily, the plumbers hadn't yet appeared—the professor seemed to think this wasn't out of the ordinary), the professor had taken Sissy and the girls back to the Antique Rat. Emmy, whose mother wasn't expecting her, decided to stay small for one more night and enjoy a second slumber party.

The tiny girls had been wild with relief. Although they had begun by giggling and eating—the usual sleepover occupations—they were so jubilant that they progressed to throwing cotton-ball pillows and running wildly between the test tubes until the professor told them, somewhat grumpily, to go to sleep.

Emmy gazed at the slumbering girls. She had gotten to know each one last night: Berit, athletic and impulsive; Lisa and Lee, friendly and almost impossible to tell apart; Merry, who was like the little sister Emmy wished she had; and Ana, the leader, the responsible one, who was more than ready to give up the job and be a kid again.

Had it been just a few days ago that Thomas had brought Miss Barmy's old cane up to the tree fort? Emmy had not wanted to look at the small carved faces then—but now she was deeply gratified to see those same faces in real life, happy and free.

Emmy felt free, too. The weight that had seemed to press down on her shoulders ever since Sissy had been wounded was gone. She glanced at the charascope, and wondered what a sample of her blood would show now.

There was a soft shuffle of feet in slippers as Professor Capybara came down the stairs and saw her looking in the charascope. "What are you studying?"

"Just a sample of my blood." Emmy slid down the

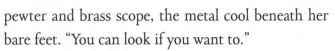

pewter and brass scope, the metal cool beneath her bare feet. "You can look if you want to."

The professor bent his head to the eyepiece. "Yes, yes—nothing unusual here—a good amount of courage, though." He lifted his head. "Were you worried that you might see something else, my dear?"

"I did see something else yesterday," Emmy said quietly. "It looked like an orange whip thing. With thorns."

The professor took another look. "Ah, yes, now I see it. But it's only a shadow."

He lifted Emmy to the eyecup, and there it was—a faint imitation of the shape she had seen before, thin and insubstantial, like a wisp of fog, or the ghostly pattern of a wake seen on the water, long after a boat had passed.

"What *is* it?" Emmy asked.

The professor shrugged. "Guilt? Shame? It's only a memory now, my dear."

Emmy nodded. She was glad it was gone, whatever it was. "But, Professor, what's going to happen to the little girls now that they've been rescued?"

"Once Sissy makes them grow, I'll call the police and tell the truth—that they came to my door last night, newly escaped from Miss Barmy, looking for shelter. And then we'll locate their families."

"But Mr. Peebles said once that all their parents were dead."

The professor nodded soberly. "Yes, perhaps—but think how glad their relatives will be, to have them back after so long!"

Emmy sat on a drooping swing in the schoolyard and swayed gently back and forth, scuffing at the worn earth as she waited for her friends to show up. It felt good to be her real size once more.

Across the street, the jewelry-store owner arrived to shake his head over the boarded-up window, unlock the door, and take down the sign that said "Closed."

A moment later the door popped open again. The man dashed out, looked wildly up and down the street, and dashed back in.

Emmy grinned. He would be calling the police about now . . . She could just imagine the conversation. "No, I don't know how they got back in the case, officer . . . No, the alarm didn't go off . . . I'm telling you, the jewels have been reset into a doll's tiara . . . No, I am *not* crazy!"

She twisted the swing, winding herself up until the chain was as tight as she could make it. She let go and whipped around and around, her legs straight out and her head back, staring at the crazily circling sky. It was so much fun she tried it on her stomach, but that made her dizzy. She stopped at last, dragging her toes, and opened her eyes to see a small rodent with its paws on its hips, looking irate.

"Are you *quite* finished? You almost kicked me."

Emmy regarded the mouse with awe, and thought carefully before she opened her mouth. She didn't want to accidentally speak a wish that she didn't mean.

"I have a question," she said at last. "How do your wishes work? I mean, on Sunday, I asked for an invitation, Joe wished to break an ankle, and Thomas wanted to be a great kicker; and you gave us all our wishes. Then, yesterday, I wanted the flies to stop bothering me, and Meg wished for a peanut-butter-and-jelly sandwich—"

"And you each got half your wish," the tan-and-white mouse interrupted. "And today you get exactly one wish—and only a quarter of it will come true—and then I'm free at last! No more wishes until next June!"

Emmy looked curiously at the small, bouncy mouse. "What happens in June?"

"The summer solstice, of course! Don't they teach you anything in school?"

"The solstice," Emmy repeated slowly. "That's something to do with the sun."

"Ding-ding-ding! We have a winner!" The wishing mouse turned a somersault and blinked up at Emmy, grinning. "See the sunburst on my head?"

Emmy looked at the light patch between its ears. "I always thought it was a star."

"The sun *is* a star," the mouse said in a lecturing tone. "And when the sun is at its highest point in the year (that's the solstice), and at the highest point in the day (that's noon), my wish-granting ability is at its highest. Now do you see?"

"Sort of," said Emmy cautiously.

"Three full wishes at noon on the day of the solstice," said the mouse impatiently. "Two half-wishes the next day, one quarter-wish the next. And after that, I suppose I could grant an eighth of a half-wish, and so on, but who would know the difference?"

Emmy frowned. "So, the day before the solstice, did you give two half-wishes?"

"Yes, of course."

"What were they?"

The tan mouse fluffed up its fur as if bored. "Someone wished that it would be a sunny day—I gave him partly cloudy. And someone else—oh, who cares. Listen, I've got things to do." The mouse ducked into a hole in the ground.

"Wait!" cried Emmy. "What about *today's* wish?"

The mouse popped its head out. "You want a wish, come back at noon exactly. And no wishing to change things that have already happened—that's against the rules."

"Can I wish for something multiplied by four?" Emmy asked quickly, but the mouse had already disappeared.

"Times four what?" said Meg, jumping onto the next swing.

Emmy explained. Then when Joe appeared, swinging along on his crutches, and Thomas came trotting up, for once without his soccer ball, Meg told it all again, while Emmy looked up at the sky through green summer leaves and tried to decide on her wish.

"I know what I'd wish for," said Thomas grumpily, after all had been explained. "That Dad wouldn't sign me up for sports camp."

Joe propped his leg on the slide and chuckled. "Better you than me, buddy."

"Are your parents back?" Meg asked, looking from one to the other.

"They drove up," said Joe, "and right away Cousin Peter told them about the two windows Thomas broke."

"Were they mad?"

Joe grinned. "Dad told Thomas he should go out for football, he had a gift, he should develop that leg, blah, blah, blah."

Emmy wondered why Thomas had wished to kick so well if he didn't like sports, but her eye was caught by a movement across the street. Emerging from the alley were Mr. and Mrs. Benson, followed closely by Peter Peebles. They stopped to look at the boarded window of the jewelry store, and the owner came out.

The children watched as the adults talked back and forth, finally shaking hands.

"Dad's agreed to pay for the window," murmured Joe. "And now . . . get ready, Tommy, here he comes."

Thomas didn't look up from the sand, where he was building something with sticks. He ripped up a handful of grass and laid it carefully on the roof of

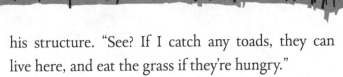

his structure. "See? If I catch any toads, they can live here, and eat the grass if they're hungry."

"Thomas! Come here a minute!"

Thomas got awkwardly to his feet and went to the little group of adults, waddling slightly. "I hear you've got quite a kick," his father said. "Want to show us?"

Thomas mumbled something that Emmy couldn't hear. She saw Mr. Benson set a ball down and point toward the far-distant soccer fields.

Thomas kicked. His father's mouth fell open.

"Incredible! Caroline, this kid's got a foot like I've never seen in my life! He needs to train it! We've got to map out a plan of action, before we waste any more time!"

"Now, Jack, calm down," said Mrs. Benson soothingly.

"He'll go to football camp—soccer camp—we'll start right away. He's got to catch up. The other kids have been playing for a long time already."

"I don't want to go to camp, Dad." Thomas wandered back to the sand pile.

"What do you mean, you don't want to go to camp? This is a great opportunity for you, son! You can be a star, you can really go places!"

"But I want to stay right here." Thomas smoothed out a road with the flat of his hand. "I want to play with turtles, and catch frogs, and play in the tree fort . . ."

"Now listen here, Thomas," said Mr. Benson, his face growing red.

". . . and dig holes, and find caterpillars, and ride my bike, and collect bottle caps . . ."

"Now, *listen . . . to me . . .*" The veins in Mr. Benson's neck pulsed. He passed a hand over his forehead, looking dazed.

". . . and maybe get a puppy, and go fishing, and build a town for toads . . ."

Thomas's father, crimson to his collar, opened his mouth—faltered, blinked twice, and went down like a stunned buffalo.

". . . and be a kid," finished Thomas, looking down at his father, who was snoring blissfully.

"Oh dear." Mrs. Benson fanned her husband with her hand. "He's been like this ever since California. I can't *think* why he keeps falling asleep. I've scheduled a doctor's appointment first thing tomorrow."

"It seems to be going around," said Peter Peebles thoughtfully. "Professor Capybara had the same trouble just two days ago. He said it was some kind of virus."

"Well, whatever it is, it only attacks him when he gets worked up about something. But Jack gets worked up an awful lot."

The children exchanged glances. "Mom," said Joe carefully, "did you see any animals in California? Like—rodents, for example? With bushy tails?"

"Oh, heavens, yes, they were all over Palm Desert. They were harmless, though. Jack even picked one up."

Thomas looked up from the sandbox. "Did it sneeze on him?"

"How did you know?" Mrs. Benson was startled. "Oh, Jack, you're awake! Now, don't get all excited again, dear. Let's get you home, and you can lie down."

"This is *awesome*," said Joe fervently, as the adults moved slowly off the playground. "He'll never scream at my soccer games again."

"Thanks to the Bushy-Tailed Snoozer Rat," said Thomas happily.

"The professor said he might find a cure soon," Emmy reminded them.

Joe grinned. "Yeah, but we don't have to mention that to Dad, right, Thomas?"

Thomas nodded, patting a sand mountain with his pudgy hands. "I don't want to play football and soccer, anyway. I just want to play kickball at recess. Billy Frank said I couldn't kick it farther than my grandma could spit, and I said I could kick it over the fence, and I bet him my favorite rubber snake, too. And now I'm going to win it back."

He gave his creation a final pat and stood up. "Do you like it?"

"What is it, Thomas?" Emmy stood beside him, looking down at the hills and roads and small stick buildings. "Is that your toad town?"

"Yup." Thomas put his sandy hands in the pockets of his shorts, looking satisfied. "I wish I had some toads to put in it, though. Some big fat ones."

A lump of brown sand suddenly lifted its head, its throat pulsing, and resolved itself into a toad. It was immensely fat. It attempted a spasmodic hop, failed, and sat stolidly, blinking its yellow eyes.

"Oh, *no*," said Emmy, with passion.

"I don't know what you're upset about," said the wishing mouse, looking at the toad critically. "It's certainly big and fat. And though 'some' isn't an exact number, I thought I was really quite generous to assume he meant 'four.'"

High in the tree fort, swaying in the good ship G.F., Emmy leaned back and studied her list. THINGS TO DO THIS SUMMER, it read at the top. The first item, to build a tree fort, had already been crossed off. She smiled as she checked off sleepover, pool party, swings, playground. Should she count sailing? She had *watched* it twice.

There was a skittering of claws overhead as two chipmunks chased through the branches, knocking down acorns that had hung on all winter long. "Hey!" Ratty looked up from one of Emmy's old alphabet books. "Do you *mind*? We're having a lesson here."

"Look, Rasty! 'A' is for 'Acorn.'" Sissy pointed to the small brown nut that had landed on the page, and laughed happily.

"It's a visual aid," called down Buck from above.

"We're only trying to help," added Chippy, dashing down to seize the acorn. He looked over Sissy's shoulder. "'C' is for '*Cat*'? What awful things are they putting in children's books nowadays? This is terrifying! It will give them nightmares!"

The Rat glared. "I don't recall asking for advice. What is this, team teaching? Just because it's popular doesn't mean that *I'm* going to jump on the bandwagon. There is such a thing as the *tried* and *true*, you know—solid teaching methods that have stood the test of time, unlike your here-today, gone-tomorrow fads—"

Emmy grinned and picked up her list again.

It didn't seem exactly right. It was incomplete, for one thing. Although she had checked off a number of things, she had done lots more things that had never even made it onto the list in the first place.

Such as? She sucked on her pencil. Such as riding in the back of a truck or staying up all night and not feeling sleepy. Walking through rodent tunnels, going to a party underground, dancing with a gopher—not a high point, but still. Stopping a burglary, escaping through pipes, and balancing on a telephone wire—that was new! Gluing someone's feet to the floor; wearing her favorite Barbie dress; winning a beauty contest. And, above all, rescuing eight friends.

Emmy stopped, struck by the number. Yes, there had been eight—the five tiny girls, and then Joe, Buck, and Ratty. And she had more friends than that, too—lots more, friends too furry to have made her original list, she realized with shame.

Emmy felt the ghost of a thorned whip stir within

her, but she shook the memory away. That had been days ago. She felt different now. Friends were friends, whether big or tiny, smooth or furry, and she wanted every one of them on her list.

In fact, Emmy realized with a sense of relief, keeping a list was kind of a bore. She lay on her stomach and happily ripped bits off her paper, letting the fragments spiral to the ground like last year's oak leaves.

"Hey, Emmy!" The shout came from below as Meg and Thomas ran down the path, with Joe crutching swiftly behind.

"Password?" Emmy demanded.

"Barmy Begone!" they shouted in unison.

Emmy let the rope ladder down. Meg and Thomas held it for Joe, so he could pull himself up more easily, and then they climbed, too, spilling onto the high platform.

"This is *so* cool up here," said Meg, rummaging in the box for the spyglass.

Joe looked at his cast. "I think my ankle is healing faster than the doctor thought it would."

"Maybe being a rat helped speed things up," Emmy suggested. "You know, a faster metabolism and all—" She broke off, gazing at Thomas.

He was reaching out a hand to Miss Barmy's old

cane, the cane she had carved, which now served as their figurehead. He traced the small wooden faces with his finger. "We did it," he said softly. "We rescued them."

"Well, Emmy did it, really," said Joe.

"But you guys rigged the line and gnawed the hole in the wall," Emmy said.

"We all helped," said Meg. "Even if it was just buckling a lunch box, or yanking on a fishing line . . ."

"Or laying pipes end to end," said Thomas, "or kicking a ball through a window."

"Some of us delivered messages," said the Rat, looking fondly at his sister.

"And one of us created a lovely song," Sissy added, smiling back.

"Everybody helped," said Emmy. "And I've thought of the perfect thing that G.F. really stands for, except . . ." She hesitated. "You'll probably think it's too sappy."

"Not Golden Fortress again," begged Joe, on his back with his good leg waving in the air.

"Nope." Emmy looked around shyly, and told her idea.

There was a little silence.

"That's kind of nice," said Meg.

"Yeah, but still sappy." Joe wiggled the sandal on the end of his foot.

"How about Gophers are Fluffy?" suggested Sissy.

"Grumpy Frogs?" This was Thomas's contribution.

"Gerbils of Flatulence?" said the Rat. "Groundhogs are Frolicsome? Glorious Flubbery?"

Emmy, laughing, leaned back against the trunk. They could call it whatever they liked. But to her, G.F. would always mean Good Friends.

It might be a little sappy—but it was the truth.

	DATE DUE		